ALWAYS BEEN *you*

LILY MILLER

Lily xoxo

ISBN: 9798517049513

Always Been You

Cover Design: Kim Bailey, Bailey Cover Boutique

Editing: Carolyn De Melo

Publicity: LitUncorked

To the remarkable women who encouraged us to follow our dream.

It is with passion, courage of conviction, and a strong sense of self that we take our next steps into the world.

Elle Woods

ONE

Olivia

This can't be happening! What is *she* doing here and where can I hide? And no, I'm not kidding. I quickly scan the room. My heart drops straight to my feet and I swear I've stopped breathing. Behind the desk? Under our antique wooden worktable? Maybe I could just slip behind my best friend Ellie, who is working beside me. Desperate times call for desperate measures - and right now I'm definitely desperate. Shit! It's too late.

"Olivia, honey! Look at you. It has been way too long."

Grace Bennett has just walked through the doors of my Reed Point flower shop and I'm pretty sure I've lost all ability to form a simple sentence.

"So, this is Bloom. It's amazing." Mrs. Bennett steps further into the store with a starry-eyed look on her face. Her heels clatter on the wood floor beneath her.

I somehow manage a smile as I take her in. She looks as beautiful and put together as I remember in her tailored navy blazer with round gold buttons, perfectly paired pants, a crisp white blouse and Prada kitten heels. Her rich brown hair is neatly styled in a bob at her shoulders and there's a warmth in her eyes that makes you want to love her. She is a rarity in Reed Point- her priorities have always been her family and their happiness, and not material things like some woman in this city. Since Reed Point has become the new, albeit smaller Hamptons, big money is everywhere, and some just love to flaunt it. *Insert eyeroll.*

"These arrangements are all absolutely stunning and I love what you have done with the space. I am so proud of what you have accomplished."

"Thank you." I inhale deeply, trying to calm myself.

I shakily look around the small room, seeing it through Mrs. Bennett's eyes. Ellie and I started Bloom three years ago. My dream of being a small business owner, now a reality.

Ellie is my lifelong best friend and now business partner, and I should add superhero to that list of titles, because she is thankfully coming to my rescue. Noticing my state of shock, Ellie has dropped the bunch of eucalyptus stems she'd been shearing and stepped out from behind the desk to save me. She takes over the conversation with Mrs. Bennett and I take advantage of the opportunity to remember how to breathe again.

"What brings you into our store, Mrs. Bennett? My name is Ellie, I co-own Bloom with Olivia. You might remember me from high school? I was in the same grade as Parker," Ellie says, shooting me the side eye and nudging my shoulder, snapping me out of my temporary brain freeze.

Geez, Olivia, get it together.

"I do remember you, Ellie. It's so nice to see you again." She adjusts her purse on her shoulder while I continue to suffer from heart palpitations.

"Well, girls, it's my 40th wedding anniversary and you know how we like to celebrate! We are having our closest friends and family over to the house for drinks and a catered dinner and I am in need of floral centerpieces - I couldn't think of anyone better for the job than you two! Do you think you can do it?"

She can't be serious. Step foot inside the Bennetts' house again? It's not happening. Has she forgotten everything that happened between her son and me?

There is no way I will risk seeing Parker again when just the sight of his mother standing in front of me is enough to twist this giant knot in my stomach. She reminds me far too much of him, with her dark hair and dark eyes and striking features. Those eyes... man, Parker's eyes. *Olivia, stop it.*

"We'd love to!" Ellie practically sings, snapping me out of my fog. She is rubbing her hands together like she just won a prize at the Reed Point fair. *Which we all know is impossible. Those stupid games are always rigged.*

I glare at her.

"Really?" Mrs. Bennett's eyes go wide, looking directly at me for my approval.

"Of course!" Ellie nearly screeches back in excitement.

What the actual EFF Ellie, are you doing? Has she lost her mind? It's the only possible explanation because otherwise my best friend is clearly a traitor! I am seeing red! If eyes could kill, Ellie would drop dead on our perfectly swept floor. I'm ready to bury her body.

I have never been able to hide my emotions, always wearing my heart on my sleeve. Mrs. Bennett can surely see my hesitation written all over my face. She takes my hand and says sweetly, "The entire family would be thrilled to see you and I would be honored if you would do this for me."

Well, I can think of one family member who wouldn't be happy to see me, but I can't say no to her. Mrs. Bennett has been nothing but thoughtful and compassionate towards me, she is one of the kindest women I've ever met. I may have spent the past eight years trying to erase her son from my mind, but I can still remember all of those happy times I spent in her family's home. And now, with her standing right in front of me, every memory Parker Bennett and I ever made is rushing back, flooding my mind.

There is no way out of this mess. I'm flustered and anxious but manage to respond, "Thank you, Mrs. Bennett." I somehow remember how to speak again. "How could we ever say no to you?"

What did I just do?! I want to bury my body alongside Ellie's.

"Perfect!" exclaims Mrs. Bennett, grabbing my hand. All of my friends have been raving about you and your elegant arrangements. I can't wait to see what you come up with."

It is no surprise to me that her friends are "raving" about Bloom. Reed Point is small enough that everyone seems to know everyone else's business - and my business is not exempt.

I've gotten used to people talking about me and my family over the years. Unfortunately, we have given them a lot to talk about. We have made it through some very hard times, but not without heartbreak, not without my world crashing into pieces thanks to my father. I haven't seen or spoken much to him since then, but that will all be changing soon.

That was then, and this is now. With time, the pieces of my life have been put back together like a puzzle and these days life is good. I only hope it will stay that way.

"Do you have a color palette you would like to stick to, or certain flowers in mind?" Ellie asks, once again rescuing me from my own head and my bad manners.

"Pink, white and green would be wonderful. Peonies and hydrangeas are my favorite. Let me see here." She circles the store, and my pounding heart seems to echo the sound of her heels against the floor. "Something *this* size and in a vase like *this* one," she says pointing to a medium size clear glass vase bursting with cut flowers we had just created this morning.

"They will be beautiful. Ellie and I will make sure of it," I answer, as confidently as possible. *'Fake it till you make it' is apparently my new motto.*

"It was lovely to see you again Olivia. You as well, Ellie. I will be in touch." I suddenly want to hug her, but I realize that would be crazy and completely awkward, so instead I reach out to shake her hand. She returns the gesture with a soft squeeze, her warm eyes meeting mine.

I watch her walk out of our store after graciously thanking us over and over again and securing her date with her Amex black card. Finally, able to breathe again, I whip around to go full fight club on Ellie.

"Jesus Ells! What were you thinking? You know I can't do this!" I move towards her, my hands planted tightly at my waist.

"Oh please, Liv, it was eight years ago and you've both begun new lives. You *need* to move on. You were eighteen! And besides, it might actually be good for you to see Parker again." Ellie finishes the transaction on the computer and returns to the large wooden worktable.

"Put the past where it belongs, make amends so you can really move on. So you can open yourself up again to love. You deserve love, Olivia. You deserve a man in your life who puts you first and gives you the feels. *All* the feels, Liv."

I roll my eyes. How the hell would she know? Neither of us are exactly experts when it comes to love. We're both in our late twenties and have yet to find "the one." Parker Bennett was the closest thing to it, and that ended a very long time ago. My chest tightens. Thinking about Parker inflicts this kind of reaction on my heart.

"And besides, do you know what this type of event will do for our business? It's the Bennetts. It's their Seaside Hotel chain... the publicity alone will take us next level."

I know she's right. The Seaside Hotel chain is listed as the place to be in almost every popular publication on the east coast. Influencers post pictures daily to their social media pages from the hotel lobbies, their rooftop pools and their luxe lobby bars. The Bennetts have been opening new boutique hotels yearly and show no signs of slowing down. Their properties are upscale and modern with luxury amenities like extensive pillow menus, custom toiletries and swanky lounges. The place to be seen, or so I've been told. Stepping foot into a Seaside Hotel means running the risk of seeing Parker. That's why I stay away.

"Olivia, there is no guarantee he will even be at the party."

I stare at her, my eyebrow raised. "Ellie, are you huffing something? Do you really think he would miss his parents' anniversary party?"

"Nope, you're right! He will definitely be there." Ellie grins and throws her hands in the air. "Can't blame a girl for trying."

Parker rarely comes home to visit since he moved to New York, but there's not a chance he would miss a family celebration. The Bennetts are close. They always have been. It had always amazed me, the way he got along with his two brothers and sister. As kids they actually loved spending time together. They always had each other's backs no matter what.

It's not the family dynamic I grew up with. My younger sister Kate and I weren't exactly tight back then, but that changed in our twenties. We needed each other to make it through the pain and embarrassment caused by our Dad. Now we are inseparable; along with Ellie, we are a three-pack. It feels good to know that I always have my two best friends to count on to bring me a bottle of my very favorite rosé when I have a bad day. After this particular bad day, though, I'm not sure one bottle will cut it.

"Ells, I'm not doing it. This is on you. You got us into this mess, and you will get us out. This is not up for negotiation."

"You are being ridiculous, Olivia."

"I don't care, Ellie!" I exclaim with a huff.

"Fine, Olivia. I'll take this one for the team. I'll do the delivery and setup alone at the estate and save you the horror of running into Parker Bennett," she states dramatically, her right hand to her forehead.

I can't help but smile. That is Ellie. She speaks her mind no matter what, never sugar-coats a thing. She also has the mouth of a trucker and just loves making me cringe with embarrassment with the innuendo that flies from her mouth. My brunette, five-foot-two bestie since middle school has stuck by me through it all - even when my family lost everything, when it would have been much easier to walk away. She is best friend goals and, apart from Kate, is the only person in my life to know what losing Parker did to me.

It is because she is the greatest friend a girl could ask for that I will not murder her and hide her body. *Joking, but I would be lying if I said the thought hadn't crossed my mind for a second time today.*

Ellie knows that taking on the Bennetts' anniversary party could be a huge win for our small business, and I can't fault her for that. I'll find a way to wipe Parker Bennett from my mind. I've done it once, I'm sure I can do it again.

It's a beautiful, sunny Friday morning and Ellie and I are busy with the Bennett order for tomorrow. Since Mrs. Bennett walked through the doors of Bloom three weeks ago, my world feels like it has been turned upside down. I am flooded with memories of the two perfect years I spent with Parker, before it all ended. I am also in dire need of a manicure after biting my nails right down to the cuticles. I know it's not a good look, but it's how I've always dealt with stress. That and a good five-mile run.

The only silver lining to this situation is that my part in the Bennett order ends here. *Thank God.* I still can't believe I said yes to this job; I must be a sucker for punishment. There is no way I will be stepping foot in their estate, though. That is all on Ellie this time, the deal we made still standing.

"Everything okay, Olivia?"

"Of course, why wouldn't it be?" I roll my eyes, jabbing a peony into the wet floral foam at the bottom of the vase.

"You just seem a little... edgy."

"The flowers have to be perfect, Ellie." I anxiously adjust three pale pink peonies and hold my breath. "This is a big deal."

"Olivia, you need to chill!" Ellie lectures me, adjusting the messy top knot that is secured with one of her signature scrunchies on the top of her head.

Since we started working together Ellie has grown accustomed to talking me off the ledge. She isn't rattled easily, where I can be a roller coaster of emotions.

It has always been a dream of mine to open and run my own business - a business that I would build from the ground up through blood, sweat and tears. I knew that I never wanted to depend on anyone in life, that I needed to be able to stand on my own two feet. It was a lesson I have learned the hard way.

When the space for the flower shop became available for lease, it only made sense to include Ellie because we did everything together anyways. We were sophomores in high school when we met and have been inseparable ever since. Having Ellie as a partner helped financially too, to get the business up and off the ground.

"You're not helping, Ellie. You of all people should know where I'm coming from." I tuck a loose strand of my hair behind my ear and narrow my eyes in her direction.

Ellie suddenly drops what she's doing, her eyes meeting mine. "Can we talk about what's really going on?"

"No," I answer defensively, hoping she'll accept my one-word answer.

"I think you might feel better if you get it out."

"I think I'll feel better when the coffee shop on the corner stops charging five dollars for a cookie. I can practically buy an entire box for almost half that price."

"Don't change the subject. I know what you're doing." Ellie rounds the table and brings me in for a hug. "You are going to be fine. You just need a few days to get over the shock of seeing his mom."

"I *am* fine, Ells," Taking a deep breath, I close my eyes and try to be fine. *I can do this.*

I pull back from Ellie's embrace. Her head is cocked to the side. She sees right through me. I'm not surprised.

"Okay Liv, if you say so." She shrugs, walking past me to fetch another vase. She's dropping the subject and I'm grateful.

I fiddle with the chartreuse hydrangeas and try to concentrate on the task at hand. Twenty-four pink, white and green floral arrangements for the Bennett party tomorrow. I have to admit, they are perfection. I really am proud of what we've created. There is no way I am going to disappoint Grace Bennett. I have put my all into her order but coming face-to-face with her son... nope, that isn't going to happen. Ellie will be driving the Bloom van to the Bennett estate tomorrow and will be placing the arrangements exactly where they need to go all by herself. I, on the other hand, will be sleeping in and enjoying the day to myself. Bennett-free.

We lock up for the day, hugging goodbye, and I wish Ellie good luck for tomorrow. Needing to clear my mind, I make my way down First Street towards the boardwalk that runs along the beach.

The laid-back beach vibe of the oceanfront streets paired with charming historical architecture set Reed Point apart from your average beach town. When I was a kid it was much quieter, but in the last decade it has grown into one of the more popular cities to visit on the east coast. At this time of year, the beginning of summer, the sycamore tree lined streets are buzzing with shoppers. On any other day I'd be one of them, window shopping the high-end boutiques and browsing the influx of pop-up shops that cater to the demand of tourists. Today though, my thoughts are too wrapped up in Parker.

How can he affect me like this after so many years? I have dated plenty of guys since our breakup, but no one has ever compared to him. I have never come close to feeling that spark like I did with Parker. With Parker, it was like gasoline to a flame. It was fire.

I make my way to the ocean and slip off my sandals. The feeling of my feet in the warm sand and the salty smell of the ocean is just what I need to clear my mind. I sit on the beach with my knees bent towards the sky and watch as the waves roll within inches of my bare feet.

My breathing slows and I feel a calm wash over me. My long golden blonde hair breezes across my face in the wind. I feel like myself again. It has always been my form of therapy to sit on the beach and listen to the waves. And it doesn't cost a penny. I have been coming here since I was a kid. My mother used to always say I was happy anytime I could see the ocean. She was right. It sets my soul free.

My life is good. I am right where I want to be. I own a cozy apartment that I'm proud to call my own. I own a successful business that turns a good profit. I spend my days at Bloom, working a job I love with my best friend by my side and I am doing it all on my own. I don't need a man to complicate things or mess with my heart. I have everything I need to be happy. *Don't I?*

But if I am totally honest with myself, I do miss having someone special in my life. Someone to come home to at the end of the day.

By the time I get back to my apartment, I feel much more relaxed. After a quick dinner and hot shower, I am tucked cozily into my queen size bed with a glass of rosé in one hand and a romance novel in the other. The perfect Friday night.

I drift to sleep thinking about how I will spend my day off tomorrow - they don't come along often. A morning run, a stop at my favorite bakery for a caramel apple croissant and maybe a lunch date with Kate. It's the beginning of summer- my favorite time of year - and the forecast for tomorrow is sun. I plan on making the most of it.

TWO

Parker

A knock on the door jolts me awake. I roll over to check the time on the clock. It's 7 a.m. on a Saturday. *Who freakin' knocks on your door this early on the weekend*? Whoever it is better have waffles and bacon.

I get out of bed, throw on my sweatpants and head for the door. I run my hand through my hair, making a half-assed attempt to look presentable.

I glance through the peephole and see Jordan, my assistant, looking wide awake and far too energetic for this time of day. It's a blessing and a curse living where you work. They always know where to find you.

My penthouse suite on the sixth floor of the Seaside Hotel has an unobstructed view of the Hudson. You can't beat living in Soho with its cobblestone streets, high end restaurants and designer stores. I have taken advantage of it all since moving to New York eight years ago.

We knew we struck gold when the previous hotel went on the market. And that's exactly when I packed my bags and made the big move from my hometown. When my dad had offered me the opportunity of opening the first Seaside Hotel in New York, I knew it was too good to turn down. Besides, I needed a distraction after everything that had happened in Reed Point. A fresh start in a new city, I thought that would do the trick. But here I am, still talking myself into that theory eight years later.

I haven't got a clue what time I made it to bed last night, but I do remember that gorgeous brunette I didn't take home. *What the hell had gotten into me?* She threw herself at me - literally. I had just taken a seat at the bar and ordered myself a scotch when she slithered onto the bar stool next to me and practically right onto my lap.

It had been a day from hell and all I wanted to do was have a quick drink and go to bed. But there she was in a low-cut dress that left nothing to the imagination. All I could come up with was a cheesy one liner: "You come here often?" *Man, I was off my game and had no idea why.* She didn't seem to mind.

I ordered her a drink and we made small talk. She had big, round dark eyes and full lips with long, wavy brown hair. She was to any man's standards a 10 and she was laying it on thick. I felt the toes of her stiletto rub along my calf as her eyes went up one side of me and down the other.

She made it clear she was mine for the night if I wanted her, but the problem was I didn't. And I was starting to realize why. I am heading home tomorrow. I am physically in New York City, but my mind is already in Reed Point. With her.

I had lived in New York for the last eight years and bringing women back to my suite has never been a problem. Relationships aren't my thing anymore, which suits me just fine. Running a multimillion-dollar hotel chain is what gets me off. And besides, no one has ever compared to her. After all these years, I'm not sure if anyone ever could.

The thought of going back home today has brought all of those memories right back to the surface. It's the reason I stay away from Reed Point. But there was no getting out of the anniversary party tonight; if I was a no-show it would break my mom's heart. I know how much she misses me, how much they all miss me, and truth be told, I miss them too. I want to see my brothers and my sister in spite of all of the memories waiting for me in Reed Point.

"Hey Jordan." I swing the door open to meet my early bird assistant. "You sure are eager this morning. You can't be human." I rub my eyes and motion him inside.

"Good morning to you too, Parker, and aren't you a vision. Late night last night?" he says sarcastically, crossing the threshold into my apartment.

"Remind me why I put up with you again?" I shake my head.

Jordan laughs and takes a seat on the couch, stretching his long legs out in front of him.

"Listen, you know your dad has been busting my balls to make sure you are out of this hotel in plenty of time to make it home by four o'clock. He has made it clear that your family, not your work, comes first this weekend. And you know your mom wants to spend a little time with you before the party. So, you my friend, need to get a move on."

"Ahh, he's got you doing his dirty work now. I see how this goes." I laugh and head to the kitchen to make myself a coffee.

"No offense, Parker, but there's no one I know with a nicer family. Why do you always seem so reluctant to go home?"

"Relax Jordan, you know I'm a momma's boy deep down. I like spending time with my family. I'm packed and will be ready to hit the road after a shower and some breakfast, so you can save the Dr. Phil shit."

I open the blinds to that view I have come to love and check on the coffee.

Honestly, Jordan is right. My family is the best. I grew up with two loving and supportive parents who still amazingly love each other after forty years of marriage. My two brothers and sister are my best friends. My older brother Liam, a hot shot lawyer, is the over-achiever of the family. He works non-stop trying to make partner at his law firm back home. Work has been, and always will be, the love of his life.

And then there is Miles. My younger brother is an actor who has a new woman on his arm weekly. He has homes all over the place: Los Angeles, Vancouver, London and he often stays in New York at the Seaside with me. He travels a lot while filming so I always love when I get to see him.

Juliette, or Jules as she prefers to be called, is the baby of the family. Like me, she works for the family business. She is head of marketing and social media for the Seaside chain and has an office at our Reed Point location with our father. I think he secretly likes having her under his wing. For the youngest member of the family, she has always been exceptional at bossing us all around. She hasn't always followed the rules, but she has matured over the years, thank fuck, and has a boyfriend who seems to make her happy enough.

"Has the email come through from Nelson?" I ask Jordan, grabbing two mugs from the cabinet above me. Nelson Baker is our corporate lawyer, he's been with the Seaside Hotel chain since the early days. He not only provides us with legal counsel, but he also provides business advice too. "Why does he have to make me wait on every small detail of this deal? I wanted to have this wrapped up before I went home to see my dad." I pour two cups of coffee and, after handing one to Jordan, sink into the armchair opposite him. I sip my liquid bliss, beginning to feel almost human.

"Nothing yet, Boss, but I'm on it. You'll hear from me the minute I know more. You know how he can be."

"This has to happen fast. I've got city inspectors ready to go in four weeks and the paperwork is still not signed." My gaze returns to the floor-to-ceiling windows and that killer view. Even after all these years, I can't get enough of it. It will be tough to leave it, but the new Seaside development means a move to Cape May – not exactly the New York vibe I've come to love, but business is business and I'm an all-in kind of guy. The thrill and the rush of turning a blank canvas into a Bennett boutique hotel is what I live for.

"That reminds me, have you booked my hotel in Cape May?"

"Yes, you are booked at the Pier Hotel in their executive suite. It's no Seaside, but you'll be right in the heart of the city. It is the best Cape May has to offer and it will work until we find you something permanent. But I gotta tell you Parker… your sex life is about to go down the drain. Unless you've developed a thing for the over 50's set you're pretty much fucked once you move there. Actually, *not* fucked may be a more accurate way of putting it."

"Don't remind me, Jordan, I've already planned the funeral for my soon-to-be murdered sex life. When I pitched this location to my dad last year, I forgot to take that into consideration." I massage the back of my neck where my muscles are tensing.

This will be our ninth Seaside property and there is no sign of it being our last. The Bennett formula has proven to work.

My dad took one small hotel inherited to him from his father and found a niche market for boutique hotels on the east coast. He has a brilliant mind for business and an instinct that has always steered him in the right direction. He has taught us to trust our gut instinct, too. If it doesn't feel right it probably isn't. My instincts are the reason I was so sure of this Cape May deal. I knew I wanted this property the minute I laid eyes on it. I can feel it, and I'm so close to closing the deal and breaking ground.

A move to the Cape will be followed by a year and a half of overseeing construction and then a grand opening to plan.

"Thanks for the coffee, Parker, I've gotta go," Jordan says, getting up and heading for the door. "I'll have your car ready for you at the entrance for 10 a.m. Good?"

"Ten o'clock is perfect. Thanks Jordan. Call me if you hear anything from Nelson. My phone will be on." I walk Jordan to the door and clap him on his shoulder. He has been my assistant since the start and he's damn good at what he does. He knows when to push me and when to give me space. He even knows I'm hungry before I do. It helps that we are close in age - he gets me.

After Jordan leaves, I hop into a hot shower. My mind drifts back to last night. How the hell did I leave that smoking hot brunette at the bar? And why? That was not me. Short flings are what I do best. No strings attached. I've had a few relationships since moving to New York, but never found anyone that could keep me interested for long. It's not that I'm a dick. I respect women and I'm always upfront and honest with them. I just haven't been able to find someone here who I can truly open up to.

With my bags packed I head down to the lobby, where I am greeted by the concierge.

"Hello Mr. Bennett, can I take your bags to the car for you? It is ready and waiting for you with cold bottles of water and your favorite clubhouse from Jimmy's."

"Thanks Charles, you've always got my back bud. How are the kids? And how's that adorable new granddaughter of yours? Got any new pictures?" I ask as we walk together to the car.

"Not today, Mr. Bennett, but I'll have some ready for you on your return. You be sure to drive safe now. We will miss you around here." Charles places my bags in the trunk and rounds the back of the car to the passenger window with a smile.

"You bet, Charles. I'm looking forward to seeing my family, I'll see you in a few days." I jump in the car, shoot Miles a quick text letting him know that I am on my way, and head for the Southern State Parkway.

Miles and I have plans to go for a quick run and catch up before the house fills with guests. It will be good to see him and I know it will be a good workout. Miles never misses a day of running and we are both competitive by nature, always wanting to outdo each other.

I have been driving for four hours when I exit the highway to Reed Point. As I drive down First Street, I feel my pulse start to quicken. I know that if I take the next right, I will be at the beach house where we spent so many days and nights together. Just the two of us. The thought of that one familiar turn is all it takes to bring everything crashing right back.

Olivia Madden.

The one girl I gave my heart to. My everything. My once upon a time.

I shake the fog from my head and continue driving to my parent's place. *Focus, Parker and keep on driving,* I tell myself.

I navigate my Audi up the long driveway and shift the gear into park. After taking my bag from the trunk, I make my way to the large front doors of the home I grew up in. Before I have the chance to knock, the door swings open.

"Hello, my sweetheart, I have missed you," my mother exclaims, greeting me at the door. "My gosh, am I happy to see you!"

"Hi Mom, I've missed you too, you look great. Are you ready for your big night?" I give her a hug and follow her into the family room.

"I am now, I have all of my boys and my Jules here with me. What more could I ask for? Your siblings are around here somewhere. I think Miles has been waiting for you." My mother beams, tidying the kitchen. "Oh, and Parker, make sure you are around for three o'clock, okay? Your dad and I miss you and I would like to spend some time with all of my children before the party starts."

"You bet, Mom. I'll see you then." I promise, pulling my suitcase towards the staircase and my childhood bedroom where I will be staying.

At nearly 10,000 square feet, the home I grew up in is a lot larger than most but it's still inviting with its warm hardwood floors, cream walls, large plush area rugs and pine wood beams in the ceiling. The walls are covered in family photos of every occasion and memory my mother can't bear to let go of. I remember the home always being full of family and friends, with my mother in her glory waiting on them hand and foot.

The spacious kitchen is situated at the back of the house with accordion windows leading out to the pool and grounds. That's where you can always count on finding my mother. Ever since I can remember she has loved to cook and bake and there was usually a fresh batch of cookies or brownies waiting for us after school. The scent would hit us as soon as we walked through the front door.

On my way up the stairs, I glance out the window at the back yard, which has been set up for the party. There are two long tables draped with white tablecloths adjacent to the pool. Party planners are busy setting the tables and arranging the chairs. There are tall round bar tables on the opposite side of the large rectangular pool in front of a bar where two bartenders are busy unloading mixes and spirits.

"Hello, son." I feel my father's strong hand on my shoulder. I turn around and give him a hug. My dad is just slightly shorter than my six-foot-two frame. He is trim and in good shape and the lines around his eyes are not so much signs of age as they are of his open heart. It is the aspect of my father's character I most admire. There is no doubt we are related. I inherited his dark features, his love of business and the Bennett charm.

"Hey Dad, it's good to see you. How are you? Has Mom spent all of your money with this party?" I tease, knowing full well my dad could never say no to my mother.

"It's good to see you too, Parker, and in answer to your question, I hope one day you too will know the pleasure of wanting to give a woman whatever she deserves." He winks and turns to see my two brothers heading in our direction. "That goes for these two knuckle heads as well."

"Parker, you made it!" Miles grabs me around the neck, pulling me into an affectionate choke hold. It is our standard greeting. "You still up for a run or do you think you can't handle me?" Miles laughs as I push him off of me and adjust the neck of my shirt.

"Handle you? I will own you. Let's go, asshole. Are you coming, Liam?"

"You guys go have your fun. Someone needs to work around here. It's good to see you, Parks." Liam, always the workaholic, turns to the den, where I'd noticed his makeshift office already set up for the weekend.

I run upstairs and change into a pair of athletic shorts and an old t-shirt and then meet Miles on the driveway. We decide to do our usual five-mile loop, which will take us along the beach.

I take notice how the weather is perfect today. Getting outside is just what I need to clear my cluttered mind. I had left my phone at home, knowing it would be too tempting to check it. I am making an effort to be present this weekend and leave work at the door.

"Tell me the latest, Miles, how's the movie going? Where are you at with it?"

"Just wrapped up filming last week and I think it's going to be a game changer for me. It's a different side to me than my fans have seen. And the chemistry with Natalie is off the charts. It's good, Parks, really good. I've got two months off and then I'm working on my next project."

"So, tell me, just *how* good was that chemistry with Natalie? She is fucking hot."

"She is more than fucking hot, but possibly the only girl I know who is totally out of my league." Miles chuckles. "She's the girl you would bring home to mom."

"Then she's totally not the girl for you, Miles." I laugh as our running shoes pound the pavement rounding the corner to the boardwalk. The ocean now in view, the waves crashing onto the smooth sandy beach.

"You're one to talk. You haven't had one decent relationship your whole adult life. You take 'smash and dash' to a whole new level," Miles says, upping his pace, making me work to catch up. My t-shirt now sticky on my skin, sweat dripping down my flushed face.

"Looks like you are getting too old for our runs there, old man. Might be time to sign up for a walking group."

I kick it into high gear. There is no way I am letting my little brother outpace me. The three of us boys have been this way since birth, always competing for first place.

We were born into a family of over-achievers.

THREE

Olivia

It is the day of the Bennett anniversary party, and my life is imploding.

When I answered the call from Ellie this morning, I knew right away that it wasn't going to be good.

She could barely make it through our phone call without heaving. She's sick- food poisoning sick - and there is no way she is leaving her bathroom today, never mind her apartment.

And you know what that means? That means the party is all on me. Shit just got real, and I feel an instant panic attack rising. I feel terrible that Ellie is sick, but this is the absolute worst timing!

"I'm so sorry this had to happen on the one day I promised I would be there for you," Elle had groaned. "Olivia, I know you must be losing your mind right now. But you've got this babe. You can do this. Just get in and get out. I bet you won't even see him."

Promising to call her later with an update, I press end on the phone call and scream into my pillow. There is no freaking way I am going to be fine today. How am I going to do this?

I jump out of bed and head for the shower. So much for my relaxing Saturday.

I shower quickly, then blow-dry my hair. I put on mascara, a smidge of blush and a pale pink lip gloss. My phone sounds, letting me know I have a text message.

ELLIE: I'm really sorry again Liv, I feel awful that I can't be there for you today. You can do this. You will be fine, I promise. And Liv, if he is there... remember it was a long time ago and a lot has changed. You are strong and you are brave. Remember how far you have come. xo

ME: Thanks Ells. You better have a bottle of wine ready for me just in case. Wish me luck xx

I slip on a pair of my nicest skinny jeans and a fitted ice blue sweater and run my hands through the long waves of my hair. I want to look my best. I am representing Bloom, after all. At least that's what I tell myself.

A hundred different versions of what could happen after stepping foot in the Bennett home race through my mind.

Best case scenario: I don't see Parker. The arrangements are all the party guests can talk about, and Bloom is later hired to do the flowers for all future seasons of *The Bachelor*.

Worst case scenario: I do see Parker. I panic, trip over a stray balloon string and land face-first in the Bennetts' anniversary cake.

There are about a hundred other scenarios that fall somewhere in the middle.

Will I see Mr. and Mrs. Bennett, or even Miles, Jules or Liam? Oh my God, will I see *Parker*? The thought of it sends me spinning. Ellie's not the only one feeling nauseous right about now.

I had run into them all over the years - minus Parker, of course. It never felt totally awkward, we would say the normal things that people say to each other, talk about the weather and such. Then we'd move on. They treated me with kindness every time, that's just the way they are.

I make myself a quick cup of coffee and a bagel while I contemplate changing my outfit. Maybe a dress with my leather jacket and heels. But heels make me nervous. I could just imagine myself taking a dive in them across their hardwood floors while carrying a centerpiece. That would just be my luck.

I check my reflection in the mirror one last time, and am happy with the way I look. I grab my purse and keys, taking a deep steadying breath before I head for the door. I won't let fear hold me back. I have come too far since then.

I drive straight to Bloom, letting the scenery distract me. It is one of my favorite times of year here in Reed Point with the azaleas and rhododendrons indicating the onset of summer. Restaurant patios are bustling and the city feels like it is coming alive after a long, cold winter slumber.

The weather is perfect today for the Bennetts as if they ordered it themselves. I smile, feeling the warmth of the sun on my face through the open window. They deserve a beautiful day to celebrate their milestone.

I park my white Prius in front of Bloom and hop out to a familiar face.

"Hey Jace, morning! What are you up to today?" Jace is a friend I met in college. We both studied business together - Jace going on to work for a local marketing firm here in Reed Point. Kate and Ellie have always tried to push us together but despite the fact that he is handsome and smart, we have never gone further than some harmless flirting.

"Hey beautiful, it's good to see you," he says through a smile, pulling me into a warm hug. "Are you heading into the shop today?"

"I am, but I'm not staying. I'm here to load up the van for an event."

"Is it just you today? Where's Ellie?"

"Ellie was supposed to be here, but she has come down with a case of Montezuma's revenge. It's pretty gross!"

"Well, why don't I help you load up the van? I don't mind. I have nowhere to be until later this afternoon."

"You know what, I'll take you up on that offer. Besides it will be nice to catch up with you." Jace follows me in and we head to the large coolers in the back of the shop, stopping to say hi to Leah, who works for us part time and when we have big events.

"These are beautiful, Olivia," Jace picks up the first arrangement and follows me out back to the van. "What's today's event?"

"It's the Bennetts' 40th anniversary party at their estate."

"Whoah, whoah back it up... are you talking about who I think you're talking about? The infamous ex?"

"Stop it, Jace. That is not what I need right now. A little less talking and a little more work from you would be great."

"Oh, I see I hit a nerve." He chuckles as we make our way back to the van with another armful of flowers.

"Ughh, you are impossible. Let's talk about you. What's the latest?" I ask, trying my best to steer the conversation in a new direction.

"Oh, you know, living the dream. Work is busy, love life is not. I'm back on the market, Olivia, now's your chance." He smirks and wraps his arm around my shoulder as we head back for the last two centerpieces.

"I'll keep that in mind, Jace." I laugh and push him away playfully. "What happened to Alexa? I thought things were going good between the two of you. I liked her, Jace. She was good for you."

"She wasn't the one, so I figured I shouldn't drag it out any longer. It wasn't fair to either of us, so I broke it off. I think she knew as well that we weren't each other's 'person.' She took it pretty well."

"I get that. And for what it's worth, I think you did the right thing. Now we need to find you a new girl." They don't come better than Jace and I often wondered why I never felt anything other than friendship towards him. He's smart, driven and handsome but I've just never felt that spark with him. "Thanks again for the help. I really appreciate it."

I walk Jace to the front door and give him a hug, then call goodbye to Leah before heading out to the delivery van. I take one last look in the small mirror in my visor and pull the van from its parking spot.

My heart is pounding as I turn into the Bennett property twenty minutes later. It feels like a lifetime ago that I last drove this boulevard, still lined with tall emerald green hedges. The iron gates are open, leading me down the crushed stone driveway. I remembered the feeling I used to get walking toward those large wooden doors with Parker after school most days.

A long time ago, this place was peace for me. It was warmth. It was the security I needed to feel when my home life was chaos. The Bennett house and the people within it would envelop me with love and comfort. Parker brought me here each day to give me that reprieve. He knew just what I needed.

Some days were spent swimming in the pool and others were spent on the large down feather sectional watching movies while his mother spoiled us with her baked treats.

Some days we would sneak away to the guest house that was nestled towards the back of the property. We couldn't keep our hands off of each other. We were magnetic.

Like a moth to a flame.

I can't ever get enough of you, he would say as he rained kisses all over me. I fell hard in his arms and only he could catch me.

He was my first in more ways than one and I have searched for that desire, that need, ever since. Searched, but never found it.

I nervously walk up the stairs to the front door, feeling my heart pound in my chest. I ring the doorbell and wait, anxiously fiddling with the hem of my sweater when the door suddenly opens to Mrs. Bennett. Happiness and warmth radiate back at me.

"Olivia, doll. Thank you for coming. I am so happy to see you." She pulls me into her slender arms, wrapping me in a hug.

I can tell she is doing what she can to put my racing pulse at ease. "Come with me. I'll show you where the arrangements should go. Cocktails and dinner will be served outside."

She leads me through the open grand foyer to the back of the house, through the kitchen and the great room. It is as beautiful as I remembered. The accordion windows are pulled open, allowing a perfect view of the meticulously set long tables by the pool. They are draped in white linen tablecloths with rows of candles of different heights. I can imagine how pretty their glow will be at night under the dark sky. There are tall heaters spaced around the tables to keep guests warm and the grounds and flower beds appear to have been freshly manicured. There are caterers, bartenders and others milling around.

"Everything looks so beautiful. Your guests are going to love it."

"Thank you, sweetheart." She beams.

Mrs. Bennett gives me instructions on where to place each centerpiece. "You are welcome to stay and join us Olivia," she tells me. "You know you have always been welcome in our home. And Ellie too, of course. Is she on her way?"

"Oh, that is too kind Mrs. Bennett," I stumble through my words. "But I won't be able to stay. Poor Ellie is sick at home and I should get back to her, and bring her some soup and Gatorade. I'll just get to work and then get out of your hair," I answer, itching to get my job done and then sneak out and put an end to this.

It is three o'clock and if I time it right, I can finish up here, drop off a care package at Ellie's and still make it back home in time for a *Housewives* marathon. What can I say, I am a sucker for trashy TV.

"That poor girl. I hope she feels better soon. And Olivia, I want to thank you again for agreeing to do this. It's so good to see you again. I hope life has been as good to you as you deserve." She smiles warmly, placing both hands on my arms, squeezing gently. For a second it feels like no time has passed.

Caught up in my thoughts, I nod with a smile that I hope doesn't look forced and then return to the van. I inhale a deep breath and begin removing the arrangements and placing them where I was instructed to, entering the home each time with a tremble in my hands and my heart at my feet.

I am just placing an arrangement on the bar when I hear my name. My spine straightens and I turn to face him.

"Olivia, are you responsible for my home smelling like fresh flowers? It is so good to see you."

"It's nice to see you too, Mr. Bennett. Happy anniversary," I stammer, my anxiety reaching its peak.

The genuine warmth in his greeting helps to calm my nerves. I smile, remembering how kind he has always been to me. He's dressed in his suit pants with a pressed white dress shirt, likely leaving his tie and blazer until the last possible minute.

"The flowers look beautiful, Olivia. My wife tells me what a great job you have done with your business. I am proud of you. Clearly you have an eye for it."

"Thank you so much," I reply, with a soft smile.

We are interrupted by Mrs. Bennett calling him into the kitchen. "Thank you again," he says as he turns towards the house. "I will have to pop by and see you for Grace's birthday."

"That would be nice. It was good to see you."

I struggle to keep my emotions in check. Mr. Bennett is a picture of contentment. I'm reminded why I was always so fond of him.

I make my way back to the van. Seeing the Bennetts again, and being back in this place where I once felt so at home-it's overwhelming. I grab the last couple of arrangements, relieved that the job is almost done. I place one on the kitchen island and the final one on the round marble table in the center of the foyer. I adjust one of the peonies and take a step back to admire our work. I pull my phone from my pocket, hoping to take a quick snap to send to Ellie, but it falls from my shaking hands to the floor. As I bend down to pick it up, I feel the energy in the room shift.

He's here.

I can feel it.

I have nowhere to hide.

I am afraid to look up. I swallow hard, feeling as though all the air is suddenly sucked from the room. Slowly, I stand up. His eyes meet mine. They lock together. There is no turning away. I feel heat rising up my neck. It's him. Parker.

He moves towards me, closing the distance between us. His dark, moody eyes on mine.

"Livy, what are you doing here?" I've always loved the way he calls me Livy, like it was reserved for just him.

"I... um... your mom hired me to do the flowers for her party. I, ..."

"Oh, that's right, I heard you opened your own business. I'm really happy for you." I chew on my bottom lip, wondering how he knows.

"Thank you," I reply, in barely a whisper. "But... I better be going." Damn, this is awkward. I need to get out of here.

He is wearing jeans and a grey Henley, and his thick dark hair is still wet from a shower. His strong angular jaw covered in stubble is the first sign I notice that he is no longer a boy. His sleeves are pushed up on his forearms revealing his toned, tanned arms and his shirt is pulled tight across his chest showing his athletic body. And those eyes. His deep brown eyes, the color of hot cocoa, sear right through me. They would trap me and never let me go if I let them. I need to go before I do something I will regret.

"Wait, Livy." Parker clears his throat and edges forward, reaching for my arm. His hand on my skin. An instant jolt of electricity passes through me at his touch, reminding me of our chemistry. "Can we talk? I'm here for the weekend. Can I see you tomorrow?"

"Parker, I don't think that's a good idea." I pull away, trying to keep space between us. I immediately miss the warmth of his touch. He smells like fresh rain and cedar and it's intoxicating. Dangerous.

"Just lunch, or coffee. I'm not asking for anything more." His mouth tips up into a gentle smile. That smile that makes me forget right from wrong.

"I'm sorry, Parker. It was nice to see you, but I really have to go." Not giving him another chance to change my mind, I turn towards the door.

"Please consider it, Livy. Meet me tomorrow. I want to see you again." The words slam into me. Every part of me wants to say yes, but I know I could never survive getting hurt again.

I pause at the door feeling that pull of energy to him. An energy I've only ever felt with Parker. It's undeniable. Why am I still here? I need to go.

I turn to him. His eyes penetrating. My lips part to answer him when we are suddenly interrupted.

"Parker, where are you?" My focus shifts to Miles at the top of the stairs calling for his brother. It shakes me back to reality.

Parker turns his glance to his brother, and, in a panic, I slip out the door.

FOUR

Parker

SHE IS GONE. I HAD A FEW BRIEF MOMENTS WITH OLIVIA AND just like that she's gone. Again.

I want to run after her, but I know it would do me no good. I know she can't be pushed, that it would only make things worse. But that doesn't mean I am giving up. There is something in me that knows I need to see her again. An ache in my bones. After all these years, it only took seeing her to reignite the spark and now everything in me wants- needs- to see her again. To touch her again.

She looked beautiful. No, beautiful isn't a strong enough word to describe Livy. She was eighteen the last time I saw her and eight years later she still has the power to destroy me. Petite at just over five feet with an out-of-this-world body that I had trouble peeling my eyes off of. Her legs in those skinny jeans and her slender waist and curvy hips.

Her full, pale pink lips and that smile that you only needed to see once to know you'd never forget. Long golden hair falling in waves far past her shoulders with sun kissed platinum highlights and her large round deep brown eyes.

I had seen her first, standing at the bottom of the stairs, and it felt like the world had stopped spinning. It took me a second to remember where I was.

Could she really be standing right in front of me, in my house, after all of these years?

I had crept her on social media over the years but her accounts were all private so I could never get very far. I knew she and Ellie had opened Bloom a few years back and I had driven past it last time I was in town, not sure if I was hoping to get a glimpse of her or not. I didn't see her. I had heard that she'd dated a few guys over the years, and it had stung me with jealousy. She was my girl once and I would always wonder what could have been if she hadn't pushed me away. I was in love with her. I would've done anything for her. It killed me when she broke up with me without warning. I never saw it coming.

I've never forgotten that day.

We had walked the beach after dinner and set up a blanket on the sand, watching the last of the vacationers leave for the day. The air was warm that night and we had stayed there for an hour, Livy lying between my legs with her back pressed against my chest. I'd wrapped my arms around her body, my cheek resting against her hair.

We watched the waves roll in and talked, in between kissing, about everything and nothing. She was quieter than usual but never in my wildest dreams would I have thought we would be over in a matter of hours.

We left the beach and drove back to her place in almost complete silence. I knew she was battling her thoughts, but I couldn't get her to tell me what was bothering her. She had been through so much, more than anyone deserved to go through at her age, but I had promised her I would be there for her every step of the way. And I meant it.

Pulling up to her house, I had put the car in park, and she turned my way with a look of defeat. She told me she couldn't see me anymore, that we weren't right for each other and she needed to end things. I was completely blindsided. My head spinning, I struggled to make sense of what she was saying. She couldn't be doing this, making this mistake. But Livy's mind was made up and there was nothing I could do to change it. We loved each other, that much I knew- but I couldn't beg her to stay. The rest of the night was pretty much a blur, except for the memory of my heart broken into pieces.

I left for New York three weeks later, after reluctantly accepting the job offer from my dad. My parents thought it would be best for me to get a change of scenery, to immerse myself in the distraction of a new city. They knew Livy and I had broken up, that couldn't be hidden, but I hadn't given them any other details. I was so damn protective of her and it felt like betraying her, to talk about something so personal with anyone else. My first instinct had been to stay and fight for her, but she wouldn't return any of my calls or texts. I stopped by her house a few times, but her mom would never let me see her, telling me that Livy wanted me to leave. I didn't know what else I could do.

So, I left for New York thinking that space was what she needed. I came back a few months later to try again. I had hoped she'd be in a better head space by then and we could work things out - but it was too late. She had moved on with another guy. I hadn't even been back in Reed Point for twelve hours when I saw her holding his hand walking down First Street. It took everything in me to not stop the car and go to her. Tell that asshole to fuck off, that she would always be mine.

As much as I wanted to, I couldn't do it. I couldn't take what was no longer mine. She, more than anyone, deserved to be happy. And if she was truly happy, then I had to let her go.

"Was that who I think it was?" Miles asks as he rounds the bottom of the stairs.

"It was Livy,"

"You saw Olivia?" My mother asks, rounding the corner from the kitchen. Her eyes widen at me, a perplexed expression covers her face.

I run my hands down the sides of my face and to the knot forming at the back of my neck. "Yes, Mom, and she just left."

"Did you speak to her?" she presses, as my eyes move from Miles to her, still wrecked with the image of Livy in my head. I am trying to commit to memory what she looked like after all of these years.

"We did, Mom, we talked but she was in a hurry to leave. Did you know she was going to be here?"

"Well honey, I booked Bloom to do the florals for the party, but I never expected to see her here in our home. I just assumed she would send someone else to do the setup. Parker, are you okay? You look light-headed."

"Yeah Parks, are you going to make it?" Miles chuckles as my mother's eyes pin him with a glare.

"Miles, your brother was in love with Olivia and it has been a long time since he's seen her. Give him a break."

"Exactly, Mom." I sigh. "It was a long time ago. It's no big deal. I just wasn't expecting to see her in our home. It caught me off guard, but I'm fine." I'm hoping the answer is enough to get my mother and my brother off my back so I can have some breathing room.

"Oh Parker, you know you have always had a thing for that girl. You've never been able to let her go. The heart wants what the heart wants, and you are powerless to stop it. You just have to go along for the ride. My advice to you, and I'm aware it is unsolicited, would be to go get her back." She smiles and turns back towards the kitchen, leaving me with that thought.

Typical. I am used to my mom guiding my siblings and I through life. Not pushing, just gentle nudges in the right direction. She has always been good at walking that line, giving us the advice we need but not orchestrating our lives for us. Her love for us is unconditional, never suffocating. And while she stops short of meddling, with four kids she has become an expert at handing out well-intentioned advice.

"What you need is a drink, Parks, let's get a sixer. Don't be getting all soft on me." Miles claps my shoulder and steers me towards the living room.

Miles isn't the type to get attached, so he would have zero clue how I feel. He has always been that way and these days it suits his movie star life perfectly. He has no problem sleeping in a different bed in a different city every night of the week. To some extent I have been living that way too. Walls up. Guarded. Never really feeling things. I'm not sure I have ever realized that until this moment, when I'm actually starting to feel something again.

Liam, Jules and my parents join us in the living room for a pre-party drink. Guests will be arriving soon and my mother insists on having some time with just the family, even if only for an hour. The family home is a gathering point for each of us, one we all like to come back to. It is probably much too large for my parents now that the four of us have moved out, but my mom doesn't hide her hope that it will one day soon be filled with spouses and grandchildren.

My sister moved out last year, leaving my parents empty nesters. She moved in with a roommate, a friend she met in college, and they live about ten minutes away in a two-bedroom apartment near the water. It is a quick commute for her to work at the Seaside or to my dad's office at the house and I know it makes my mom happy to have her nearby. Her boyfriend Alex is a nice enough guy, from what I've heard. I don't know him well because I'm not around much. But Liam gave him the stamp of approval after a good couple of months of hazing, so that works for me.

"There will be no talk of business today, do you hear me? I want to know what is new in all of your lives." My mother places her cup of hot tea on the side table, looking at each of us in turn. She is used to family gatherings veering off into discussions with our dad about the Seaside.

"I'll sum it up really quick for you, Mom," Miles begins. "Liam is working 24/7 and hasn't gotten laid in a year. Jules is still dating Alex and wondering when and if he'll ever put a ring on it and Parker is enjoying the many amenities that the Seaside penthouse has to offer, if you know what I mean."

I raise my middle finger at him with a smirk.

"Miles, mind your manners. I don't need to hear about any of my sons' sex lives or lack thereof," my mom shoots back.

"Whatever, Miles. You have a list thirty pages long of women you have discarded from your contacts," my sister snaps back. "I shudder at the thought of the tally."

My mother takes a deep breath, while simultaneously giving a death stare to my sister. It's an impressive bit of multi-tasking.

"And what about you, how did the movie go?" she asks Miles, turning her attention to him. "I know you said Natalie Landon is so sweet to work with. It's nice to know she has a good head on her shoulders. I know how those Hollywood types can be."

"It went great. Natalie made it easy. She was never demanding with the crew or other actors, she's a true professional and she works hard. I've got two months off before I start filming in Iowa, which I think will be cool. I'm planning a beach vacation in a few weeks and then I'll start prepping for my next role."

"That sounds wonderful, son. I'm thinking a trip to visit you in Iowa sounds like a great plan. What do you think, Grace?

It would be nice to visit a state we have never been to and we could see Miles at the same time."

"I would love that, honey. Now Liam, what's been going on with you? Is there anyone special in your life?" My mom is many wonderful things, but she isn't exactly subtle at times. We all know she is practically hearing the patter of tiny feet on the hardwood floors already.

"Nope, mom and I like it that way. I have zero time to worry about someone else. It's just me and Murphy and he keeps me plenty warm at night," Liam jokes, referring to his 80-pound golden retriever. "And besides, work is busy. I have a big case I'm working on and it's not an easy one."

I am only half-listening to what is happening around me. My mind is stuck on Livy, plotting what my next move should be.

I know it will be an uphill battle, but when I want something, I can be relentless. I don't have her phone number or her home address, but I know where she works. My mind is made up, I will go there tomorrow and talk her into seeing me. Stalking is not a good look, I know, but if it gets me more time with Livy then I will be the best damn stalker there is. I shake my head. *What the hell is wrong with me?*

Realizing that guests will be arriving in forty-five minutes, mom sends us off to get ready for the night.

I am staying in my childhood bedroom, which hasn't been altered since I left home. There is a row of old soccer trophies lining a shelf and a few souvenirs from family trips that feel like a lifetime ago. A wood desk full of old textbooks rests underneath the window.

I flop myself onto the double bed that I have long since outgrown, reach for my laptop and type Livy's name, hoping she's eased up on her privacy settings since the last time I checked. It's like Fort Knox trying to dig up anything on Livy. I also check her Facebook page, but have no luck there either. I try her sister Kate's social media accounts and find that she is under lock and key too. *Dammit!*

I give up and get dressed in my navy suit and white dress shirt and head downstairs for a drink. The party has begun, and the house is full of family and friends. I'm determined to have a good night so I hit the bar for a tumbler of whiskey and start making my rounds.

OLIVIA

STANDING IN FRONT OF MY FULL-LENGTH MIRROR, I ADJUST MY Lululemon running shorts and then make sure my ear buds are securely in place. Some people run to lose weight, some people run for a cause and some run to balance their minds. I am definitely the latter. I leave my cell phone at home, not wanting to answer the onslaught of texts pouring in from Ellie, and Kate. Both are clearly dying to know how the Bennett delivery went and if I had run into you-know-who while I was there. I'm not ready to be grilled just yet.

I had come straight home after swapping the Bloom van for my Prius, thankfully avoiding bumping into anyone I know. I washed my face with warm water to remove the little makeup I wore, threw my hair in a ponytail and changed into my running clothes. My body was still buzzing from seeing him, excitement rushing through my veins.

I had often wondered if the day would come where I'd see Parker again, and what it would feel like if it did. Now I know. The few moments we spent together reminded me of what that boy could do to me. His lips on mine, his hard body, my name falling off of his tongue. In an instant, it all came rushing back. He is still just as gorgeous, even more so. I didn't know how that was possible or even fair. Every part of me wanted to know what he felt like again, tasted like, but I couldn't let him get to me. He was an addiction I know I could never kick.

I leave my apartment and head out on my usual five-mile route towards the beach. The warm, dry air against my skin feels like comfort and my tension-filled muscles begin to release. My racing mind slows as I get closer to the water and I feel a calm wash over me as the ocean waves draw closer. I run along the beach towards the park then take a detour through town, feeling the air pump through my lungs.

I pick up the pace as my apartment comes into view, pushing my breathless body the last two blocks home. I slow to jog as I round the front of my building, feeling that runner's high that my body has come to know and crave since I began running in college.

Once inside, I scroll through my texts and emails, finding one particular text I knew would be waiting for me. It's from Ellie, wanting to know how the event went. I have avoided her long enough. I owe her the full story, so I shoot her a quick text back. I plan on heading to her place next so I can tell her all about it when I see her.

ME: Hey Ells, bringing you Gatorade and soup. See you in 30.

ELLIE: It's about time! You're holding out on me. Your best friend status is in jeopardy, woman.

ME: Not nice, Ells. *eyeroll*

ELLIE: See you soon. Kate is en route too. You didn't think she was going to miss this did you?

ME: You two suck so bad.

After a quick shower I throw on a pair of tights and an oversized sweater and tie my hair in a top knot. Good enough. I hop in my car and head to Ellie's, making a quick stop at Whole Foods for the care package. I snag a parking spot in front of her building and head up the stairs to her fourplex.

Kate and Ellie are lounging on the couch when I arrive, looking at me like they are ready for an inquisition. I decide to drag it out a little longer, heading into the kitchen and pouring the soup I had just bought into a bowl. I find a spoon in a drawer and bring both into the living room, interrupting their conversation.

"Does she look okay to you?"

"I'm not sure. You?"

"I don't think she looks okay."

Kate and Ellie whisper talk back and forth as I drop myself into the armchair across from the sofa the two are sitting on.

"I'm right here, and I have two fully functional ears. I can hear you."

"Well then for the love of God spill it now!" Kate demands as she pours me a glass of Pinot Grigio from the open bottle on the living room table.

"For the love of God, you are killing us! Dish now," Ellie adds, taking her first slurp of the chicken noodle soup.

"Okay, I'm not sure where to even start."

"Before you get into it, we just need to know... Did you see him?" my sister questions me, her brown eyes wide with anticipation.

"I did, you guys. I saw Parker."

"Oh em gee!" They both squeal.

"Okay, start at the beginning. We want all the deets."

"I can't believe I actually saw him after all this time," I sigh, dropping my head in my hands, remembering how ridiculously gorgeous he looked. I gulp down a mouthful of my wine and start to fill them in on my day.

"First, work: The event set up went smoothly and Mrs. Bennett loved what we did, Ells. She was so happy and the house looked so beautiful. She couldn't stop thanking me. Mr. Bennett even commented on how wonderful the house smelled. It was stunning."

"Please tell me you remembered to take photos for social?" Ellie asks, looking like a little color is returning back to her face after drinking half of the soup.

"I did Ells, I took so many and they are going to be amazing. Her house is magazine-worthy, so the flower arrangements looked even more impressive. I wish you could have seen the backyard. It looked magical; what fairy tales are made of. I am so proud of us, Ellie. Taking on this event was the right thing to do."

"Was it the right thing to do because of the publicity we are going to get or because you ran into Parker?" Ellie smirks. "Now get to the good stuff."

"You guys, I'm falling asleep with all this talk about flowers. Get on with it. Get to the part where he took you upstairs to his childhood bedroom and you slept together for old times' sake." Kate grins, clearly enjoying this.

"Seriously Kate, gross." I can't help but laugh. This is a different side of Kate than I'm used to. My sister is normally more reserved. She is a kindergarten teacher, and that is her true passion in life. She treats her students like they are her own and her classroom is always lively and full of creativity. We've grown very close in recent years, but I usually save the details of my sex life - or lack thereof- for Ellie.

I replay it all for them both, from the second Parker and I locked eyes until the minute I bolted through the door. They both groaned when I admitted that part, but I have no regrets. Whatever this is between us, it won't go any further. He lives in New York City; he likes his fast-paced life in a big city with lights and action. I've heard all types of action, which turns my stomach. I, on the other hand, am the exact opposite. I know I could never leave Reed Point. Leaving my family, my sister, Ellie and Bloom is not an option. And having my heart broken by my now playboy ex is not something I'm interested in chancing.

"It was nice to see him, but it wasn't what you guys think," I lie.

"Oh, come on, you've got to be kidding me. There had to be sparks. You go all wiggy every time his name is brought up." Ellie mocks, pointing her spoon at me like it's a weapon.

"I do not," I lie again. "It's all in the past. You guys are making this into a bigger deal than it is."

"At least tell us what he looked like. Was he fuckable?" Ellie always cuts right to the chase.

"Stop! He looked good. Okay, he looked better than good, but that doesn't mean I want to go back down that road." I insist. The lies just keep on coming like word vomit.

"Don't you think this could be fate, Liv, that you two ran into each other after all these years?" Kate questions me, a glimmer of hope in her eyes. I consider her question.

"I don't believe in fate anymore. It was bound to happen at some point."

"Did he ask to see you again?" Kate pushes, not letting it go. This is the question I had hoped they wouldn't ask. I know they will be all over me once they hear my answer.

"Yes, but I told him no. I hardly see the point in that. He's happy in New York and I'm happy here. And I would have to be crazy to take a chance on him. Come on, you've both heard the rumors of all the women he's been with. It wouldn't be good for either one of us to go down that road again just to go our separate ways."

"They're rumors, Olivia. You of all people should know about judging people without knowing the facts. Don't you think you should at least hear what he has to say? I really think you should re-consider, Liv. If you really feel like this is no big deal, then what's the harm in meeting him?" Ellie pushes.

"It's not going to happen. Time to give up, girls."

They stop pushing me, but I know it won't be for long. These two know me better than anyone and I'm sure they can see right through me, like a perfectly clean window.

I push all thoughts of Parker from my mind. He is my past. That's where he needs to stay.

One thing I know for sure - I can't fall for Parker Bennett a second time.

FIVE

Parker

I AM SITTING WITH MY FAMILY AT ONE OF THE LONG rectangular tables by the pool, the quiet hum of conversation occasionally broken by a peal of laughter or the clinking of glasses. We have finished dinner and are on to dessert.

The sky has darkened but the backyard is glowing under the mini lights wrapping the trees, the tall space heaters keeping guests warm. Candles surround the flowers running the length of the table. Seeing the flowers make my thoughts drift back to Livy. I'm trying to be present, to enjoy the evening, but the truth is I can't get her out of my mind.

Sitting across from me, my father's arm is draped behind my mother's back. They look so happy. It's enviable.

"Parker, let's get a drink," Hunter says from behind me, clutching my shoulder. Hunter and I have been close friends since our days playing soccer and football together in junior high. Back when we were teenagers, he was pretty much a fixture in our house, practically a part of the family.

I rise from my seat and follow Hunter to the bar where we find Jules ordering herself a glass of Riesling. I order us each a scotch on the rocks and hand one tumbler to Hunter.

"Hey Jules, drinks are on me tonight. Order whatever you like." Hunter jokes as we stand together at the open bar.

"Seriously Hunter, no wonder you are single with lines like that." Jules rolls her eyes and takes a sip of her drink.

Hunter laughs it off. He has known my sister for years and their banter is like a well-rehearsed routine. Jules knows that every now and then Hunter needs to be put in his place and she has no problem being the one to do it.

"So, Parks have you heard any word on the Cape May project?" she asks. "I know Dad is anxious about it but won't dare ask today and break Mom's *'no business talk at my anniversary party'* rule."

The sound of annoyance in my voice is evident in my reply to Jules. "Nothing yet. I keep checking my phone and not a word from Nelson. Jordan is on it, though, so I guess I just have to be patient."

"Like you even know the meaning of that word, Parker," Jules jokes. Even I have to admit she's right.

"What word? There are so many words Parker doesn't know, Jules. You need to be more specific." Liam laughs, nudging me as he joins us at the bar. “Did you tell Hunter who you ran into today?”

“No. Are you holding out on me?” Hunter smirks with one brow raised in my direction.

Not wanting to answer this question, I try to play it off as matter of fact as I can, “I ran into Olivia today before the party. My mom hired her to do the flowers.”

“Olivia Madden?” Hunter asks.

“Yes, Olivia Madden,” I respond. I didn’t plan on getting into this tonight.

“Interesting choice of florists by Mrs. B.” Hunter shoots me a questioning look. “So, how did that go?”

I’m not sure how much I want to say. Hunter can be a tough crowd. Besides, I don’t even know if I’ll be able to get Livy to talk to me.

“It was good to see her and that’s all you’re getting from me on this subject.” I take a long sip of the cold, oaky liquid, leaving my mouth feeling dry after it’s gone.

“Fuck, Parker. You really want to go down that road again? I remember the aftermath she left in her wake. You were fucked up for months,” Hunter says.

“Yeah Parker, I had to binge drink with you for a solid week after she dumped you. Wait, maybe it’s not such a bad idea, going back down that road,” Miles teases. “I’m always up for drinks.”

“You boys are complete tools. I can’t take another second. Since when did being loved by someone become such torture? You guys need to grow up." Jules turns and walks away, but not before rolling her eyes so hard I'm thinking it must have hurt.

"What's got Jules running away from you three fuck nuts?" Liam interjects, arriving at the bar.

"It's nothing. But what isn't nothing are our plans for tomorrow night. Where are we going? It's Parker's last night in town so let's make it a good one," Hunter announces.

"Why don't we hit up Catch 21? I can text Jonathan now and ask him to reserve us a table," Miles offers.

Catch 21 is one of Reed Point's newest hot spots, right on the beach. Our buddy Jonathan is the night manager, which helps because it's typically pretty busy. You can't beat the view of the ocean from the expansive patio covered in string lights.

We agree to meet for drinks, but in the back of my mind I know that might change depending on what happens with Livy tomorrow. I have one more day here before I head back to New York and it feels like the clock is ticking.

I take my seat at the table to finish the lemon thing that was served for desert when my dad catches my eye. He appears distracted, his mind somewhere else, and from the way he is looking in my direction. It may have something to do with me. My mother has left the table to mingle with guests, so he takes the opportunity to check in with me. He does that with each of us kids every so often, reminding us that he is always there with an ear and a shoulder.

"How's New York, son?" he asks, taking the empty seat next to me. "You know the hours you spend at the office are going to catch up with you. Life is short, Parker, you don't want to work it away."

"With all due respect, Dad, I think I learned about hard work from the best. You are the hardest working man that I know. Even Liam takes second place to you."

"You're right, son, I have worked very hard for everything I have in life, but you are forgetting one very important thing. I have your mother."

I wait for him to elaborate because I know more is coming. My father is a man of many words when he wants to be, and I can tell by his tone that on this occasion he wants to be.

"Parker, I do work very hard, but I come home every day to someone who loves and supports me and that makes it all worth it. Your mother and I worry about you. We just want what is best for you, we want you to be happy and fulfilled in your life. And we know how much happier you can be sharing your life with someone who loves you and cares about you."

"I am happy, Dad. I love my job and I'm happy doing what I do." I am trying hard to convince one of the only people on the planet who can see right through me.

"Think about what I said, Parker. Life is better with balance. You will find your work so much more fulfilling if you have someone to share in your successes." My father stands and places his strong hand on my shoulder. "I love you, son."

"I love you too, Dad."

I watch him make his way to my mother, who is busy mingling with her guests. He rests his hand on her lower back and kisses her temple. I think about the truth bomb he just dropped in my lap and wonder if I'm ready to settle down.

SIX

Olivia

I'M FORTY-FIVE MINUTES LATE WHEN I FINALLY ARRIVE AT Bloom. I was tossing and turning all night and slept right through my alarm. I have been replaying the conversation with Kate and Ellie over and over in my mind.

Were they right? Should I meet him and see what he has to say?

Even if I did decide to see him, I don't have his number. What was I going to do? Show up on his parents' doorstep like a desperate teenager? I wish Parker was all I had to worry about.

The timing could not have been worse, or more bizarre, seeing Parker after all of these years just as I was about to see my dad for the first time in ages as well. If this is the universe's idea of a joke, I'm definitely not laughing.

Seeing my dad feels bittersweet. I'm conflicted about it. Some days I am happy at the thought of having him back with our family and others I feel like I will never get past the grudge that I've been holding onto all of these years. Tight.

Watching my father dragged through a lengthy trial for months in a courtroom and on the six o'clock news every night, and then sentenced and taken away in handcuffs is not something you forget about.

"Look what the cat dragged in! You look rough." Ellie eyes me as I make my way to the back office to drop my purse and coat.

"Thanks Ells, so sweet of you to say. I blame you and the wine last night. Mostly you, though." I hang my jean jacket on the hook and take my cell phone from my purse, sliding it into my back pocket. Blaming my appearance on the wine I drank last night is a lot easier than telling her I was up all-night thinking of Parker.

Ellie laughs and pulls me in for a hug as I meet her at the large wooden worktable that we had found on one of our antique treasure shopping sprees.

I know I don't look my best, but I'm not exactly a hot mess either. My long hair is tied back into a ponytail and I'm wearing a pair of my favorite skinny jeans with a clean white t-shirt. I did what I could with my concealer to hide my tired eyes this morning and added a pop of color to my lips to brighten my face.

"I didn't mean it. You're always beautiful, but you do look like you have a lot more on your mind than you need. Want to talk?"

"Honestly, not really. I thought a lot about what you said last night and while I do appreciate your advice, I'm not going to do it. I'm not going to see Parker. I can't, Ellie." I bite my lip, hoping she will leave it alone.

"Olivia, I'm not going to push you. I said what I wanted to say last night and ultimately, it's your decision. You are a smart girl and perfectly capable of doing what's best for you. I'm dropping it."

I adjust my ponytail and smile, silently thanking Ellie for not pushing the subject. She can be feisty, so I realize that I dodged a bullet with this.

"There *is* something I want to talk to you about though, Liv and then we can drop the heavy topics and get to work. We talked a lot about Parker last night, but I know you have a lot going on right now with your dad as well. How's everyone holding up?"

She is right. As much as I try not to let it bother me, my Dad's return is consuming my mind just as much as Parker is right now. I know I need to have a talk with my mom about it sooner or later.

"I've been avoiding the subject at all costs with my mom. It's hard. You know she and I don't exactly see eye to eye when it comes to my dad. That hasn't changed, and it may never will."

"My mother has been waiting for this day to come and naively believes it will be just like it used to be. One big happy family. I, on the other hand, just can't get there. I still blame my father for ruining my life. There is so much hurt in my heart, Ellie. "

I run the tips of my fingers along the grain of the wood table, going back in time in my head.

We had lost our home. My mother had to sell our house to cover legal bills and the fine my dad was ordered to pay. So we moved to a new city forty-five minutes away, to a smaller, older home we could afford. I was forced into a whole new life, one I never asked for.

I lost trust in people, mostly in my father, and that spilled over into other relationships. I spent more time with my mother as most of the time she was barely able to function, not getting out of bed for days at a time, leaving me to do the cooking and the cleaning. Someone had to take care of Kate, so I assumed that responsibility, too, making sure she went to school every day on time, had clean clothes and did her homework. There was a huge void in my life all of a sudden when my dad left too. I was emotional and on edge a lot of the time. Then there were the stares and the talk and the whispers that were directed my way daily. I was *that girl.* I hated being *that girl.*

"I'm sorry, Olivia. You didn't deserve any of it and it wasn't fair. You know what you need? I'm not taking no for an answer. You need a night out with just us girls. I'll call Kate and make a reso, and we can have dinner and drinks and dance the night away. It will be so much fun."

"I actually think that sounds like a great idea. Let's do it." I'm not going to argue with her because I know she's right. I could use a night out.

Ellie beams. "I'm happy you said yes and made my life easy. I was fully prepared to harass you all day long if I had to. Just be warned: I will do what it takes to get you to come out and have a good time. Physical force, getting you drunk- you name it, and I will get the job done!"

I laugh and shake my head. "Seems a little excessive but I believe it. If I remember right, that's exactly how you talked me into that truly embarrassing karaoke performance the last time we had a girls' night out."

"Not even a bit too excessive. And for the record, nobody does Mariah like you do."

I exhale with a shake of my head and throw up my hands, making my way to the desk. I need to check on our orders for the day and make sure they have all been filled. Meanwhile Ellie makes her way to the coolers to check stock for next week.

It's Sunday, so it's a short workday and I'm hoping to sneak in a nap before we head out tonight. We close the shop at three o'clock so I should have plenty of time to go home, nap, shower and change for the night.

The bell above the door chimes, signalling we have a customer. I call out to Ellie from the back room letting her know I will just be a second as I make my way to the front of the shop. My eyes catch Ellie's.

"Ummm... I think he's here for you." Ellie stammers, looking towards the door.

I turn my head in the direction of her gaze and we lock eyes.

Oh My God. What is he doing here?

"Parker?"

I swallow hard, stopping dead in my tracks. My eyes not leaving his because they can't when he looks at me that way.

His eyes warm and a slow smile curves his lips. I first notice his hands in the pockets of his fitted jeans and my eyes move up his body to his short sleeve t-shirt stretched across his hard chest. He is the kind of guy that girls fantasize about.

He catches me eyeing him and my cheeks turn a shade of pink that must match the tulips on the display next to me. I'm sure he can hear my heart beating through my chest from where he's standing. He shifts his gaze down towards my mouth and a shiver shoots down my spine, remembering his lips on mine and how good it felt. No one else has kissed me with such heat and passion.

"Hi Livy. I hope it's okay that I'm here. I didn't know how else to reach you." Parker searches my eyes. He looks nervous, waiting to see how I will react.

"I think this is a good time for me to do that delivery," Ellie interrupts, although I think we had both forgotten she was in the room with us.

"Parker, what are you doing here?" I ask, the question comes out sounding sharper than I'd intended. I didn't mean to come off as rude, but his presence makes me anxious.

"I wanted to see for myself what all the talk is about. From what I hear Bloom is the only place in the city to buy flowers and apparently after my parents' party you are the talk of the town. I'm proud of you, Livy. This is amazing."

I feel my cheeks turn an even brighter shade of pink at Parker's genuine compliment. I've never been a girl who needs the praise of other people but coming from Parker it means something.

"I also wanted to see you, Liv. I needed to see if there was any chance you changed your mind about meeting me." He takes his hands from his pockets and I suddenly am wishing he would put them right back. His hands unnerve me, I want them on me. It was better when I couldn't see them.

"Livy, I promise it's just two old friends catching up. Nothing more." He runs his hand though his thick, dark chestnut hair and I die. His hair is short on the sides and long on top and when he runs his fingers through it, it falls over his forehead, making me want to put my hands through it and push it back.

"Parker, I can't. I'm sorry."

"You can't or you won't, Livy?" he asks firmly, taking a step towards me, closing the distance between us.

"Why does that matter Parker? It's just semantics." I want to take a step back, but my body betrays me, leaving my feet planted to the floor beneath them.

"It matters to me Livy. If you already have plans that's one thing, but if you are just refusing to see me, well then, that's another."

"After all of this time, what would be the point? You live in New York and you seem to be happy and I live here. I'm happy too, Parker. We've both moved on. Why rock the boat?"

"Look Livy, seeing you yesterday did something to me, and I haven't been able to stop thinking of you since. Can you honestly say you felt nothing for me yesterday after seeing me again? Because if you can, I will leave, and I won't bother you again. Can you?" He looks at me with his piercing dark eyes knowing full well what he does to me.

I fidget with the hem of my shirt. Parker knows me better than anyone, so I'm sure he knows I am flustered. I'm sure it is also obvious that I am fighting the urge to run my hands up his hard body and press my lips to his mouth. He looks so damn good that I wonder how he could still be single. How has someone not made him hers? I think again about all the women he'd been with in New York. I am not going to add my name to that list.

"Parker, of course I felt something seeing you yesterday, you were my first love. I will always feel something for you and that will never change, but that doesn't mean it's a good idea for us to talk again. I'm sure you can understand that."

I take a deep breath, noticing the frustration in his face. It almost breaks me to see him feeling rejected, but I have to stick to the decision I've made. Parker has the power to wreck me and I need to protect my heart at all costs, even if it means watching him walk away.

"Livy, I really wish you would reconsider. I'm in Reed Point until tomorrow morning if you change your mind. Can I at least give you my number, just in case?"

"It won't be necessary," I reply, shifting my gaze to my feet.

"Come on, Livy," he pleads as he moves closer and I can feel my body stiffen. I can see he's not going to give up, so I walk the few steps to the desk and grab a pen and a note pad, handing them to him. He scribbles something down and gives it back to me, brushing his fingers over mine. A spark lights beneath my skin, reminding me yet again of our connection.

"It was good to see you Livy." He flashes me a devastating grin, his eyes on mine, and for a moment I'm certain that he knows exactly what I'm thinking about.

I watch Parker walk away, my eyes travelling from his broad shoulders down to his perfect ass in those jeans. Adrenaline courses through me as the door closes behind him. I'm hoping I didn't just make the biggest mistake of my life. I look at the piece of paper folded in my hand and see that he'd written something else on it, too.

I won't give up, Parker xx

This man. Shivers are rolling over my body from this man and he hasn't even touched me yet.

ELLIE: We'll be there in 10. Be ready.

ME: Can't wait. I'm Ready! See you soon.

I put on my gold hoop earrings and a bangle and run my fingers through my hair to loosen the waves. I'm looking forward to tonight, to getting out *and* to getting out of my head.

I had managed to sneak in a 45-minute nap after work and a shower. I also had time to call my mom to see if there is any news on my dad's return. She still hasn't heard. Figures. My mother was used to being kept in the dark and being the last to know when it came to him, but she never gives up. I struggle to understand why. How it is possible to turn a blind eye to the lies and the stories he spun.

I know when the time comes, I will need more in a husband than my father ever gave my mother.

Honesty.

Loyalty.

Devotion.

Time.

I won't settle for anything less.

I check the time on my phone. The girls should be here any minute. It was decided without my input that Kate would be driving tonight so Ellie could get me drunk. I went with it because it was easier than arguing. Especially with Ellie. I never win.

I grab my cell phone and purse and make my way to the street to wait for them. It's a warm, clear night and I have to admit, it feels good to be out of the house. I plan on drinking just enough that I forget Parker Bennett ever walked back into my life.

SEVEN

Olivia

WE ARE SEATED AT THE LAST TABLE AVAILABLE AT THE NEWEST restaurant on the beach. It is packed with people sitting inside and outside at the most beautiful patio in Reed Point, covered in Edison lights and fire tables. Our table is indoors, on the edge of what will turn into a makeshift dance floor right in front of a long marble bar extending across the entire back wall.

I'm glad I agreed to a night out. I typically prefer a cozy night in with a glass of wine and some bad reality TV or a book, but this is nice for a change and definitely needed.

Ellie orders us a round of drinks to get the night started and I know I'm going to have to pace myself if I want to keep up with her.

"Kate, give us the goods. How did your whack-a-do speed dating lunch go today? I still can't believe you did that. Was it full of crazy cat women and gamer nerds? Please tell me you took a shower before meeting us tonight," Ellie teases, looking beautiful in a black strapless top and high-waisted skinny jeans, her hair in waves down her back.

"Leave me alone, you bully. Stop being so judgey. It wasn't all bad. There were some nice guys there."

"Like who?" I ask, narrowing my eyes at her.

"Well, there was a fireman, and an art teacher and this one guy who refused to tell me what he did for a living. He said the topic was 'off limits.'"

"What the fuck, Kate, are you kidding me? He's either a serial killer who wants to wear your skin as a jacket or he's a stripper," Ellie teases.

"Ooh let him be a stripper, did he have a hot body?" I add. "Oh wait, I got ahead of myself there. How would you know unless you took him to the washroom and undressed him and had dirty washroom sex? So... did you?"

"Really?" Kate rolls her eyes at me.

"Seriously Kate, did that not concern you at all? Talk about a red flag. Please tell me you filed a police report on that creep. How about the fire fighter? Did he talk about his hose and what he wanted to do to you with it?"

"Oh, for the love of God, Ellie. Could you be anymore cliché? He was a gentleman and never once talked about his hose, but there was this one guy who barely spoke English and he kept calling me Kitty. But it got really weird when he asked me to remove one shoe."

"What? Why? Please tell me there's more to this story." I rub my hands together, eager to hear the rest.

"Oh my gosh, this is so embarrassing." Kate covers her face with her hands. "It took me forever to figure it out."

"Jesus, no Kate! Did he want to check your feet out before committing to a date with you?"

Kate erupts in a fit of laughter, barely able to get the words out. "He had a foot fetish, you guys! He wanted to do sex stuff to my feet!"

We all lose it at this point.

"Sex stuff? I can't take it. What does that even mean? No wait, never mind, I don't want to know," I say as our waiter, with apparently impeccable timing, arrives with our drinks.

"Please tell us that you will never sign up for another one of these crazy town shit shows again. Stop the speed dating!" Ellie announces, clinking her glass to ours in cheers. We all take a sip.

"And then how would I entertain you?" Kate smirks, resting her chin on her hands, looking gorgeous.

Kate has always been the popular one, the girl with the social life and a line-up of guys who wanted to date her. She never studied because school just didn't interest her. She was a C student who preferred to skip with her friends and head down to the park or the secluded area of the beach. She has always been carefree and rolls with the punches, a dreamer at heart. I have always been the polar opposite. I'm quieter with a type A personality; I prefer things put in their place. I'm happy with a good book in a quiet space. In high school, I kept to my group of friends who enjoyed theatre and dance. I auditioned every semester for the school play and always won the role I was working for. I rarely broke the rules, whereas my sister felt rules were made to be broken.

There was one exception.

Sneaking out to meet Parker became a regular occurrence when I was 17. He would wait for me under my bedroom window after my parents went to sleep. My room was at the front of the house and down a long hallway from my parents, which made it easy to slip out without them hearing me. The home I grew up in was big - not Bennett estate big, but still pretty impressive. It sat on a one-acre lot, with a kidney-shaped pool in the backyard and lush, perfectly manicured hedges for privacy. I loved living in that house. Until the day it was no longer ours.

Parker and I would stay out late into the night, talking for hours. I wanted to know everything there was to know about the boy who looked at me like I'd hung the stars. It was only a matter of time before we took things further. We couldn't keep our hands off each other, our self-control was non-existent back then. We were love drunk teenagers.

One night in particular is etched in my mind forever. We had met as usual beneath my window and ran hand-in-hand to his pickup that was parked just down the street from my house. I think we both knew that night would be different, that it would change us both. It would change everything.

He parked the truck at a viewpoint that overlooked the dunes by the ocean and smoothed a blanket over the bed of his truck. The hot July night air hung thick all around and it felt like there was nothing else in the world but us and our beating hearts. We laid together on our backs in the dark staring up at the onyx sky counting stars and making silent wishes on the falling ones.

I still remember him leaning over to kiss me, one hand on my cheek and the other hand pressing into my hip. Our bodies pressed together as my arms wrapped around him, pulling him into me. I wanted it and I could feel he wanted it too.

We are written in the stars, Livy. He whispered in my ear and I was gone. Drowning so far in the depths of Parker that I never wanted to come up for air.

Ours hands were touching, grabbing, taking whatever we could get from one another. Our clothes were off in seconds, our mouths greedily tasting each other. We drew apart for a moment and his eyes locked on mine, making sure this was what I wanted. He was so sweet and kind. He didn't want me to feel pressured but there was nothing on that earth that I wanted more. He slid himself into me slowly, his eyes never leaving mine. I closed my eyes, the emotions running though me with such intensity it all went black and I saw stars. Beautiful bright white stars that rivalled the ones in the sky. He rocked back and forth taking it slow like he was afraid to hurt me. I asked for more and he gave it to me, harder and harder until we both came undone. I remember feeling the adrenaline pumping through my veins as he collapsed over top of me and whispered, he loved me. It was perfect. Our perfect moment, and I've never been able to erase it from my mind.

He brought me home later that night and we sat in each other's arms by the pool, not wanting to say goodbye. Once we started kissing, I never wanted to stop.

"Hello? Earth to Olivia!"

I'm jolted from the memory at the sound of my sister's voice.

"Ellie and I were just saying that looks like Jace at the bar, wearing the black button up?"

I look to my left, at the crowded bar. "Oh. Yeah, it is him," I reply. "Do you guys mind if I run over for a second? I should go say hi."

"If you don't, one of us will. Olivia, I don't get it, he is seriously hot. Look at him. How have you not slept with him yet? You have some major willpower that I don't have." I could be wrong, but Ellie might be drooling as she says it.

"It's not like that between us. We are just friends. There's just never been that spark. I'll be back in a minute."

I make my way to the bar to where Jace is standing with a friend. The girls are right, he does look good. Handsome in a pair of dark jeans, his black dress shirt with the sleeves rolled to his forearms, showing off his caramel-colored skin.

When I first met him in college, Jace was seeing a pretty girl named Faith; she was two years younger than us, from Rhode Island. It is probably one of the reasons we have never dated. It was impossible not to like her. Faith and I hit it off right away, spending Friday nights at the pub on campus with Jace and a group of friends we all had in common. Unfortunately for Jace, Faith had big plans and once she graduated from college, she packed her bags and her VW and moved to the west coast. A long-distance relationship worked for a minute but eventually it fizzled and Jace broke things off.

"Jace." I beam, surprising him from behind.

"Hey Liv. It's really nice to see you. You look beautiful." He wraps his arms around me, pulling me close. "Who are you here with?"

"Kate and Ellie." I motion to our table where they are sitting, clearly amused about something. Ellie's head is thrown back in a roaring laugh while Kate looks like she is on the verge of tears. "An emergency girls' night was apparently on their agenda today, so here we are."

"Nice. It's good to see you here and not working the night away. Hey, let me buy you a drink. Pick your passion." He motions to the bartender and I order a gin and tonic. He then introduces me to his friend Matt, who is standing next to us in a deep discussion with a blonde who is very obviously a fan of the push-up bra and wing tipped eyeliner. *I'm not usually this judgmental. I swear.*

"Are you guys waiting on a table or sitting at the bar?" I ask him. "I'm sure we could ask the waitress if she could squish you two in with us at our table if you want?" I know it's girls' night, but I also know the two single girls at my table wouldn't mind. The question is whether we can peel Matt away.

"That sounds fun, but busting in on girls' night also sounds dangerous."

"Trust me Jace, there will be no complaints and besides, the more the merrier, right?" I glance around the restaurant looking for our waitress to ask her for two more chairs.

The bartender hands me my drink and Jace and I raise our tumblers, toasting to a good night and great friends. My open V-neck sweater slips off my shoulder and down my arm. Jace reaches to draw it back on my shoulder just as my eyes move towards the main entrance of the restaurant. My heart seizes and my knees go weak as I brace myself on the bar. I am staring right at that beautiful man who once stole my heart, the heart that no one since him has been able to claim.

Parker is here, looking sexier than ever, with a look in his eyes that tells me I'm in serious trouble.

Parker

She notices me as soon as I walk into Catch 21. My eyes find hers immediately, along with the asshole who has his hands all over her. To say it annoys the fuck out of me is an understatement.

Who the hell is this guy and why is she with him?

Part of me wants to walk right over there and tell him to get the hell away from her, but I fight the urge, knowing that would only make me look like a jackass.

The room - full of people dining, drinking and out for a good time – falls silent in my head. It's just her and I alone in the space. Her full lips part and fall open as she meets my gaze. Her big, cocoa colored eyes wide with shock.

She looks good enough to eat in her off-the-shoulder sweater dress and high heel boots that end at her knees, her golden hair flowing in waves down her back. I try to keep my cool and keep myself together, giving her a half smile as I walk to my table behind Miles, Liam and Hunter, my hands clenched into tight fists. I will let the air settle between us before I make my move.

We are seated at our table inside and I make sure to take the seat that gives me the best view of the restaurant and Livy. The guys haven't noticed her yet and I'm hoping it will stay that way for as long as possible to avoid the questions and most likely a lengthy interrogation.

Our server comes to the table and Hunter is quick to order us a round of shots. Miles flirts with the waitress, who brings us our drinks a few minutes later.

"Easy on the tequila shots, Hunter. It's Sunday and Monday will come quick. Some of us have to actually work," Liam barks, lifting an eyebrow.

"Jesus, Liam, take your balls out of your purse and shoot the fucking tequila." Miles laughs, rolling his eyes at our older brother.

"What would you know about work, Miles? You play make-believe for a living."

"For fuck sakes. We get together how many times a year and I have to listen to you two bitch?" Hunter takes a pull of his beer, annoyance crossing his face. He looks to me, changing the subject. "Parker, any news on the Cape May project? Is it a done deal yet?"

"This deal has been breaking my balls, but I finally heard from Jordan a few hours ago. Nelson called him to confirm that it's all been settled, and we can start construction next month. The signed contracts are being sent to Dad's office tomorrow. Liam, will you have time tomorrow to go over them?"

"Yeah, I'll check in with Dad tomorrow and sort it out. I'll text you when I have a chance to look it over. This is going to be good, Parker. That location is prime, and I plan on taking full advantage of it."

"Great news, brother. I think this calls for another round of shots. The Bennetts are taking over," Miles announces, looking over his shoulder to flag down our server.

"What's going on with you, Hunter? Your dad still breathing down your neck?" I ask.

Hunter had followed in his dad's footsteps working at the family business, holding a title there that he never had to work for. His is a classic case of Peter Pan syndrome, a boy who, despite being in his late 20s now, still doesn't really want to grow up. Hunter works hard but plays much harder. He spends his money on expensive toys and on girls with expensive tastes and seems to have no interest in settling down.

We played on the same high-level football and soccer teams for years, Hunter always wanting the win no matter the cost. He collected red cards like they held value and could be traded. At school, Hunter walked the halls like the trust fund kid he was. Everyone knew him and wanted to be part of his circle, but most had it all wrong. Deep down, Hunter isn't the bad boy that he portrayed. He is good at his core and a loyal friend who would do anything for you. He just likes the rush of pushing boundaries and taking things too far.

I spend the next hour stealing glances in her direction. It's taken every ounce of willpower I have not to look her way every three seconds. Watching Livy at her table eating dinner with her sister, Ellie and the two guys from the bar is driving me out of my mind. The jealousy claws at me even though I know I have no right. In all honesty my eyes haven't left her for more than two minutes at a time. I've caught her stares my way too, giving me a glimmer of hope.

How could she forget that connection we shared?

There's little doubt in mind that if it felt that strong for me, it had to have felt that way to her too.

"Parker, did you hear a word I said? What the hell is the matter with you tonight?" Hunter questions me from across the table. Seeing how distracted I am, he turns his head, following my stare. A second later, he spins back around back to me with an amused grin on his face. *Busted.*

"Are you serious, Parks? Olivia?" Hunter challenges. "What is it with you and her? You've had your eyes focused that way all night. Are you two back on?"

"No, it's not like that." Raising the tumbler to my mouth, I shoot back the gold liquid, feeling the burn down my throat. I decide there is no point in talking about it. Even if I told him everything- that I was going for it, that I was determined to make Livy mine - he would never believe that I might be ready to settle down with one woman. I barely understand myself.

Livy is different. She is different than any other girl that I've ever been with. As soon as I saw her again the other day, I knew that I had to have her. Whatever happened in the past, whatever heartbreak there was between us, it doesn't change the fact that she is my girl. The girl. She always has been, and always will be. There is no other option. And I won't stop until she knows it. "Well then what *is* it like?" Hunter asks. "I've only seen you look like this once before and we know how that ended. Are you sure you know what you are doing? I just don't want to see you get hurt again."

"I just saw her for the first time in eight years and I'm trying to figure this out. You know how it was between us." I notice that Livy is getting up from her seat and walking towards the open patio.

"You always did have an intense connection, but you lead two different lives now. You live in New York. You love women. Plural. Do you honestly think you could leave it all behind for a high school crush?"

It takes me no longer than three seconds to make up my mind.

"I guess we are going to find out."

I stand up from my chair and follow Livy to the patio. I'm not giving up on her and I refuse to walk away. I won't go back home without a fight.

EIGHT

Parker

I FIND HER ON THE PATIO, HER BACK TO ME, THE FULL MOON shining down on her like a spotlight through the clear black sky. Her body aglow like it should be. A star. My star.

I move towards her, fumbling the words in my mind that I want to say to her. I need to get this right. I sense her body stiffen and know that she can feel me inches behind her. I'm so close I can smell her citrus and vanilla scent that has always driven me wild. The air is warmer than usual for this time of year and the energy between us is undeniable.

"Do you remember that night, Parker? You kissed me for the first time on this beach underneath this same sky?" Livy hasn't moved, but she knows it is me behind her without even turning her head. I place my hands on the railing on either side of her, closing her in, my chest so close to her delicate back. My lips almost brushing her ear.

"How could I ever forget my beautiful girl? I had wanted that kiss since the first minute I saw you," My mouth is so close to her skin, it takes everything in me not to taste her. I watch goosebumps shiver across her skin, an admission that her body gives mine. She is coming back to me. My girl, letting me in.

"You were that wild boy that I was scared to hand my heart over to. But I never could resist you. And you knew it."

"I think you have it all wrong. It was me who could never resist you, and nothing has changed after all of these years, Livy." I want to say more but I know I need to go slowly with her. I remove my hands from either side of her, letting the words I just confessed sink in.

I move beside her, resting my arms on the railing. I look out into the ocean, feel the salty, warm air all around us. Our shoulders touch, but it still isn't close enough for me. I want more. I want all of her.

"Oh Parker, you've got the world at your fingertips in New York. You don't want a small-town girl like me." The words drifting from her lips, her eyes still on the ocean.

"I ran away to that big city to try to forget about you. I've been with other women Livy, I am no saint, but I would never lie to you. As much as I tried to let you go, I couldn't. I compare every woman I meet to you and none come close. It's you, Livy. It always has been. Do you believe me?"

She turns to face me finally, her dark gold-flecked eyes meeting mine. "Believing you has never been the issue. It's just not that simple. So much has happened between us and we are not the same people we once were. This is all too much. Why would we put ourselves through this?"

"Why wouldn't we? What if it was all worth it in the end?" I brush a loose strand of hair from her flushed cheek. "Come with me, Livy." I take her hand in mine and lead her towards the three steps that lead down to the beach.

"Where are you taking me, Parker? I can't just leave my friends inside."

"Don't worry, beautiful, we won't be long. Do you trust me?"

"You better not give me reason not to." Livy answers back with a hint of humor in her eyes.

I give her my best smile, the one that I know used to drive her crazy, stopping at the edge of the boardwalk where the stone meets the sand.

"Take off your boots." I tell her instead of asking. Both barefoot, I take her hand back in mine. It killed me to let it go in the first place. It seems she didn't want to let go of my hand either.

The sun begins to set as we walk through the sand, away from the sounds and lights of the restaurant. I need to have her all to myself, no distractions, and I am hoping that leading her in this direction will help to remind her of how good we were together. So many memories live in this sand, on this beach, at our spot.

We walk hand-in-hand, our toes sinking into the fine white quartz sand. Hulking dunes are in the distance, the beach stretched as wide as a football field. It's just the two of us, under the stars and the moonlight.

"Do you ever come back here?" I see the tension in her face when I ask the question, feel it in her fingers that are still laced in mine. We continue to walk towards the homes that line White Harbor beach.

"I run the boardwalk often and come to the beach to think, but I never come this far. I ... um." She looks down, stopping the conversation from going any further. We both know the direction we are walking towards and what it means.

"Tell me about you, Livy," I ask, directing the conversation to safer ground. "What do you like to do these days? Do you still write? You always blew my mind with your writing."

"I do. Mostly journaling now, but lately the words haven't been coming as easily as they should."

"Maybe what you are missing is a little inspiration? Something new and exciting to write about." I squeeze her hand and give her a gentle nudge. Her lips curl a soft smile. I'm getting somewhere with her. I can feel the tension slipping away from her body.

"I'll keep that in mind when I'm struggling with writer's block. Enough about me, tell me about New York. Is living in a big city as amazing as I imagine it to be?" Livy was never comfortable talking about herself. She was always more interested in learning about the people around her. She genuinely cares about the people in her life, it's one of the qualities that I always loved the most about her.

"At first it was, it's easy to get caught up in the lights and the action of the big city. They're right, you know, when they say it's the city that never sleeps. But that can get stale pretty quick. I'm looking forward to a change."

"A change?"

"We recently acquired a new property in Cape May, and I am overseeing it. I'll be moving there next month when we start construction and eventually will launch the new hotel. I'm looking forward to being closer to home, to my friends and family."

"That sounds amazing, Parker. I'm really proud of you. You've accomplished so much. But I'm not surprised." She finally glances my way with a sweet smile.

I swallow hard, not knowing if I really want the answer to my next question, but I have to know before I can take this any further.

"I know it's none of my business, Liv, but I have to ask. Are you seeing that guy you were with at the bar tonight?"

Her smile widens and she lets out a cute laugh as she turns in my direction, catching me staring at her. For a second she looks like the girl I used to know. The girl who I had tried to forget for a very long time.

Does she have any idea what she does to me?

Her sweater shifts down her arm, exposing her bare shoulder. Without thinking, I reach out to gently lift it back in place, my fingers brushing against her smooth skin. A flush creeps up her face.

"Jace? No. He's just a good friend that I met in college. He's a great guy, but there's never been anything more between us. I'm not seeing anyone right now. Bloom is my only focus."

I exhale a deep breath. I've never been a very religious person, but I find myself thanking God she's not with the guy.

"Good, because I didn't want to have to kick his ass." Livy side-eyes me with a smirk and we both laugh.

We continue walking hand-in-hand, in silence, the salty ocean breeze moving through her long hair. I brush the loose strands from her face, tucking them behind her ear. She stops walking and blinks up at me. She stands there speechless, but still manages a soft smile, and I feel the mood shifting around us.

"I've missed you, Livy, and I didn't realize how much until yesterday, seeing you again." I want to kiss her, but I need to be sure that she wants it just as badly as I do. I will give her all the time she needs, she's worth waiting for.

I run my fingers down the side of her jaw, and her gaze turns down towards the sand. She is breathtaking and vulnerable and suddenly I don't want this night to ever end.

She tries to pull her hand from mine, but I hold it tighter and gently pull her along, continuing to walk in the direction of our secret spot. She seems lost in her thoughts. I can see the confusion in her eyes, and I decide not to push her.

"I think we should let the others know where we are, but I left my phone in my purse at the table. I don't want Ellie and my sister to worry about me. Maybe we should walk back."

"I'll handle it. I'll text Liam now to tell him where we are and ask him to find the girls and let them know."

I let go of her hand and I instantly miss the warmth of her. I quickly text Liam to let him know, adding that we could be gone awhile. He shoots me a text back almost instantly, likely already on his phone working, letting me know that he has it covered.

"Done. Liam will let the girls know. They are cancelling the Amber Alert," I joke, wanting to see that smile again, the one that can take me to my knees. She shakes her head and chuckles as I return her hand to mine.

"Always the funny man, Parker."

"Is that your way of telling me how handsome I am?"

"Are you flirting with me?"

"Is it working?" I wink and flash her my sexiest smile.

We are just seconds away from our spot, the beach house, so close I can see the veranda and the white-washed grey shingles, worn from the salty air and the sun.

It belongs to my family, passed down by my grandparents, and typically sits empty for much of the year. In the summer, we all take turns staying there, often coming together as a family on holidays like the Fourth of July, setting up tables in the sand for our annual clam bake.

Livy and I reach the path leading up to the beach house where we used to hide away from the world. This is where we came to be alone together, just the two of us. The walls of the small coastal home are bursting with memories. The veranda just steps away with a porch swing, red Adirondack chairs around a fire table, and a hot tub with an ocean view.

"Will you sit with me?" I motion towards the veranda. Livy nods and follows me towards the swing where we sit, our legs touching. I can't help but notice her toned bare legs on display since taking off her tall suede boots. It's taking everything in me not to run my fingers down them.

"I think the last time I sat on this porch swing with you I was eighteen and had just snuck out of my bedroom window. It's mind-blowing that we never got caught considering how many times we did that." She laughs a little, looking out into the ocean, the porch swing swaying gently.

"It's true. There could be an AC/DC concert at the foot of their bed and I'm pretty sure your parents would sleep right through it. It's actually impressive." We both laugh as she curls her knees up into her chest.

"I see you are still friends with Hunter. I saw him with you at the restaurant." I pick up on her attempt to shift the conversation from her parents. I want to ask her about her family and especially how her dad is, but I can see she isn't comfortable with the subject, so I leave it.

"Yup, still friends. I love him, but you know Hunter. He hasn't changed much. He's still kind of like a two-year-old, just with slightly smaller tantrums and a much bigger bank account."

I feel her body stiffen beside me and I'm curious why, worried she's re-thinking being here with me. She inhales deeply but doesn't move to leave.

"Does he ever visit you in New York?" she asks.

"He does. He heads my way every couple of months. We'll hit up a Yankee's game and he'll stay with me at my suite."

"Suite? Where do you live? Do I even want to know the answer?"

"Very funny. I live in the penthouse at the Seaside. It's not the Playboy mansion."

"Are you sure about that? Never mind, I don't want to know. I'm sorry Parker, I shouldn't have said anything. It's none of my business." Her eyes offer up a silent apology as she looks my way.

"I'm an open book Livy, it's okay. You can ask me anything. I'll never lie to you. So tell me more about Bloom. What made you decide to open a flower shop?"

"Flowers bring me joy. They always have, ever since I was a little girl working with my mother in her garden. We spent hours there, bringing seeds to life, and those are some of my fondest childhood memories. She used to say that gardening was an act of love of the purest form, that it made you look forward to each new season bringing change and new hope. I figured if I could take my joy of flowers and turn it into a business that gave me financial freedom, I could be happy. It's been a lot of hard work and late nights but somehow Ellie and I did it. It's been profitable enough to support the two of us."

"You should be proud of yourself. It's not easy to build a profitable business from the ground up."

"Thanks. You've always been supportive. Remember that time you supported my decision to get bangs? You really should have broken up with me right then and there. I didn't even want to be seen in public with myself, but for some reason you willingly did." Her mouth curves into a smile at the memory. She looks so damn pretty.

"Even with those horrific bangs - and they really were horrific - you were still the prettiest girl in the room. You always have been." She blushes again, and with a shaky breath stands up from the swing and walks towards the glass railing of the veranda, gripping it tightly.

I follow her so that we are standing next to each other, both leaning against the railing looking out to the ocean.

"Parker, you are killing me. I don't know what to do with myself right now. I'm scared. You come back into my life out of nowhere and make me feel things that I thought I'd never feel again. I could never survive losing this again. My heart couldn't take it. "

Biting her bottom lip, she turns to me and our eyes lock.

"This is worth taking a chance on. I'll prove it to you." I search her eyes, and they blaze right through me. They darken and her lips part and I can feel the desire pulsing through my veins. She wants this just as bad as I do. Swallowing my nerves, I reach for her. I've never wanted anything more in my life than her right now.

I run my hand to the back of her neck, pulling her into me, praying that I'm right and that she wants this too.

My forehead drops to meet hers, my lips hovering over her full open mouth.

"I want to give us one more shot. I want to take this chance with you." The words barely leaving my lips before I move in closer.

Our lips crash together as I pull her face towards mine, kissing her like I've never kissed her before. I press her back into the railing, my other hand moving to her hip and pulling her body into mine. I angle my mouth, deepening the kiss, needing more, and she whimpers in concession.

Our tongues sweep each other's over and over, frantic and feral like we could never get enough.

She tastes so fucking good.

I untangle my fingers from her hair, running them down the angle of her jaw, my other hand sliding from her hip up her ribcage to her neck to meet my other hand. I grasp her jaw with both of my hands as I run my tongue along her bottom lip, and she smiles with a sexy smile. I am so turned on right now.

A soft moan escapes her lips and it nearly does me in. My dick twitches behind my zipper, hard as a rock.

"I love your mouth," she whispers.

"I have a list about four pages long of what I love about your body. Jesus Livy, you drive me wild."

She smiles that sexy smile and I kiss her again, pushing my body into hers, showing her what she does to me. She winds her fingers through my hair, kissing me harder, sending a wave of heat up my spine. I don't remember a kiss ever feeling like this with anyone else but her. She tastes sweet, like an oaky vanilla wine. I can't stop.

Her warm body feels so good up against mine as I press into her, my dick hard against her stomach, her back still pinned against the railing. I thread my fingers through her hair and tip her head back, granting me access to her long, delicate neck. I trail kisses from her ear down her jaw and into the hollow of her neck. I slowly pull the neck of her sweater down over her tanned shoulder as I run my tongue across her collarbone, covering her in soft kisses.

Livy whimpers and drags her nails across my back to my shoulders, whispering my name in a low voice.

I groan. "Fuck Liv, you feel so good. I never want to let you go." I run my hand down her ribcage and back to her hip, feeling her curves, wishing it was her skin I was touching. I want to rip this sweater from her body and devour her. I trace my hand up her stomach to her breast. She stills.

"Parker, I can't." She presses her hands against my chest, pushing me gently back. Her eyes are suddenly scared and vulnerable.

"This feels so good, but what happens tomorrow? You are more than just one night to me. I can't do this and go ahead and get my heart broken all over again."

"I meant what I said, Livy. I miss you and I want you. Let's try to see where this goes."

"And how are we supposed to do that? You are heading back to New York in the morning. There is no point. This will only end in heartbreak and my heart can't take it again." She straightens the neckline of her sweater, her chest rising and falling with each heavy breath.

"I need to go back to the restaurant, Parker. I want you to take me back." She slips out of the space I've closed her into and walks towards the beach, away from me. Like a tidal wave out of nowhere, it hits me that I've lost her. My gaze remains on Livy, waiting for her to change her mind, to reconsider. She looks at me over her shoulder, her eyes pleading."Please, Parker."

"Livy, I..."

"Don't, Parker. I don't want you making any promises you can't keep. Let's just pretend this never happened and we can go back to the way things were. It's for the best."

I nod because there isn't much more I can do. I can't force her to want to be here with me, so I follow her off the veranda and in the direction of the restaurant, trying to retrace how this perfect night fell apart so quickly.

We walk back to the restaurant in silence, my stomach churning with the thought of never seeing her again. I pushed her too far too soon. I fucked it up and I'm pissed at myself. I see her eyes fill with tears and it nearly breaks me in two. It kills me to see her so upset.

We arrive back at the restaurant and stop to put on our shoes before going inside. I run a hand over my face, taking a deep breath, then decide she needs to know exactly how I feel. I turn to face her, my voice full of certainty, "I need you to know, Livy, that I can't forget tonight. There's no way I ever could. What happened between us means something to me. *You* mean something to me. I hope you will change your mind and give us a shot."

She looks at me like she wants to say something, but then changes her mind. Her hand reaches for the railing on the stairs and emotion fills her eyes.

She turns and walks into the restaurant. I catch my breath that I didn't realize I was holding and follow her inside.

So, this is it? This is how it ends?

Not a chance.

NINE

Olivia

ON A SCALE OF ONE TO TEN OF ROYALLY SCREWING THINGS UP, I am at an eleven. I kissed him. I actually flipping kissed him. I did more than just kiss him if I am being honest with myself.

What was I thinking? Okay, I wasn't.

How could I have been when he looked so good, smelled so good, felt so good? My pulse quickens, remembering last night. Shit, I need a distraction from the hotness that is Parker. And fast.

Whatever this is between us, it can't go anywhere. He doesn't even live in the same zip code as me and he's probably halfway home to New York by now. Plus, we are complete opposites. I'm ready to settle down in Reed Point while he is still the epitome of a bachelor. The thought turns my stomach.

I run my fingers over my lips remembering the way he kissed me, the memory seared in my mind. I have never in all my life been kissed like that and the way he touched me set my body on fire. His muscular body, hard and toned, those thick arms that I could have stayed wrapped up in all night long. *Why is it suddenly hot in here?*

I sigh, trying and failing to shake the memory from my mind. He looked so sexy in his fitted button up shirt with the sleeves rolled up, tempting me all night with his tanned, toned forearms. *Why is that particular body part such a turn on?*

No one has ever made me feel the way that Parker does, and I hope that I didn't make the biggest mistake of my life leaving him last night.

I take a sip of my coffee as the morning sun peers through my window, feeling the sleepless night I had just endured. I found my phone and my purse waiting for me inside my apartment when I arrived back home last night. Thankfully, the girls had dropped them off at some point in the night using the touchscreen keypad I had installed after locking myself out of the house one too many times. Kate, Ellie and my mother all know the code in case of an emergency.

I am scrolling through my phone, trying to distract myself at the bar in my kitchen, when a text pops up from Ellie.

ELLIE: So whose bed did you wake up in this morning?

ME: If I told you I'd have to kill you ;)

ELLIE: Spill it Loosey Liv.

ME: This angel slept in her own bed all by herself. Now apologize right now.

ELLIE: WTF! You didn't hit that? You let that man get away? You must be regretting that decision this morning.

ME: You would know, you're the queen of morning regrets. I've seen you walk into work in the same clothes you had on the night before more times than I can count. It's not a good look.

ELLIE: That depends on who you ask. I say it's called living the good life, Liv. You should try it sometime. I guess you found your purse and phone?

ME: Got them, thanks. See you at work. Gotta go, you're breaking up. Service sucks here, Byeee!

By the time Parker and I made it back to the restaurant last night, our friends were already gone, which was a good thing because I wasn't in the mood for company. I also felt a bit embarrassed after ditching my friends to follow a guy I knew I could never have.

Parker had offered to drive me home and since it was that or a taxi, I accepted. It was a quiet and awkward ride. I did my best to avoid eye contact by staring out my window, wanting to get back to my apartment as fast as possible.

He was a perfect gentleman though, walking me right to my doorstep. He didn't push me to talk, or try to kiss me goodbye, but the wrecked look in his dark eyes as I said goodnight almost broke me.

I went inside and closed the door behind me, then slid my back down the cool wood to the floor in tears.

Mondays are my favorite day at Bloom, a chance to get organized and plan our week. I contemplated taking today off, but decided the distraction will be good for me. I also didn't want to make Ellie shoulder the day's workload, so I stopped feeling sorry for myself, got myself ready and made the 10-minute drive to Bloom.

We need to put several orders through to our suppliers for some bigger events coming up, including a launch party for a new local up-and-coming magazine that has been getting a ton of buzz. We are excited to be included in the launch and about the publicity it could bring to Bloom, potentially expanding our clientele to the east coast. The magazine had agreed to a feature article about us in their new publication.

The phone rings and Ellie gets to it before I do, so I continue to go through our orders for the week. After a few minutes, she ends the call and meets me at the worktable where I've set up a makeshift desk to sift through outstanding contracts.

"That was Meadow Flowers. Our order is ready, but they can't deliver because their delivery truck has a flat tire. One of us needs to do the pickup if we are going to make that deadline. You or me, let's rock-paper-scissors."

"I'll save you the childish games that you get way too excited over and do the pickup." I roll my eyes and get back to work. I need to finish up what I'm doing and reply to two more emails before I take off.

"I see what you are doing Liv, planning your escape so you don't have to tell me what happened last night. You dined and dashed on me, remember? So you kind of owe me after being the world's shittiest date."

"I know, I'm so sorry Ells, I do feel really bad about that. Trust me, I had no idea that was going to happen. Actually, now that I think about it, you're at least partially to blame for ordering us a few too many drinks." I grin at her, knowing full well it wasn't the drinks.

"Okay, okay, you are forgiven," Ellie concedes. "But only because I desperately need to find out what happened."

"I got caught up in the moment. We walked the beach hand-in-hand and we ended up at his beach house." I drop my pen on the table in front of me and push the tips of my fingers into my temples. I squeeze my eyes shut and back open, inhaling a deep breath. "You know what that beach house means to us. It was like every single memory of the two of us together came rushing back."

I fill her in on the rest of the night and watch her expression shift from excitement to disappointment when I get to the part about how the night ended.

"That must have been pretty overwhelming. I can only imagine what it was like for you, being back there after all this time. But I still don't understand why you stopped it. Parker is hot as fuck. Like Leonardo DiCaprio hot, Liv." Ellie walks to the coolers, then returns to our worktable with an armload of tulips.

"What's not to understand? He's leaving today to go back to New York. He is probably halfway there by now. There's no way for this to work. As hot as he is, it would have been one amazing night followed by my heart shattering to pieces having to watch him go. And then I got nervous, too, that it would have meant way more to me than it would to him."

"I get that, but it doesn't have to be so black and white. Sometimes you have to put your heart out there and take chances in life. Stop trying to control everything around you and listen to what your heart wants. I guarantee you it wants Parker's dick." Oh my God. Did she really just say that? "It's not over for the two of you, I just know it. Maybe it's worth the risk," she says convincingly, wiggling her brows.

Could Ellie be right? I mean, not about the dick part. Maybe I need to stop listening to what my head is telling me and start listening to my heart.

I grab my purse from the desk and am fumbling inside for my keys, when I hear the bell chime at the front door. I look up from my search and my stomach does a cartwheel.

Parker just walked into Bloom.

"Parker, what are you doing here? You are supposed to be heading home right now. Is everything okay?" He looks from me to Ellie.

"Hey Ellie, I'm sorry to bug you two at work but I'm hoping I can talk to Livy for a second."

He looks hotter than hell in a pair of faded grey jeans and a white t-shirt. It takes everything in me to tear my eyes from his body. This is a really bad idea.

Ellie grins, giving him a once-over, and nods Parker's way, disappearing into the back room and leaving the two of us alone in the storefront.

"Hey," Parker says in a low voice and moves closer to me. "Can we talk?"

"Sure." The word falls off my tongue so quickly I don't have time to take it back.

"I'm not going back to New York until I convince you that this can work between us." His sexy dark eyes narrow and I get the feeling he's ready to convince me if he needs to.

"This can't all be done in a day, Parker." *But I want you to stay.*

"Livy, hear me out. I'm not leaving you. I'm staying right here in Reed Point. I'm extending my trip. My assistant is boxing up my things as we speak and shipping them to me. After last night, leaving isn't an option. It has all been sorted. I've already moved into the beach house."

The beach house.

Our spot.

I am completely speechless, letting his words sink in. I am also totally aware of the relief I feel suddenly rush over my body. It is clear in this moment that I want him to stay, to get to know him again. We could take it slow. That thought makes me laugh. Take it slow, when all I want to do is take his clothes off and feel every inch of his chiseled body. *Good luck with that.*

"Why do you have a smirk on your face?" Parker asks me, and I notice he's smiling now too. It makes him look even sexier, and I have to suppress the urge to kiss that smile from his gorgeous face.

I bite my bottom lip trying to hide the hot blush I feel covering my cheeks, wondering if he knows that I'm fantasizing about him right now.

"No reason." I clear my throat.

"You were thinking about me and how much you can't resist all of this," Parker says through a laugh, motioning to himself with a silly Vanna White-like gesture.

"Nice try." *If he only knew what I wanted to do to him right now.*

"Come for lunch with me today."

"That sounds nice, but I was just heading to our wholesaler to pick up an order we need for tomorrow." I reach for my purse, happy for an excuse to end this now, before I do something I may regret.

"Perfect, let me come with you. I'll keep you company."

I shake my head. "I'm sure you have more important things to do than be my assistant for the day."

"When the boss is as hot as you, it would be my pleasure to assist in any way you need." Ohmygod ohmygod ohmygod.

"It sounds like we would have to get HR involved." I smile, feeling a tingle deep down in my belly.

"Let's risk it. Grab your keys, where are we going?" *Dammit!* How can I say no to that?

"Fine, you win - but don't make me regret this, Parker."

"I'm on my best behavior, unless you'd prefer that I wasn't - that would be okay with me too," he says, holding up his hands.

I turn towards the back room so he can't see my face. I'm fighting an enormous smile, slipping so easily into the easy banter we have always shared. He follows me out the back door to the van and we hop in and hit the road. There was no way he wasn't coming with me. I am no match to his power of persuasion and never have been.

Parker reaches for the radio from where he sits in the passenger seat. "Are you still a die-hard country fan?"

"Yes, I'm a one trick pony when it comes to music."

He finds a country station and turns up the volume just a little so we can still hear each other talk. I sneak a peak in his direction. God, he's so handsome. His right arm is draped out the open window, and he looks so relaxed and easy going, like he doesn't have a care in the world. He's always been that way, and I've always been envious of how he is able to just live in the moment.

He shifts his gaze to me, catching me staring. "So, tell me what a day in the life of Olivia Madden looks like?"

"What do you want to know?" I have made up my mind that I want to be here with him and get to know him all over again, but I'm nervous. There is so much we no longer know about each other and it scares me that he might not be into me now in the same way he was. I hardly live a glamorous life – unlike him, running an upscale hotel in a gigantic, busy city.

"I want to know everything Livy. What makes you happy, what makes you unhappy, what you like to do in your spare time? Is there a certain extremely handsome man you are interested in?" He winks with a grin.

"Well, let me see... I love a good 5-mile run, I'm still not a morning person, I take a hot yoga class on Wednesday nights and if I was interested in a man, he would be tall, dark and very funny." I glance in his direction and find him smiling this adorably smug grin.

"I could probably help you out with that last part. I know a guy." *Good God*! He is charming and funny, and our chemistry is undeniable. He is edging his way back into my heart with every second.

"You probably could," I say, in a tone just above a whisper. "How about you, Parker? Tell me all about the lavish life you lead."

"You make it sound like I'm hanging with famous celebrities every night. I work non-stop, barely see my friends and if I'm out, nine times out of ten, it's for a business meeting."

That isn't the answer I was expecting, and it surprises me. What about the parties, the nightclubs, all the women?

"Then what keeps you there?" I want to ask him about the women he has dated but I quickly lose my nerve and go with something safer.

"I've been starting to question that myself the last couple of months. Don't get me wrong, it has been a great experience and I've learned a lot, but I miss my family, I miss having genuine connections."

"Hopefully you'll find that in Cape May."

"I am hoping I find that with you."

I instantly feel a tingling low in my stomach. *Is this really happening? oh my god oh my god.*

My heart is beating so fast that I'm thankful I am sitting down. I try my best to pull myself together. How do I respond to that?

"Okay." *Okay?* Shit, Lamest response ever. I cringe inwardly. If I could throw myself from this moving van and survive I probably would.

We drive for another fifteen minutes and I mentally pat myself on the back for managing to avoid making an ass of myself yet again. We park in the loading bay of Meadow Flowers and Parker follows me inside, insistent on helping. Mabel greets us at the door. She and her husband have owned this business for forty years and are my favorite suppliers. They are both in their late 60s and sweet as pie. They remind me of my grandparents.

"Hi Olivia! And oh my - who is this gorgeous man with you?" Mabel eyes Parker, drinking him in. "Hello handsome, I'm Mabel."

She extends her right hand and Parker takes it, raising it to his lips for a kiss. Just when I thought he couldn't possibly be more adorable. I stand aside so I can watch this go down.

"Hi Mabel, Parker Bennett and it's a pleasure to meet you," he says with a twinkle in his eyes.

"Oh sweetheart, it is nice to meet you too. Olivia, where have you been hiding him?"

"Parker is my assistant for today. I..."

He interrupts me before I can finish my sentence.

"I think what Olivia is trying to say is that I'm the best darn assistant she's ever had, and that she thinks I'm easy on the eyes too."

I roll my eyes and laugh. Mabel, I notice, is eating him up.

Dammit, Parker, could you be any more adorable?

I review the order before signing off, then thank Mabel and return to the van where the last of the flowers are being loaded into the back. I start the engine and we head back into town.

We make it back to Bloom just before four o'clock and Parker helps me unload the truck. Even with his help it takes about thirty minutes, making me even happier that I accepted. Suddenly starving, we realize that we skipped lunch. He leans on the counter, one foot crossed over the other, and drinks from the water bottle I just handed him. I catch myself staring, watching his Adam's apple move along his throat. He can even make drinking water look sexy.

"Let me take you for dinner, Livy. We could go for Italian."

"Are you not as tired as I am?"

"I've got a better idea. How about I grab takeout and I'll meet you back at your place? You can head home and shower and put your feet up until I get there? Sound good?"

I know what my answer *should* be, but my heart wants to say yes. If I'm being honest, my heart wants to say yes to a hell of a lot more than just dinner. I think back to Ellie's advice about taking risks occasionally. Before I can talk myself out of it, I give in. "That sounds great actually. I'm in."

His eyes light up and his mouth lifts into a wide smile. “Okay, give me your phone.”

“Why do you want my phone?” I ask suspiciously, but unlock it and hand it over, nonetheless.

I watch his thumbs fly across the keypad. “Parker, what are you up to?”

“I’m just making sure you added me into your contacts. I’m texting myself your number.”

Parker leans in and presses a soft kiss to my cheek, and I melt. How am I ever going to restrain myself tonight after fantasizing about him all day? Instinctively, I start to run through a list in my mind of all the reasons we shouldn’t be alone together, but then stop myself. For once in my life I decide to ignore all of my own second guessing. After spending the day with Parker, I know without a doubt, that I need to take a chance on him.

I watch him walk out the door and only minutes later, my phone vibrates in my back pocket indicating a message. I pull the device from my pocket and my screen lights up. It’s a text from Parker.

PARKER: Excited to have dinner with you Livy. See you soon ;)

I literally LOL, he has changed his name in my contacts to LOVER.

What am I going to do with this man?

I HOP OUT OF A HOT SHOWER AND SLATHER MYSELF FROM head to toe in my favorite vanilla body lotion. I pull my hair out from the top knot I swept it up in to keep it from getting wet and throw on a pair of jeans and a tank top. I don't want to look like I'm trying too hard. I add some blush, a pale pink lip gloss and am finishing up with a touch of mascara just as I hear a knock on my door.

Suddenly nervous, I run my hands through my hair one last time and open the door to my apartment.

"Honey, I'm home!" Parker announces as he strides through the door with take-out boxes in hand.

Don't get ahead of yourself, Olivia.

My body immediately warms at the idea of us making a life together, but I need to stop that kind of thinking right now. It feels like I'm standing at the edge of a cliff and at any moment I might jump right off. I don't know how it's possible to feel this strongly so soon. But then again, it's Parker- my first love and the only man I have ever given my heart to. I can picture a life with him, and I like the way it looks. This is moving so fast and it's scary, but it also feels good. Too good to stop.

"What's for dinner?"

"Thai food because I know it's your fave." Parker winks and carries the food to the counter.

"You remembered?"

"I haven't forgotten a thing, Livy. Try me."

"Challenge accepted." I grin and lean back against the kitchen counter, trying to think of a question I can stump him with. "Okay, what is my favorite movie of all time?"

"Easy. You love rom-coms. It's *Sweet Home Alabama."*

"How do you remember that, Parker?"

"You made me watch it more than a few times with you. I can probably recite the whole movie to you right now. Try me again."

I tap my finger against my bottom lip, trying to come up with another question while busying myself in the kitchen finding forks and knives to eat with. I'm looking anywhere I can but at Parker, the energy between us making it hard for me to breathe. I place the cutlery on the counter next to the take-out boxes and walk back to the cupboard to fetch us two plates. I place them down next to the Thai food and lean back against the counter.

"Okay... What am I most afraid of?"

"Easy again. You hate spiders. You are equally as terrified seeing a spider in a picture as you are seeing the real thing." He moves towards me, placing his hands on the counter on either side of me, boxing me in. His legs are open, my body between them. There's a shift in his eyes as he moves closer. His breath runs over my cheek and his lips land at the shell of my ear. A shiver runs up my spine.

"Am I right?" His voice is low. He follows with a kiss to my earlobe. I swallow hard because that was possibly the sexiest moment of my life.

Parker pulls back, putting a little bit of distance between us so he can look me in the eyes. I'm still caged between his legs, and my heart begins to beat faster.

His eyes capture mine and there's something different in them. They are suddenly dark and hooded and full of need. I stop myself from pulling his mouth into mine like I want to.

"God, Livy. I've missed you."

"Parker..." I whisper.

"I'm going to kiss you Livy and I'm warning you that if I start, I probably won't be able to stop." He's asking for permission. My body reacts, a pulse throbbing through my veins. I want to cross this line with him. I want to give us another shot.

"Then kiss me, and please don't stop."

He kisses me hard, his mouth crashing into mine. There's nothing sweet or careful about this kiss. It's greedy and frantic and I lose all control. He angles his mouth to take the kiss deeper and his tongue finds mine, pushing and pulling. He's kissing me like he could never get enough and it's driving me wild.

My hands explore his body, desperate to feel every inch of him. I run them down his back, digging my nails into the fabric of his t-shirt. A deep moan rumbles from the back of his throat. My hands travel back up under his t-shirt, removing it and revealing his tanned, toned body that I've been dying to get my hands on. Hard lines cover his torso, his abdomen. He's a work of art. His t-shirt falls to the floor in a puddle.

My eyes fall closed as he kisses me again. This time the kiss is softer and sweeter, and it dawns on me that I'm completely present in the moment, not over-thinking, not worrying. I'm giving in to what my heart wants. I feel fearless for the first time in a long time. I feel myself letting go. I need tonight. There's nothing more I want than to be with him.

His hands grip my hips, and he lifts me easily up onto the counter, never breaking our kiss. He pulls me closer, nudging his knee between my legs. His arousal grinds into me. His hands roam my body eventually finding my breasts and I moan, unable to stop myself.

"Is this okay, Livy?"

"Yes, Parker."

"You're so damn beautiful Livy. I've been wanting to do this all day."

"I want you Parker. I want all of you."

I don't care what happens after tonight. I want him now. I need him now. I just hope I will be enough. A pang of nerves suddenly hits as I remember that Parker is much more experienced than I am with sex. I push the feeling away and will myself back into the moment with him.

I run my fingers down the hard planes of his abdomen, almost drooling at the sight of his muscular body. I drop my head to his pecs, running my tongue along his nipple and gently pulling it into my mouth. I move to his other nipple, taking it in my teeth. His eyes close and his head falls back. I press a kiss to the centre of his chest and another at the base of his neck as he reaches for the hem of my tank.

He moves my shirt up my body and lowers his mouth to trail kisses up my ribcage. My body hums with desire, begging for more. He takes my shirt over my head and slides the strap of my bra down my arm. He peppers kisses over my collarbone and up to my lips where his mouth meets mine again. He pulls at my bottom lip with his teeth while pulling my hips into his, grinding his erection into me again.

"Parker," I breathe. "I've waited so long for this. I need to feel you inside of me."

"Are you sure you want this? Because there's nothing I want more right now than to be inside you."

"Yes," I whisper in a plea.

Parker grabs my behind and pulls my hips up to his, lifting me from the counter as I wrap my legs and arms around him. He carries me down the narrow hallway, peering through doors looking for my bedroom.

"Last one on the right," I manage to say into his mouth between kisses.

He finds it and lowers me onto the bed. His seductive gaze sears through me. His body hovering over mine, he lowers his head to my chest. He pulls the cup of my black lace bra down and circles my nipple with his tongue. My eyes close and my back arches into him, loving the feel of his warm breath on my body. He sucks and teases and tastes me, sealing his mouth over my nipple. I moan softly, letting him know how good it feels. He pulls his mouth away and moves to my other nipple, giving it the same attention.

"I want your clothes off, Livy."

God, I want that too.

"What are you waiting for?"

He reaches his hand beneath my back and unclasps my bra, throwing it to the floor. He presses a path of soft kisses down my torso and reaches for the button on my jeans. He unzips them, sitting back on his knees, and pulls them off of me, leaving me feeling vulnerable in nothing but my black lace thong.

"Fuck Livy, if I knew you were wearing these under your clothes all day, this would have happened sooner. You are so fucking perfect." And I feel that way with him. He makes me feel like I'm the most beautiful girl in the world. Any insecurities I have about my body are gone.

"Now it's your turn, Parker. Pants off. Now."

I decide that I want to be the one to take them off, so I sit up on my knees and begin to unbutton his jeans. He moves to stand at the edge of the bed and pushes them down to the ground. I'm given a perfect view of his toned, lean abs and the lines on his torso shaped in that sexy V disappearing into his boxer briefs. My gaze moves to his broad chest and thick arms that I want to be wrapped up in. He takes it one step further and slides his fingers into the waistband of his briefs, bringing them to the floor.

Holy Shit.

He climbs back on top of me, the weight of his body against mine. He takes my breast in his hands and rolls my nipple between his thumb and finger. I can feel it tighten into a soft peak, sending shockwaves up my spine.

Parker lowers his body to mine, grinding himself between my legs. All that separates us is one thin layer of lace. His strong arms flex and tense on either side of me as he holds his upper body above me. I run the tips of my fingers up and down them, watching a trail of goosebumps cover his smooth, bronzed skin.

"Can you feel what you do to me?" Parker growls in a low, sexy voice that turns me on even more.

"I can feel it."

He pulls back to his knees and reaches for my thong, pulling it down over my legs. He runs his fingers up my thighs and my body trembles in anticipation.

"Parker, I can't take it anymore. I need to feel you."

"I'm not rushing this. Be patient, baby. You feel so good."

I can barely breathe. The connection between the two of us is so strong. I've never felt like this with anyone else.

Having his body wrapped around mine makes me feel safe and whole in a way I haven't felt in a very long time. I want to move faster and at the same time I never want this to end. I could stay here in his arms forever and be totally content. I want to take a vacation in Parkerland.

I thread my hands through his thick, dark hair, pulling him closer. I need his body on mine, skin on skin.

He kisses me with those full lips that I want to devour as I wrap my legs around his hips, arching my body into him. Needing the friction, needing him inside of me. He moans the sexiest sound, and I can't wait another second.

"I need you now, Parker."

"Hold on, Livy."

He reaches for his jeans on the floor and takes a condom from his pocket, tears the package open with his teeth and rolls it on. He braces himself over me, guiding his length inside of me slowly. Our bodies join together. I lift my hips to take him deeper, feeling every inch of him. His dark eyes lock with mine.

"You feel so good," he groans. "Damn, I've missed you."

"Don't stop Parker, it feels too good."

We rock back and forth, our bodies finding a perfect rhythm. I dig my fingernails into his back as he drives into me harder, bringing me closer to the edge. He lowers his mouth to my collarbone, kissing the hollow of my neck and moves up to my ear, placing open mouthed kisses over the sensitive skin behind it. My body shivers and I tilt my head back to give him more access. I'm about to come undone.

I graze the soft, smooth skin on his shoulder with my teeth, the intensity taking me over.

"Yes," I cry.

I can feel he is right there with me. He laces my hand in his, pinning it above my head as he quickens his pace only to slow it right down again. I grasp his hip in frustration with my other hand, trying to speed up the motion. He finally gives into me, giving me exactly what I want. My body tightens around him and I feel my release starting to build deep in my belly. I squeeze my eyes shut and ride out the bliss that takes over my entire body. The orgasm hits me hard, with such force that I feel it right down to my toes. He pulses inside of me and his body tenses as I try to catch my breath. With one last push, he loses all control and collapses on top of me. He gently brushes a loose strand of my wild hair from my cheek and kisses me behind my ear.

When I open my eyes, he's watching me like there's nothing else in the world to look at. He grins and my heart flutters in my chest.

"Are you okay?" he whispers.

"I've never been better."

He rolls onto his side and gathers me into his warm body. I instantly want the weight of his body back on me. He lifts my chin and his dreamy eyes gaze into mine. "That was incredible."

"It was. It's always been that way between us."

Parker nods in agreement and, a warm smile lifts the corner of his lips.

"I want you to know that tonight means everything to me, Livy. This is right where I want to be. Right here with you. I understand if you need more time, but I need you to know that."

I blink back at him, eyes wide. I let his words sink in, words that set my heart on fire. I want to tell him that it means everything to me too, but when I part my lips, the words don't come.

He pulls my face into his, our foreheads together.

"You don't have to say a word right now. It's okay." He sweeps his finger along the edge of my jaw.

"We do need to eat something though. Should we pull ourselves from this bed and tackle the Thai food?"

I laugh. "Yeah, I think we worked up quite the appetite."

TEN

Parker

Livy looks lost in a dream, her long, dark eyelashes casting a shadow on her cheeks, her pale pink lips still swollen from last night. The morning light filters through the sheer curtains in her bedroom, leaving its glow over her.

I lay beside her, taking in the perfect view. I'm usually not one to stick around but literally all I want to do is stay here beside her and stare at her breathtaking face.

Never in my wildest dreams would I have expected to be here, lying in bed with Livy, but here we are after all these years and nothing has ever felt so right.

I sit up, carefully untwining our bodies so as not to wake her. I look down at her again. The bed sheet covers her naked body up to her chest. She is on her side with the sheet pulled tight, revealing the curve of her hip. I had forgotten how good it feels to be inside her. There is no coming down from this high. As much I'd like to stay here in bed all day with her, I know if I don't get up now, I'll have my hands all over her again. And after what we did last night, I know she could use the rest.

We barely got through dinner last night before winding up back in her bed. We couldn't keep our hands off each other, making up for the eight long years we had been apart. We moved from the kitchen counter to her couch to her bed, finally falling asleep in each other's arms just after midnight. It was the best sleep of my life having her warm soft body wrapped up in mine, which is surprising considering I have gotten so used to sleeping alone. I liked listening to the sound of her even breathing as she fell asleep on my chest, her body nestled into mine.

One night with Olivia, I knew now, would never be enough.

I fight the urge to wake her up, to put my hands and mouth all over her body, and instead slip out of bed and pull on my boxer briefs. We both have to work today so I make my way to her kitchen to make us breakfast. This girl deserves to experience my culinary skills.

I fumble through her cabinets to find what I need and get to work, trying to be as quiet as I can. Luckily for me, her kitchen is fully stocked with groceries and top of the line pots and pans. She could basically host her own cooking show in this place. I have everything I need to wow her with one of my famous breakfasts.

First up, coffee. Once that's brewing, I throw the bacon in a pan and get to work on the pancakes.

I'm anxious for Livy to wake up, hoping she's not having second thoughts about last night. I had hoped like hell we would end up in bed together when she agreed to have dinner with me, but I never imagined it would be as incredible as it was.

But does she feel the same?

What if it wasn't as incredible for her? What if she regrets it? I can't believe I've already started picturing a life with her. Fucking white picket fence and all. *Who the hell am I?*

"He cooks, too." Livy is standing in the entrance of the kitchen wearing only my t-shirt that lands just above her knees. Her hair is in a messy bun thing on her head and she's leaning against the wall with a slow smile curving her lips. Her eyes trail down my bare chest as I catch her ogling me and I fucking love that she looks at me like that.

"I hope you're hungry. Coffee is made too."

"You've come a long way." She looks incredible standing there in just my t-shirt and I drink her in. "I'm not sure the boy I used to know could boil water."

She tries to duck past me in the small kitchen, making a beeline for the coffee maker, and I can't resist pulling her to me by her hips. Her back curves perfectly into my chest.

I nibble on her ear and then press a kiss to the side of her face, wanting her to know what just the sight of her does to me.

"You are killing me in that t-shirt right now. You are every one of my fantasies come to life." I growl in her ear and she giggles, the sweetest sound. I pull her tighter into me and she tilts her head back so her lips can reach mine, kissing me slowly. I breath in her familiar scent. I want it on my clothes, on my bed sheets, everywhere.

I release her reluctantly to finish cooking our breakfast and she pours two cups of coffee, one for each of us.

"How do you like your coffee?"

"Black works. Thanks babe." The word slips effortlessly from my mouth. I'm not sure what we are yet to each other, but I know I can't rush things. We made so much progress last night and I don't want to lose that. I want to keep this moving forward.

I plate the pancakes and bacon for the two of us and place them on her small round dining table. She sits and I take the seat beside her so I can be closer to her. My knee leans against hers as I sit back into my chair.

"So, what's your plan for today?" I'm really hoping to get more time with her. Last night was a breakthrough for us and I want her to know that I'm committed to seeing where we can go from here.

"Ellie and I have that event today to prep for so it's going to be a long one. How about you?"

"I guess I'll resign my position as your number one assistant and head into the office. I'm sure there's a lot to catch up on considering I haven't bothered to check my emails for a full twenty-four hours." I'm starting to not even recognize myself. It feels surprisingly good to focus on something other than work.

"I hope I'll be able to get all my work done without you." She grins before taking a sip of her coffee.

"I can be on call in case of a flower catastrophe," I joke, noticing Livy's smile doesn't quite reach her eyes.

She picks at the pancakes on her plate with her fork before nervously asking me, "Parker, can I ask you something?"

"Ask me anything Livy, I'll tell you anything you want to know. I'm an open book when it comes to you." I look her in the eyes, hoping she will see that I mean it.

"Have you really thought your decision through to stay here for a while? I don't want to come between you and your work."

I want to put her mind at ease, to reassure her that I can work effectively from here for a little while. I don't want her to think for a second that being here with her is an inconvenience.

"I absolutely have. There's nothing I do behind my desk in New York that I can't do from here. Besides, it will be good to work along-side my dad and Jules for a while. It's long overdue, actually. I've been meaning to come back and work with the Reed Point team, and now have an added incentive to stay... a very sexy incentive." I wink and nudge her foot with my toes under the table.

"Now let's talk about tonight. Can I see you later?" I turn to face her in my seat. I drop my hand to her thigh, gently squeezing it. I swing her body to face me, leaning forward to kiss her. "Dinner with me? Let me take you out somewhere nice."

"I would love that, Parker," she answers with very little hesitation in her voice and I can't help but lean into her again, pressing another slow kiss to her lips. I can't get enough of her mouth on mine.

"Perfect, I'll pick you up at seven."

I grab her empty plate and her coffee mug and straighten up the kitchen as she watches me from her chair with a playful look on her face. Her tanned bare legs stretch out in front of her, toned from her daily runs. My dick takes notice too.

"I think we should add housekeeper to your list of jobs, right after floral assistant and chef."

"Don't forget to add sex machine to that list too," I joke. We both laugh as she tosses her napkin at me and I turn around to adjust what is currently happening in my briefs.

"Time for a quick shower before work? We can save water and shower together. It would only be the right thing to do for the environment. You know, save the earth." I stick out my bottom lip and flash her my best puppy dog eyes.

"I'm sure that's what you are worried about." She rolls her eyes. "I *do* have to take a shower. Whether or not you join me is up to you."

Livy reaches for the hem of her t-shirt -my t-shirt- and pulls it over her head in the sexiest way possible, giving me the most unbelievable view of her bare back and that ass that I can't get enough of. This might be the best Tuesday of my life.

I'M IN THE MIDDLE OF A MEETING THAT SEEMS TO BE LASTING all day. I keep reminding myself to focus on the conversation going on around me, but my mind keeps drifting to Livy lying naked on her bed, Livy dripping wet in the shower and the best night of sex of my life. Talking business usually amps me up but today I'm short on patience. This meeting needs to end before I lose it completely. The thought of stabbing my eye out with my pencil comes briefly to mind.

I discreetly tap out a text to Livy to see how her day is going.

Can't wait for our date tonight. Get ready, it's going to be fun xo

I lock my phone and place it on the boardroom table. I'm sitting across from my father and Liam and my father's secretary Erin, discussing the Cape May project. Liam went over the contracts yesterday, so we are signing off on them today. Everything seems to be in order, so we are breathing a little easier and excited to get started on construction.

We have yet to address the elephant in the room, the question of why I chose to put off my return to New York. I can tell that they are wondering and waiting for me to bring up the subject but I'm enjoying watching them squirm. I really have no problem sharing my news about Livy with my family, but I thought it would be best to do it after we finished talking shop.

My mind continues to wander to last night, in particular to one moment that is stamped in my mind, when Livy said *I want you Parker. I want all of you.* The lust in those heart-breaker eyes and her shallow breathing as she gave herself over to me. My dick perks up in my pants just thinking about it. I send him a message to chill and calm down. *Now's not the time.*

I'm interrupted by a knock at the office door as my sister Jules walks in and takes a seat at the long rectangular cherry wood table. This table holds many memories for me. My mom used to bring me and my brothers and sister to the office on weekends to visit my dad and we would sit around this table and watch him work. All these years later, I still remember the pride on his face when I started working for his company.

"Good morning, Juliette. Do you need me for something?" My father asks as Jules sits down on a leather swivel chair beside me.

"No, I'm good Dad. I just needed a break from my computer. I knew you were all in a meeting, so I thought I'd drop by. I also wanted to know why my brother here extended his stay?" Jules eyes me with a smirk.

"Leave it to Jules to be the only one in the room with the balls to ask," Liam teases, clearly waiting for my answer.

I clear my throat. "I spent some time with Olivia over the weekend and I'm not ready to leave her. I thought I would stay at the beach house for a few weeks and work from here. I want to see where it goes with the two of us."

"It must have been quite the weekend if you are willing to stay here longer than forty-eight hours. Please spare us the details though," Jules warns, swiveling in her seat.

If they only knew.

"Son, it's no secret that we adore Olivia, we always have. You stay here as long as you need. The beach house is yours."

"Thanks, Dad. I don't want you to worry. I won't let my personal life get in the way of work. Everything is running smoothly with Cape May and Jordan has New York under control. I will check in with him throughout the day."

"I know how hard you work. I'm not concerned for a second that your tasks will suffer - in fact I am elated that you are finally prioritizing what's really important in life. Your mother and I have been waiting for the day when you found someone who makes you realize that there is more to life than work. I hope things work out between the two of you."

"I've always liked her, and Dad is right, you do work too much," Liam adds. "And let's face it: we all figured you'd end up with her, it was only a matter of time. You just seem to be the last one to figure it out."

"Woah, slow down. This is all brand new, and Livy is still nervous. I'm going to have to take things slow with her."

"All the best things in life take time, son. Have patience and I'm sure she'll come around and learn to trust you." My father's eyes meet mine from across the table and I can tell he is speaking from experience.

"Guys, I'd love to stay and help plan the wedding, but I've got work to do. Parker, go get your girl. I'll be at my office if something pops up with the Cape May project and you need my help." Liam pushes his chair back and stands, patting our dad on his shoulder before leaving the room.

"Just an idea, Parks. If you really want to win her over, you should give James a call. He is always offering up his vacation home for us to use. It's so beautiful there and I bet Livy would love that little town with all those cute shops and galleries. You should give him a call and see if you can stay there for a night or two."

"That's a great idea, Jules. I think I might just do that." James is my cousin and owns a beautiful vacation property right on the ocean with a private dock and a sexy 32-foot Sea Ray

Sundancer, a cruiser boat with a small cabin below and a lounge area up top. My sister is right, Livy would love it there.

My phone vibrates on the table and my heart just about jumps through my chest. I realize immediately that I'm hoping to see Livy's name. I pick it up but am disappointed to see a text from Jordan. It has been an hour since I messaged Livy and no response. I hope she's just busy. She seemed okay this morning when I left her. I pray she is not having second thoughts.

I decide to shoot her another text, not able to stop myself.

Is it weird that I miss you already? Can't wait to see you. ;)

I spend the rest of the day lining up meetings with our architects and project managers for Cape May. I've taken over a spare office that we use as a shared space whenever Liam or I need a place to work. It is a busy afternoon playing catch-up after all the work I missed the day before, and I end up skipping lunch. I've checked my phone at least a thousand times this afternoon and still no reply from Livy.

I pick up the phone to call Jordan when I'm interrupted by a knock at my door.

"Come in."

Jules walks in with a paper bag in her hand.

"I haven't seen you leave your office all day so I figured I would pick you up some lunch. Hope you are hungry, it's a turkey clubhouse from my favourite place down the block."

"You are one hundred percent my favorite sister."

"I'm your only sister you dimwit." She moves into the office, hands me the bag with the sandwich and sits in one of the chairs opposite my desk.

"Everything okay? You seem a little distracted."

I'm not sure my sister is the one I want to talk to about this, but I need some advice because I feel like I'm losing my mind. This weekend has been a rollercoaster of emotions and I can feel the stress of it all like a rock in the pit of my stomach.

"It's Livy."

"I figured as much. Want to talk about it?"

"Not really. But kind of. Okay, I guess I do." *Fuck, I'm really losing it.*

"Everything was so good this morning when I left her, but I've texted her twice today and no response. I feel like I'm coming undone. I'm hoping she's not regretting last night." I can feel the vein pulsing in my neck, and I try to rub the tension away with my fingers.

"I've never seen you like this over a woman, Parker. She is really under your skin."

I lean back into my chair and rub both of my hands over my face. Jules is right, I've never felt this way before about a woman. Ever. Correction- about any other woman.

"If it's Livy that you want, then go get her. Why are you still here?" She says, lifting her brow.

I ponder the question for all of five seconds then sit up straight in my chair and shut my computer. I want Livy.

"You're a smart cookie, Jules. Why the hell am I still here? Tell Dad I left for the day and I'll see him tomorrow. Love you, Jules."

"Love you too, Parks."

I finish my sandwich because a guy has to eat, grab my laptop and my keys and throw on my suit jacket. I glance at the pile of paperwork on my desk still needing my attention. It will have to wait.

I head out the door with one thing on my mind: finding Livy and getting her back in my arms where she belongs. I've lost her once before and I'm not going to make that same mistake twice.

SOMETHING IS OFF WITH LIVY. I JUST KNOW IT. MY MIND IS racing with reasons she might be shutting down on me as I drive to the first place I think she might be. Bloom. It's four o'clock and she is supposed to be working until six.

I park my car and head into the shop to find Ellie working by herself on an arrangement. She stops what she's doing and greets me with a cautious smile.

"Hey Ellie, how's your day going?" I'd like to cut right to the chase and ask her where Livy is, but I manage to remember my manners first.

"Hey Parker. You look nice in your suit. Working at the office today?"

"I am, and thanks. Hey, is Livy around?"

"She's not, I'm afraid. She just left for a break."

"Do you know where she could be?" My throat tightens all of a sudden.

"I don't know exactly, she just said that she needed some fresh air." Ellie stops what she is doing and wipes her hands down the apron she's wearing. "Are you guys okay? I mean, I know it's none of my business, but she seemed quiet today, like something was on her mind."

I feel my jaw pulse, then tense. "Ellie, I've got it bad for that girl. I'm all in but I think she's having a harder time accepting me back in her life."

"That's not surprising. She is cautious, especially when it comes to her heart. She has been through way more than your average 28-year-old and trust doesn't come easy to her. She just needs time to sort it all out in her mind. You mean something to her. You always have, so it makes everything more complicated."

"I'll give her all the time she needs but I'm not giving up." It dawns on me that I know exactly where to find her.

"I can do that. Thanks Ellie, for the talk. I've got to run."

"Anytime. I'm one hundred percent Team Parkey."

I stare at her with a confused look on my face. "You're team *what*?"

"Team Parkey. You know, Parker and Livy smashed together. Or do you think Larker's better? I'm still working out the kinks."

I roll my eyes and chuckle. "The smashing part sounds good. Thanks, Ellie. Have a good night."

I race out of Bloom and head on foot straight to the spot where I'm positive she will be. I make my way down First Street towards the ocean, taking in the quiet streets and fresh ocean air. Walking through New York is like an assault to your senses. The masses of people, the bright lights, the sounds and the energy all coming at you at once. I loved all of that for a while, I fed off it, but being back here now has made me realize how much I miss this place. A slower paced life, Sunday dinners with my family and dare I say it, even watching my children play in my parents' pool one day all suddenly sound very appealing to me.

There's a light breeze as I approach the beach. The sun is bright, the air dry and warm. I stop where the concrete gives way to the sand, remove my dress shoes and take in the view, the shoreline stretching on for miles. Then I spot her. Livy. She's sitting in the sand, her knees pulled tightly against her body. My girl has always come to the beach to think and clear her mind and as anxious as I feel right now, seeing her gazing at the ocean, makes me smile.

I move closer to her, feeling the knot in my stomach getting tighter as the distance closes between us. There's a chance that she wants to call off whatever this is between us. I flinch at the thought, but I'm not going down without a fight.

I sit down beside her, noticing how deep in thought she is. Her brows are knit together, her lips pierced in a straight line.

"Hey Liv, mind if I sit with you?" I cross my long legs at the ankle, not caring that my Armani suit is getting dirty in the sand.

"How did you find me here?" She shifts her gaze to me, asking the question like it amazes her. She looks beautiful, with the sun's rays casting bright lines across her face. She looks so small, so delicate and lost in her thoughts.

"I remember your love of the ocean. I also remember that when you need time to yourself this is where you come. I remember everything about you, Livy. I know how much you like the feel of the warm sand between your toes and the sounds of the waves crashing in. I know how it centers and calms you being near the ocean. When I didn't hear back from you today and didn't find you at work, I knew you would be here." I watch her intently as she tucks a few loose strands of her hair behind her ear. There is something she wants to say, I can tell the words are on the tip of her tongue.

"Talk to me, Livy. What's on your mind?"

"I'm sorry, Parker, I didn't mean to ignore you, but the last two days with you have been a lot for me to take in. Don't take that the wrong way, I've loved spending time with you again. I'm just scared to let you back into my life only to lose you again. I know I couldn't take the heartache."

"Why do you think you will lose me?"

"Parker, we lead two different lives. I don't know any other way to say it. How *can* it work? We'd just be playing house for a few short weeks and then you'll be gone again. My feelings for you are already so strong. I can't imagine the way I will feel about you in a couple of weeks when you decide you need to go back to your life in New York. It will crush me."

My heart leaps in my chest. Her admission that she feels strongly for me is all I needed to hear.

"Livy, I'm not leaving you. We will figure this out together. In three days, you have managed to change everything for me and when I think about my future now, you're all I see."

"That's what scares me, Parker. Will I be enough for you when the passion and excitement wear off? How will I fit into your world? You know I have a past, Parker, one that you probably don't want attached to your family's last name."

This is a topic I've known we would need to discuss at some point, but I haven't wanted to ruin the momentum we have going. I have so many questions, but above all I just want to be there for her, and I need her to understand this.

"Is that what this is really about? You think I'm embarrassed by your past? Do you not know me at all? I was right by your side when it all went down, and it never changed a thing for me." I feel my jaw tense as I struggle to understand where this is all coming from.

"What about your family? Do you really think they want their successful son dating the daughter of a convicted felon? They have a well-respected name; they don't need my past tarnishing it."

She looks down, avoiding eye contact with me as she streams the warm sand through her fingers. She has it all wrong. My parents are two of the most understanding and non-judgmental people around. They know about the mess Livy's dad got himself into. Hell, it was front-page news, everyone in Reed Point at the time knew what had happened. It never changed my parents' opinion of Livy, though. I don't know why she would think it would.

"Livy, my parents couldn't give a shit about any of that. They would never judge you for what your father did. My parents love you; they would want nothing more than to see me with you. Think about it - have they ever given you any reason for you to believe that they have doubts about you?"

I pause to let what I said sink in. She needs to know that the past is in the past and no one from my family is judging her - or ever has.

"Just accept it Liv, I'm here to stay. I'm not just walking away from this. I should have fought harder for us the first time." I watch her expression soften and I reach for her hand, lacing our fingers together.

"Do you have any idea how crazy I am about you? I haven't been able to get you off of my mind since the second I saw you at my parents' house. You are all I can think about. I want you Livy. I want us. You have to trust me. I promise you I won't hurt you."

"I believe you, Parker." Her brown eyes shimmer, her hair golden in the sun. My eyes drift to her lips I'm dying to kiss.

"Livy let's do this. I promise you I will never hurt you. I..."

"Kiss me, Parker."

My heart hammers in my chest as I cup her face in my hands and pull her mouth to mine. I seal my lips to hers, angling my chin to take the kiss deeper. She tastes salty like the ocean. She wraps one hand around the back of my neck and runs the other through my hair. My hands find her waist and I lift her body to mine, her legs straddling my waist as she sits on my lap. My dick throbs, pushing against her center.

I fist my hands into her hair and the sexiest sound slips from her mouth. I love the little noises she makes. Her lips part as she takes in a breath and I run my tongue across the length of her bottom lip. Her lips curve up in a smile and I can't help but smile back into our kiss.

My hands travel down to the small of her back and I dig my hands into her hips, pulling her closer to me. My hands glide over her ass and I kiss her hard. I want to be inside of her, to feel her skin against mine. A low groan rumbles from my throat.

"Don't stop kissing me," she pleads, her voice breathy.

She doesn't have to ask me twice.

I can feel her body starting to completely relax and a rush of heat washes over me. I need to feel more of her. I want to lay her down and take her right here on this beach.

"Livy," I moan as I break the kiss. "It's taking everything in me right now to not rip off your clothes, but we are at a public beach. Unless you want to be ticketed for public indecency, we better stop. Come with me to the beach house."

She laughs and leans back a little, making me immediately miss her body on mine. I take her hand in mine and kiss the tips of her fingers. The sound of her laughter is one of the best things I've heard all day. It's almost as good as her response.

"Hurry Parker, let's go."

ELEVEN

Olivia

I don't think I've ever run that fast. Parker has my hand in his and we are laughing and stumbling through the sand on our way to his car. We stop for kisses along the way, not able to get enough of each other.

"Please tell me that you aren't planning to go back to work today Livy?"

"Not a chance." I will text Ellie when we get to the car and ask her for a favor. There are only a couple of hours left in the workday so I'm confident she can handle it. And even if she couldn't handle it, at this point, I would ask her to close the shop and sell it rather than leave Parker now.

We reach the pavement and Parker slips on his dress shoes. I finally get a good look at him in his navy suit and crisp white dress shirt and think to myself that if I died today, I'd die a happy woman. He looks expensive. The suit is tailored to perfection, fitted in all the right places, and looks like it costs more than my entire wardrobe. This man is the definition of sexy.

"Where did you park?"

"Back at Bloom. I came to find you, but you obviously weren't there. Ellie told me you went for a break and needed fresh air. I ran to the beach hoping my instincts were right."

"You really haven't forgotten a thing about me." I feel my cheeks warm at the realization. I am amazed that after all these years Parker remembers the little details that make me who I am. He sweeps the tips of his fingers across my forehead, tucking loose strands of my hair behind my ear.

"No, I haven't, and I probably never will." He pulls me in close to him and presses a kiss to the top of my head.

"Now let's go. I need to get you out of these clothes right now." We race through the streets, his hand in mine, to get to his car, ignoring stares from strangers along the way. We must look like a couple of criminals fleeing the scene of a crime.

Finally, we are at his car. Parker opens the passenger door for me, backing me into the leather seat with his mouth on mine. He breaks the kiss, flashing me a devastatingly handsome smile.

"You are perfect, Livy."

My heart thunders in my chest. He shuts my door, rounds the front of the car, and gets in the driver's seat.

We reach the beach house in record speed. We stumble to the door in each other's arms kissing and touching, our breathing ragged. It takes Parker three attempts to unlock the front door. I'm sure it didn't help that my lips were basically glued to his.

The door slams shut behind us and Parker pulls me towards him, lifting me by my waist and then turning, pinning me against the door. My ankles lock around him and he pushes his body into mine.

"Kiss me, Parker."

He has one arm under my bottom and his other hand is pressed against the door by my ear. He kisses me hard with hunger in his eyes and my arms snake around his neck, deepening the kiss. His tongue finds mine and his hand breaks from the wall moving to my jaw. He grasps my jaw in his hand and angles my chin higher, trailing kisses down my neck. The feel of his warm mouth on my neck sends a tingling sensation over my body.

"What are you doing to me, Parker?" I breathe the words into his ear, my body on fire. He nips the side of my jaw then runs his tongue across the mark his teeth leave on my flesh. The warmth of his mouth soothes my skin. Parker breaks the kiss and finds my eyes.

"Exactly what you want me to do. I'm going to make you feel so good Livy."

I shudder, knowing just what Parker can do to me. I close my eyes, willing him for another kiss and because he knows me so well, he claims my mouth with his.

I reach for the front of his shirt, unbuttoning it one by one, resisting the urge to tear it off his body. I drag it down over his broad shoulders and it falls to the floor. I roam my hands over his hard pecs, loving the feel of his muscles that he seems to have perfected at the gym.

"I love your body, Parker. You are so damn sexy. I will never get enough of it as long as I live." I've wanted someone to make me feel this way for such a long time. The intense desire and need for him courses through my body. It feels like an addiction that I never want to break.

"Take your shirt off," Parker commands in a voice that should be illegal it's that sexy. I quickly pull it over my head. This new demanding side of him is turning me on, and I want more of it. *Holy Shit*.

"Bra. Now," he demands again, pulling my back just far enough from the door that I can reach the hooks. I unhook the clasp as he pulls the straps away from my shoulders, letting it drop to the floor. His hand palms one breast, his thumb trailing across my nipple before he dips down to take it in his mouth. I run my hand through his hair, gripping it at the base of his neck, trying to relieve the mounting pleasure between my legs.

"God Parker." The feel of his breath on my skin and his arousal pulsing into my center is intoxicating.

"I want you in my bed now." His eyes narrow and he looks at me like I am everything he has ever wanted.

He steadies both of his arms under my thighs and carries me to the bedroom. He stops at the foot of the bed and I slither my legs from around him and down his body, so I am standing in front of him. I go up on my toes so I can reach his mouth and I kiss him with force. My hands travel down his abs to his belt buckle and I unfasten it, removing his pants. His hands are by his sides, fisted, fighting to stay in control.

My fingers find the waistband of his briefs and I tug them down to the floor. His erection springs free. I straighten and stare at every inch of skin that is displayed in front of me, feeling my heartbeat race. A sexy grin slips across his lips.

"Do you like what you see?"

"You're incredible." There is no other word that comes close to describing him. He has the perfect athletic build, just the way I like it. His muscles are defined, long and lean and powerful. His arms strong and smooth. My eyes narrow on a vein that I can't help but notice runs down both of his arms from his forearm to his wrist.

"Livy you are so God damn beautiful, I could just stare at you all day."

I grasp his hard length in my hand, stroking up and down. He closes his eyes and I watch his Adam's apple move as he swallows hard. I rake my nails with my other hand up his hip, and his jaw tightens as I pump faster.

"Shit Livy, that feels so good." He brushes the tip of my chin with his thumb. "But you need to stop. It feels too good and I want you."

He lifts me by my hips and lowers me onto the king size bed. It's covered with a plush white down comforter, soft blue and white pillows against the headboard. The weight of his body stills on mine. I arch my back, pushing my hips into his as he sucks my bottom lip into his mouth. Sucking and teasing me and chasing it with his tongue. My eyes roll shut.

He leans back and gets to work on my jeans, peeling them from my body, then does the same to my white lace thong. We're both finally totally bare.

"You are sexy as fuck, Liv." His eyes run over my body from my knees up to my mouth and he growls, taking my nipple between his lips. He sucks and licks and circles it before moving to the other. The stubble over his jaw tickles my skin.

"God, I've missed you," I say, my hands trailing up his back to his neck. His mouth stays firmly in place, just where I want it. He knows exactly how to drive me out of my mind.

His fingers move down my body before he slides two inside of me, moving them back and forth, slowly pushing them in deeper. Every nerve ending is on fire and I want to feel him inside of me right now. He keeps pushing and his thumb moves in tiny circles.

"I'm almost there, Parker. I'm so close. I want you inside of me," I beg.

He begins to reach for the nightstand to get a condom when I stop him.

"I'm on the pill, Parker, and I trust you. I want to feel all of you."

"I trust you too, baby. Only if you're sure?"

"I'm sure, Parker. Stop talking."

Parker smirks and flattens his hand against my thigh pushing it open as he places a kiss to the swell of my breast.

He's taking his time teasing me and the anticipation is almost too much. My thighs fall open and he positions himself between my legs, sliding his tip up and down before pushing inside. I pull him in closer by his muscular ass, needing as much of him as I can get. A low moan escapes him. It feels too good like this.

"Are you sure you want this?"

"Please don't stop. I don't want you to stop."

My hips rise to take him in deeper. I wrap my legs around his hips and my hands around his neck. He moans louder, increasing the pace. He moves harder and faster until my entire body trembles with pleasure.

He changes the angle and finds that sweet spot. He moves faster and I know he's right there with me.

"That's it, baby. I've got you."

My eyes squeeze shut as I cry out his name and ride out the intense rush that takes over me. He follows me over the edge, his muscles clenching as he releases into me. My name escapes his lips in a low moan. He drops his face into my neck, kissing the sensitive skin behind my ear, that spot he knows I love. We both struggle to catch our breaths.

"You're all mine, Livy. All mine."

He kisses my shoulder and lifts his upper body. He hovers over me, holding himself up on his forearms.

We catch our breath and look at one other. The look in his eyes is different now. I can feel the shift between us. I wonder if he feels it too. I've only ever felt this way with him, and I know it's love. I'm falling so fast for this man. I should be nervous and scared, trying to plan my escape. Instead, my heart is bursting in my chest and I know I never want to leave this.

"I love having you in my bed." He says it softly against my lips.

"I love being in it."

His eyes turn serious and the corners of his mouth tip up. "Can I just keep you here twenty-four seven? Seriously, Livy. Let's do it. We can pick up some of your things tomorrow and you can stay here with me."

I can see myself here with Parker. It's funny, I am so used to being on my own that I never thought I'd actually consider sharing my life with anyone else. But being here in Parker's arms makes me feel so safe and protected.

"I think that can be arranged."

Parker smiles and rolls me over so I'm on top of him now. "Can you tell how happy I am?"

"I can - and I can feel it too." I giggle and glance down at the situation happening between us. He's inside of me and still hard as steel.

"*You* need something to eat! I'm making us dinner."

"Excuse me. Since when do you cook?"

"Have you already forgotten my Michelin quality breakfast this morning?" He tickles my ribs and I squirm, letting out a high-pitched squeal. Our bodies finally separate and I feel the loss immediately.

"How could I forget? But making breakfast and cooking dinner are two completely different skills."

"Hey, I'm not just skilled in the bedroom you know. This meal will blow your mind. Come on, I'll pour you a glass of wine and you can relax while I cook. I'll let you ogle my body all you want."

I can't help the smile that lights up my face. He smiles back, threading his fingers through mine, and presses an open-mouthed kiss against my lips. He breaks the kiss and I give him my best pouty face to let him know I wasn't ready for it to end.

"If you keep looking at me like that Liv, we are never going anywhere but this bed." He raises his brow and kisses me slowly. "And I wouldn't complain, by the way."

I feel the mattress dip, watching Parker rise from the bed. I follow, throwing one of his t-shirts over my head as he whips on a pair of his joggers and we head to the kitchen.

On the way to the kitchen, I stop and look at a bookcase covered in family photos. There's a photo of Parker with Liam and Miles on a football field, arms around each other's shoulders, beaming. There's another of Parker with his family that looks like it was taken on a vacation. They are standing together on a pier, all smiles. Parker appears to be laughing. They are all so darn good looking. There are some serious good genes in that family. I start to imagine what our kids would look like. I bet they'd be diaper box photo worthy.

Woah, I really need to slow down. What just happened there?

Parker calls me into the kitchen and hands me a glass of wine. He has pancetta chopped into cubes on a cutting board on the counter and a large pot of water waiting to boil on the stove.

"What are you making me?"

"My dad's famous carbonara. You will love it, it's delicious."

"I bet I will. What's also delicious is you cooking for me in nothing but your joggers."

He eyes me with a cocky grin. He clearly likes it when I stroke his ego, and I'm more than happy to oblige.

There's something so insanely hot about a guy in just a slim fitted pair of joggers slung low on his hips with no shirt and bare feet. Especially with a body like Parker's. I'm enjoying the view. *Who could blame me?*

"What can I do to help?"

"Nothing babe, I've got this." Parker cracks two eggs into a bowl and adds a little salt and pepper. "What are your plans for the week?"

"It's going to be another busy one. Besides that, I have yoga Wednesday night with the Ellie and Kate and at some point, I need to make time for my mom." Just the thought of my mom reminds me of what I will be facing soon. I need to check in with her and make sure she is emotionally ready to see my dad again. The subject of my father hasn't come up yet with Parker beyond our conversation at the beach and I'm dreading it. I know he must be wondering where my family and I are at with it all.

"How's your mom doing? I could go with you to see her if you like. It would be nice to see her again. Unless you would prefer I didn't tag along?"

It's really sweet of him to offer. Parker and my mother always got along well. She liked him for me, and I know she was disappointed when I called things off with him. On one hand it would be nice to have him with me for moral support, but on the other it feels like it's too much too soon. I don't really want to talk about my mom right now, knowing where it will inevitably lead, so I decide to brush over the subject.

"She's fine. Can I think about it?"

"Of course you can."

"So work is pretty busy? It seems like you two have done one hell of a job with growing the business. Have you ever considered expanding?" Parker stirs the pancetta that is sizzling in the pan with a wooden spoon.

"We've talked about it and it's something we both are interested in pursuing. We mostly just haven't found a location that would work. The capital we would need is also a bit of an issue. Well, it's a major issue."

"I'd be happy to help you. I have the resources to scout for a location beyond Reed Point. We could look together."

"That's a really nice offer but I know you have a lot on your plate right now." I decide I need to do something to help with dinner, so I begin to set the table. He grabs me by the waist, pulling me into him. His shirtless body wrapped around me is making it really hard to think straight.

"You know I'm being serious. I would do anything to help you."

"You might have to pinch me. I don't believe you're real."

I've always done things on my own because I've had to. After my dad left, it fell on me to take care of Kate, and for the most part, my mom too. My dad had built a very successful business, but I was never really able to learn from him. He went to prison the summer before I started college. He was convicted of tax evasion and money laundering, both federal offenses, and sentenced to nine years in prison. He was also convicted of mail and wire fraud, both adding hefty jail time. On top of that he was required to pay a substantial penalty. It was the reason we lost our home.

I opened Bloom with Ellie soon after we graduated college with very little knowledge of how to start a business. It would have been nice to have my father around to guide me, but after what he did to land himself in prison, I wasn't sure he was the right person to be taking advice from anyway.

Parker plates the pasta, and we sit down together to eat. As promised, it is unreal, and he agrees to give me the recipe. Cooking is something I've always enjoyed, and I've gotten pretty good at it over the years. It's cooking for one that I find not too appealing, so more often than not I just order in or pick up something on my way home from work. Sitting at the dining table with Parker, I realize I am already planning out the meals I want to make for him.

After dinner, Parker offers to drive me to my apartment to pick up a few things, including my swimsuit. He isn't happy when I leave my apartment with just a duffle bag of essentials. I'm sure he would rent a U-Haul in a split second to empty out my apartment if I let him.

We make it back to the beach house and Parker insists I unpack my things, even though I let him know I am happy to live out of my duffle bag. He's not having it. As soon as my stuff is tucked away in a drawer, we change into our swimsuits, pour two glasses of wine and hop into the hot tub.

It's a warm, clear evening. The sun hasn't quite set, and the beach is almost completely empty, giving us our privacy. The house is nestled into the far end of the beach in a small residential area just before the dunes meet the sand. It is far enough away from everything to allow for privacy, but still close enough to the street, with its cute restaurants and coffee shops to make it convenient.

I take a sip of my wine and admire the perfect view from the deck overlooking the ocean. It's undeniably beautiful, but my favorite view is actually sitting across from me with water running down his chest. His feet are tangled with mine at the bottom of the tub. He has a cheeky grin on his face, so I decide to try and kiss it off.

I move slowly through the steaming water, never taking my eyes off of his. I run my hands up his hard pecs to his neck and place a soft kiss on the edge of his mouth. I straddle his waist as he pulls my slippery body in closer, his two hands cupping my ass. I run my fingertips up his neck towards his jaw and his lips part. He angles his chin and I press a long slow kiss to his lips.

"You're amazing, Livy."

"You think so?"

"I know so." His voice is low and sexy, kiss talking in between kisses. Our mouths never leave each other.

I feel his hands move up to the strings of my bikini across my lower back and he gently tugs. He then finds the strings at the back of my neck and he tugs those too, removing my top. His hands move immediately to cup my breasts.

I remember where we are, and I'm flooded with memories. This beach house was our hiding spot when we were kids. It was our special place we would run to be together, just the two of us. We were here when he told me he loved me for the first time. The memory brings a smile to my face. He notices and breaks the kiss.

"Do I make you happy?"

"So happy, Parker," I say softly and kiss him again.

"I want you back, Liv." He palms my cheek with his hand.

"I'm already yours."

We quickly remove his swim trunks and my bikini bottoms, and I straddle his waist again. I sink down on his length and rock back and forth. The water spilling over the edge of the tub. It feels so good. Parker's gorgeous cocoa eyes have darkened, and his head falls back. I run my nose along the column of his neck and glide my tongue along the sharp edge of his jaw. His lips part and as he moans, I capture the sound in my mouth. His fingers dig into my hips as he lifts me over and over again.

"So good, Liv. Fuck. So good."

My body stiffens and I can feel Parker swell inside of me. Exhilaration grips me and aftershocks take over. It just keeps on getting better with him. I'm not sure how that is even possible.

He holds me close to his chest, running his fingers up and down my spine. Once our bodies are no longer joined, Parker wraps me in a towel and takes me to bed.

He pulls the covers back and we both drop our towels to the floor and crawl in. He nuzzles me into his side, and I rest my head on his chest. He covers us both to our waists with the down blanket and I listen to his breathing, synching mine to his.

He turns out the lights.

My eyes are heavy, and my body is in a complete state of bliss.

I drift into sleep.

TWELVE

Parker

I WAKE UP TO LIVY'S FINGERTIPS DRAWING CIRCLES ON MY chest. She's propped up on her forearm, her gaze following the pattern she's drawing around and around. Her thigh is hooked over mine.

"Good morning, beautiful."

"Hi you." She continues running her fingers over my skin and I like the way it feels. A lot.

I wish we didn't have to work today. I can think of a million things I'd rather be doing. All involving Livy.

Yesterday was amazing and I want more of that. It crosses my mind to ask her to take the day off with me, but I have a better idea. A weekend away. Just the two of us. I decide to keep it to myself for now, until I can make plans.

"Did we sleep in?"

"Nope, we are good babe. It's seven thirty." I run my hand over her smooth skin watching it pebble under my touch. "I'm sorry I fell asleep on you last night. You were so cozy and warm and the hot tub made me feel so relaxed," She says, kissing the center of my chest. I roll her over to her side so we can face each other.

"I just want to stay here a little longer with you. I like having you in my arms. I could stay like this forever Livy."

I realize I can't keep her in this bed with me forever, but I'm going to drag it out as long as I can. This all feels so right. Like this is where we belong. It feels like we are starting again where we left off. She feels like home.

I link my fingers through hers and kiss each one of her knuckles. I love how small and soft her hands are compared to mine. I can wrap my hand around hers completely. I turn her hand over to kiss the four small freckles on her wrist that I've always loved. I first noticed them when we sat together in class back in high school.

"I still can't believe I fell asleep on you. I haven't slept that well in years."

"I'm happy you got a good sleep. I moved you around a few times in the middle of the night to get closer to you and you slept right through it all. You even slept through my attempt at seducing you."

Livy giggles. "Oh God Parker, I'm so embarrassed."

"Don't be. It was cute. I love how soundly you slept curled up beside me."

Sleeping in bed with someone is not something I'm used to. I don't typically let it get that far. It always feels too intimate and then the waking up part in the morning next to someone you really aren't interested in, just seems like it would be awkward. With Livy it's different. I like the intimacy, and the feelings that come with it.

My vibrating phone on the nightstand attempts to interrupts us, but I ignore it. I'm enjoying lying in bed with Livy way too much. I obviously have zero self-restraint when it comes to her and instead of getting out of bed like I know I should, I bring her in closer.

"Do you need to get that?"

"Nope."

"Are you sure? What if it's important? It could be work."

"What could be more important than this right now? I'm not moving. I'm way too comfortable." I smooth a few loose strands of hair over her ear and lean in to kiss her cheekbone.

She's silent all of a sudden and I'm not sure why.

"What just happened Livy? Something is on your mind."

"It's nothing."

"It doesn't feel like nothing. Let me in, Liv. What's going on in that pretty head of yours?" Livy has always internalized her thoughts and that scares me. I need her to open up to me if this is ever going to work between us. I need to know what she needs and wants from me.

"It's just.... Well. What exactly are we, Parker? Are we exclusive?" She's chewing on her bottom lip and I can tell that she is nervous.

"Well, there's no way I'm sharing you with anyone else, so we better be. That's what you want, right?"

"Of course, it is. This all just happened so fast. I mean, five days ago you were only a memory to me. It's a lot to take in, but I'm happy with you. And for the record, I don't share either."

I laugh and kiss her, trying to reassure her that she's the only one I want. It's hard to believe that she has chosen me again. That I got *that* lucky. There's a small part of me that still worries that she could change her mind like she did the first time. I push those worries away, not wanting to burst this bubble we are in right now.

I press a kiss to her shoulder and reach for my phone to snap a pic and capture the moment. I slide my lock screen to access the camera and hold it up over top of us.

"What are you doing? Are you seriously taking a photo of us right now? You can't take a picture of me looking like this. I'm sure my hair looks like there is something nesting in it."

"Do you honestly not know how beautiful you are to wake up to?"

I snap a photo as she buries her head into my neck and then snap another of me kissing the top of her head. The picture shows her profile and her smile pressed into my neck. Her cheeks pink and her slender fingers across my bare chest. She looks beautiful and happy and, in that moment, I know that I'm the reason for her happiness. These will come in handy when I can't be with her.

"I have an idea, Livy."

"That sounds dangerous. What is it?"

"I would like to take you on a date. Like, a proper date. Our first date now that we are official."

"We've already had our first date. Do you not remember taking me to that burger shack and then a movie?" Of course I did. I still remember how nervous I was, thinking that I couldn't believe a girl like her had agreed to go on a date with me.

"I do. But that was before. We need another first date. I want to take you out like you deserve. I want all of Reed Point to know you are mine."

"You are ridiculous."

"Is that a yes then?"

"It's a yes, I would love to go on a second first date with you." She runs the pads of her fingers up my arm to my shoulder. My body reacts in a shudder and a smile covers my mouth. I'm going to have to get us both out of bed before I do what I really want to do to her and make her come. Over and over again.

My phone vibrates again, and I reluctantly pick it up from where it lays beside me on the bed sheet. There's a text from my mother inviting me for dinner tonight with the rest of the family. It sounds nice, but I really want to take Livy out.

"Everything okay?" Livy asks.

"Yeah, it's just my mom. It's an invite for dinner tonight at the house. She's having my brothers and sister over."

"I bet she's pretty happy to have you around for longer than a weekend. You should go."

"I'd rather be with you. Besides, it's date night and I have plans for us."

"You can't already have plans for us, Parker. You just decided less than five minutes ago to take me on a date. We can do it Thursday night. I'm not going anywhere."

"Or... you could come with me tonight to my parents' place and we could still do our date night on Thursday?"

A look of hesitance crosses her face and she's pulled her bottom lip under her teeth. It's her automatic response when she's nervous, I bet she has no idea she's even doing it. It's cute and it drives me crazy. I bring her hand up to my face and place her palm on my cheek. I brush the back of her hand with my knuckles.

"What have you told your family? Do they know about us?"

"My dad does. So do Miles, Liam and Jules. I mean, they know I decided to stay here because of you, but that's about it. I haven't talked to my mom yet, but I plan on doing that the next time I speak to her."

"What did they say? Were they supportive of your decision to stay here because of me?"

"They are. Honestly, they are surprised it took us this long to find our way back to each other." I take her hand from my face and kiss the tips of her fingers. One at a time. She still looks uncertain.

"How does your dad feel about you working from here? Is he concerned that you're not in New York?"

"Not at all. I want you to stop worrying. He offered me the beach house for as long as I need. Livy, I don't want you to worry about my family. I promise they would love to see you tonight. But we don't need to go. I'm fine telling my mom I have plans."

"I'll go. But will you promise to run it by your mother first and make sure it's okay?"

"Yes baby, I promise." I can't help but smile at her, she makes me so damn happy.

I flip her onto her back, my arms braced on either side of her face. Her hair is spread out all around her. She's looks like a fucking goddess. I center myself between her legs.

"We have to get ready for work. We don't have time," Livy says, but she reaches for me, running the tips of her fingers down the back of my neck.

"I can be quick. I will probably embarrass myself with just how quick. I want you so bad, Liv."

I nudge her legs open with my knee and move my body in between hers. Her lips part and her eyes lock with mine.

"Parker...." Livy brings her hands to my face, dragging her nails through the scruff of my beard. Her beautiful eyes flutter closed, and I'm lost in her. So damn lost.

I'm so far gone for this girl I may never be able to be found.

And nothing could make me happier.

I TAKE A BITE OF MY CARAMEL APPLE CROISSANT AND WAIT FOR the light to turn green. This is probably the best croissant I've had in my life. Before saying goodbye, Livy and I stopped at her favorite bakery on our way to Bloom and she convinced me I needed to try one. A coffee shop breakfast was all we had time for after our marathon of morning sex. I'm not complaining.

I press the command button on the steering wheel and ask the system to call my mom. I need to let her know I'm bringing Livy to dinner tonight. I have a feeling I'm going to make her day with this news.

"Hello?"

"Hi Mom, it's Parker."

"Hi honey, how are you?"

"I'm good. Do you have a minute?"

"Of course. I'm always available to talk to my boy. It's good to hear your voice. Your dad and I would love to see you. Can you make dinner tonight?"

"I can. Thanks for the invite mom. I -" She interrupts me before I have a chance to tell her about Livy.

"Oh fantastic. I know it's short notice, but I was hoping it would work out. This means I will have all of my kids around the dinner table with me tonight. Jules is bringing Alex too."

"Sounds nice, Mom," I say, turning right onto First street. "I am actually calling to let you know I will be bringing someone too. I invited Olivia. I hope that's okay with you."

"Oh my, Parker, things must be going well for you to be bringing her to dinner. You have no idea how happy this makes me. She is always welcome, you know that."

"Thanks Mom, and I know. It was important to Livy that I ask. I think she's feeling a little nervous to see everyone again." I stop at a red light and take a long sip of my coffee.

"I can understand that. Her life was upside down when we last had her at family gatherings. But you know your father and I will do our best to make her feel at ease. She's a sweet girl and I think she's good for you."

"Thanks Mom."

"So, I assume things are going well between the two of you?"

"I think I'm making progress. She's worried about the distance between us. I mean, her living here in Reed Point and me living in New York or Cape May or wherever my job takes me. She owns a business here that she loves, and it's successful. She hasn't said it, but I don't think she would want to leave it. So, we have a huge challenge on our hands and she's not sure it can work between us. I can't blame her."

"Oh Parker. You need to reassure her that it's all possible. It just means that you're going to have to put in an extra effort. It's normal for her to have doubts and insecurities. It won't be *as* easy for the two of you as it would for a couple who live in the same city, but you can figure it all out together. Take it one day at a time and be patient with her."

"Thanks for the advice, Mom." I grab my sunglasses from below the arm rest, slipping them on so I can see through the searing sunlight.

"I'm always here for you. I love you, Parker."

"I love you too. See you tonight. Bye Mom."

I end the call and park my Audi in front of the Godiva store. I want to buy Livy things. I want to spoil her. I think chocolates are a good start. After all, I can't exactly buy her flowers. I'm assuming Livy hasn't lost her sweet tooth. She never used to go a day without chocolate of some sort, so I think it's a safe bet. I browse around the store before deciding on two boxes from their Gold collection and the woman behind the counter wraps them up with a large red bow. I arrange to have them sent to Bloom this afternoon with a note.

I head into the office and say a quick hello to Erin at reception.

"Good morning, Parker."

"Morning, Erin. How's your day going?"

"Well, thank you. You know, it's really nice to see you in the office. And I can tell your father is really happy to have you here."

"It's good to be here. Thanks, Erin."

"Don't forget you have a meeting with your father and Liam at two o'clock."

"Got it, I'll be there."

I lock myself in my office. I have a lot of work to get done if I'm going to sneak away with Livy for the weekend.

I skim through my emails for anything urgent before calling Jordan. He's been good about not emailing and texting me too often. He seems to be managing well on his own, which is making this a good trial run for when I leave the NYC hotel permanently. He's proving he is capable of taking over there.

There's an email from Nelson wanting to set up a meeting with the architect in three weeks and go over a few design issues before the construction starts. It reminds me that I don't have a lot of time here with Livy. There's a pit in my stomach all of a sudden at the thought of leaving. I need to stop thinking about that and get back to work.

I shoot Nelson an email letting him know my arrival date in three weeks and the rest of my morning is spent reviewing the development plans for Cape May. The project is running smoothly and on schedule, thanks in large part to a great team that I know I can count on.

The day flies by. It's four o'clock and I've wrapped up my last conference call. I spent a good part of my day running numbers with my father and now my brain hurts, and my eyes are sore. I'll put in another hour at the office before I go home to shower and change to pick up Livy.

My phone vibrates on my desk and I check the screen. It's a text from Livy. I open it immediately, feeling like a giddy high schooler.

OLIVIA: The chocolates are sweet Parker, but not as sweet as you. I'm feeling pretty spoiled. Thank you xx

I text her back right away.

ME: I'm happy you like them. I miss you btw. I'll pick you up at six o'clock. My mom is excited to see you. xo

I watch the dots on my screen bounce as she's typing out her response.

OLIVIA: I miss you too ;)

I lean back in my chair, my hands clasped behind my neck. Images of Livy float through my mind: her sweet smile, sexy eyes and tanned olive skin.

I can't help but smile. I think I might be winning her over.

THIRTEEN

Olivia

I TRANSFER THE FRESHLY BAKED PEANUT BUTTER COOKIES THAT have been cooling on a rack in my kitchen onto a serving plate. My mother taught my sister and I to never show up for a dinner empty-handed, so I rushed back to my apartment after work and got started on the cookies. Ellie is here helping me, she insisted on it. I'm pretty sure she thinks I'm a flight risk and may possibly try to cancel on dinner tonight. She's definitely in full support of Parker and I dating.

In my rush, half the cookies slide off of the plate and I frantically rearrange them, so they look somewhat presentable.

"Olivia, relax. You've got time. I don't know why you are acting so fidgety. You are just going for dinner at the Bennetts' and you've known them most of your life. It's going to be fine. And besides, it's hardly torture hanging out with all of those pretty faces. I've always wondered - do you think they sit around talking about how good looking they all are? I mean, with each other?"

"I don't really want to know what happens in your brain, Ellie, because it seems like a scary place to be. Did you just hear yourself? You are ridiculous."

"What? They're all so damn hot. It's not normal. What do they eat? Do you think it could be something they eat?"

"I'm not even answering that." I roll my eyes and swat her with my tea towel.

"Listen Liv, I've been your best friend for a gazillion years. I *know* you. I haven't seen you this happy in a very long time and Parker is clearly into you. Like, really into you, and it almost makes me envious. I mean, if I was actually into all that romance crap and wanted the same hot guy in my bed every night." Ellie shakes her head, crossing her eyes in a silly face. "Seriously, he's been so sweet to you and he really is trying. Don't overthink this like we both know you tend to do with everything in your life."

"I know, you're right Ells. I've just fallen so hard for him and I'm really scared to lose him again." My eyes look to the floor, feeling the weight of my confession. Admitting that out loud to Ellie feels like a big deal to me.

Ellie places her hand on my forearm.

"I've seen the way he looks at you. He feels the same way, Liv. I know it. Just be yourself tonight. And if you really need me to bust you out of there, slip into the bathroom and text me our exit word 'Pineapple.' I've been working on new material ever since Kate began her speed dating escapades.

I'm sure it's just a matter of time before one of the speed dater whack-a-dos insists on pulling out his joystick too soon and I need to bust her out of her date."

"Joystick? Again, Ells Bells, your brain scares me sometimes."

"Really Liv, Do I need to spell it out for you?" Ellie motions an alarmingly obscene hand gesture.

I try to shake the image out of my head, throwing my hands over my eyes and moving my head side to side.

"Come with me, Liv. Let's get you changed for dinner. Parker is going to be here soon."

I follow her to my bedroom and watch her rifle through my closet. I don't really need her help choosing the right outfit but having Ellie here is a good distraction. We decide on a white silk blouse tucked into my nicest pair of skinny jeans. A touch of dry shampoo through my hair and some lip gloss and I'm ready.

"You look beautiful. My job here is done." Ellie wraps her arms around me in a hug and I walk her to the door. I'm grateful she insisted on coming home with me. I fought her on it at first but having her here is exactly what I needed.

I throw a few things into my purse and check the time on my phone. There's a notification from Parker. He texted to let me know he left the beach house and is on his way to pick me up. I'm anxious, so instead of pacing a hole in the floor in my apartment, I decide to wait for him outside. I toss my purse over my shoulder, juggle the plate of cookies and the fresh flowers I put together for Parker's mom, and head out the door.

A light breeze touches my skin, easing the butterflies deep in my belly. I take a few deep breaths, attempting to further calm my nerves.

It's been a long time since I've "met" the parents. Technically I know I've already met Parker's family, but a lot of time has passed. It also doesn't help that they know my past. They lived through it in a lot of ways with me. I'm praying it's not a topic of conversation tonight considering I haven't even discussed it with Parker.

Parker's Audi pulls up in front of my building. He parks and rounds the front of the car to greet me. He has changed out of the suit he left the house in this morning and is now wearing a pair of jeans and a dark button up shirt. His hair is styled, and his jaw is covered in stubble. Exactly the way I like it. He may not be a male model, but I swear he could be. My girl parts agree with me.

He walks confidently and with purpose towards me. He always does. And when he looks at me, there's an intensity - he's got a hold on me and I can't look away. It's happening now, I feel his gaze sear right through me.

God, he's gorgeous.

His smile widens as he approaches. "Hey babe," he places his hand on my cheek and kisses me. "You look beautiful." He wraps his arm around my waist and folds me into his firm chest.

"Thank you. You look pretty good yourself." *And by pretty good, I mean super-hot.*

“Did you wear these jeans to torture me? You kill me in these. How am I supposed to keep my hands off of you tonight?”

“You will just have to manage. Do you think you can behave?” I tease him with a heated stare.

“Livy, you are too tempting and way too damn sexy for your own good. I can’t make you any promises I’m not prepared to keep.”

“You are so bad.”

“Who, me? Nah.” He winks then covers my mouth with his.

“Let me take these for you. Did you bake these? They smell amazing.” Parker reaches for the plate of cookies.

“I did. I hope your family likes peanut butter.”

“They will love them. When did you have time?”

“I quickly baked them after work. Ellie helped me. I didn’t want to show up empty-handed.” He takes the cookies and flowers from my hands.

“You are amazing, Livy. You’re hot *and* you bake.”

He flirts and I feel a giddy smile threatening to break free. There he goes again sweeping me off my feet. With anyone else it would feel like a line but with Parker it’s genuine. He puts the flowers and cookies into the trunk and then returns to open my door. Before I get in, he grabs me by the waist pulling me in for a kiss, our bodies pressed tight together.

“I’ve waited all day to do this,” Parker states in almost a growl.

“Was it worth it?”

"More than worth it, but I'll need to kiss you again to be sure." *That definitely works for me.*

We eventually settle into our seats. Parker pulls away from the curb and quickly reaches his arm across the seat and settles his hand at the nape of my neck. He has one hand on the steering wheel while the fingers of his other hand rub gentle circles on my skin, making it hot under his touch. His scent permeates the air around me. He smells so good.

"Nervous babe?"

"A little, but this is helping." I close my eyes and rock my head back and forth against his fingers letting him know I appreciate his touch.

"Good. I'm really happy you said yes, by the way."

I'm not sure how to answer that so I stretch my arm across the console to his thigh and give it a squeeze.

"Thank you again for the chocolates. That was really thoughtful of you. I've never had anyone send me something before. I have to admit I really liked it."

"What kind of assholes have you been dating, Livy?"

"I guess I haven't been very good at choosing men. Other than you, of course." Parker is right. The men I've dated since him, and there've only been a few, have been more concerned with themselves than with me. I never felt like I was a priority with my last two boyfriends and they certainly never bothered to send me gifts. It's a nice change to have someone always thinking about me.

"Thankfully you won't have to look anymore. You've got me now." I feel my smile widen at the thought. And while I'm scared to death that this could end between us at any moment, my heart squeezes at the thought that Parker could really be the one.

Ten minutes later, he pulls into his parents' long driveway and parks behind three other cars.

"Looks like everyone is here." It's a reminder that it isn't just the two of us having dinner tonight and I take a deep breath. He opens his door and walks around the front of the car to open mine, helping me to my feet. He must sense that my nerves are getting the best of me because he gently kisses my cheek and rubs his thumb over my jaw.

"You don't need to worry about a thing. My family already knows and loves you. I promise." I nod and reach for his hand. He lowers his lips to mine once more before drawing back with warmth in his eyes.

"Give me a sec, I'll grab the stuff from the trunk."

He walks to the back of the car and grabs the cookies and bouquet of flowers. I take the plate from his grasp and he carries the flowers. I feel his hand settle on the curve of my back as he ushers me to the front door. I'm pretty sure he has purposely placed it there to put me at ease.

We walk into the sounds of chatter and laughter coming from the back of the house where the kitchen is. We are greeted by Mr. Bennett as he rounds the corner by the staircase. His face lights up when he sees us, and the knots that have twisted in my stomach begin to unravel. He walks directly towards me and pulls me in for a warm embrace.

"It's so nice to see you, Olivia."

"It's nice to see you too, Mr. Bennett."

"I've known you way too long for you to be calling me Mr. Bennett. Please call me Michael."

"I'll try my best." I smile as he directs us to the kitchen. Mrs. Bennett is busy at the stove and Miles and Liam are deep in discussion at the end of the long rectangular island in the center of the kitchen. Jules is the first to spot us.

"Yay, you both made it." She jumps off her stool, where she is sitting next to a man I assume is her boyfriend and beelines it over to us. She gives Parker a quick hug. "Hey Parks." She then turns her attention to me.

"I'm so happy you could make it, Olivia. It's so nice to see you again." She glances down towards the plate of cookies I'm holding. "Did you make these? They look amazing."

"I did. I made them after work today. It's really nice to see you too, Jules."

She takes the plate of cookies from me and carries it to the counter. I've always loved her energy. She's been upbeat and energetic since I met her when she was about fourteen. Even then she had a way of making you want to get to know her better, just to be in her presence. She has dark hair, like her brothers, that rests just below her shoulders, but her eyes are lighter. She's a good mix of both her parents.

"Oh, my goodness, these look so good, Olivia! You didn't have to do this but I'm glad you did because peanut butter is my favorite. Come here, honey, give me a hug."

Parker's mom draws me in for a hug and then does the same to Parker. She takes her son in with an affectionate smile. "Keep on doing whatever it is you are doing, Olivia, because my baby looks happier than he has in ages." Parker chuckles and hands the flowers to his mom.

"Mom, these are from Olivia." He hands his mother the bouquet and she dips her nose into the fresh flowers, enjoying the scent. Parker eyes me with a smile spreading across his face.

Mrs. Bennett wraps her arms around me and pulls me into another embrace. She thanks me for the flowers, and I offer to put them in a vase for her. It makes me wonder why I was ever nervous to come here tonight. That familiar welcoming feeling, the one I had come to know when we were kids, is already encompassing me. I take in Parker's parents' house: The happy family memories adorning the walls, fresh baked goods in cloches on the kitchen counter and this family that was built on love. My mind wanders, and I think about my family. There weren't many memories made in the home my mother lives in now. The ones we did make there are mostly painful ones that I have tried hard to bury.

"Bring those cookies over here. I need one now." Miles' huge six-foot-something frame stretches over the counter reaching for the plate, pulling it towards him.

"God, Miles you are such a child. No one would ever think that I'm the youngest in this family because you act like a five-year old. I should get you a glass of milk to go with your cookie."

"That would be nice, Jules. Thanks for making yourself useful."

Miles takes a bite out of the cookie and smirks, a slightly devious smile.

I love their family dynamic, the way they are so easy around each other. Yes, they're family but it's something more. They joke and tease each other, but there is an unconditional love between them, and the banter is definitely entertaining.

"These flipping cookies are unreal, Olivia. Holy Shit!"

"Language, Miles."

"Sorry, Mom." Miles stands from his chair and gives me a hug, followed by Liam. They both remind me so much of Parker with their dark hair and athletic builds and wide smiles. They fill up a room when they are all together with their broad frames and big, endearing personalities. The three of them are all so incredibly handsome, it's almost hard to take when they are all in a room together.

Jules introduces me to her boyfriend, Alex, who's currently in med school. Jules is always so boisterous and outgoing, so I'm surprised to find that Alex seems quiet and kind of reserved. They seem like a bit of an odd fit, but Parker has mentioned that she seems happy with him.

"Let's leave the women to chat and have a drink in the living room, boys," Mr. Bennett suggests.

Parker hangs back for a moment, pulling me to his side. He kisses the top of my head, whispering into my hair. "Do you want me to stay with you? I don't mind."

I tilt my head up to look him in his eyes and let him know I will be fine. He kisses my cheek and pulls back with a grin. I can't help but look at him and see the boy I fell in love with. He leaves me in the kitchen feeling light-headed and full of emotions. Jules hands me a glass of wine and I follow her to the kitchen island where Mrs. Bennett is working on dinner.

"You know, we are all really glad you are here. You are a good influence on my brother. He's different around you. He seems so happy. Not that he isn't usually happy, but it's different. He's relaxed and settled, less wound up.

"Jules is right, you know my boy is crazy about you. I've never seen him so smitten."

I feel my cheeks warm and I know they've turned a bright shade of pink. "I'm just as crazy about him. It's still so hard to believe that we are back together after so many years."

"Oh honey, we are so excited for the two of you. It's nice to have you back in our lives. I hope to see a lot more of you."

"It's good to be here." I bring the wine glass to my lips to try to hide the enormous smile that is covering my face.

I turn my attention to Parker's sister. She was just a kid the last time we spent time together and I genuinely would like to get to know her better. "Jules, I hear you work for your dad now. How do you like it?"

"I love it. I love what I do and it's nice to see my dad every day, but sometimes the stresses of a family business can get to you."

"Well, if you ever need a stress reliever, you could join me at my yoga class. You might like it. I go Wednesday nights with my sister and my best friend. You would love them. It would be fun."

"That sounds great. I would love that. I'm free tomorrow if that works?"

"It works! I can pick you up and we can go together."

"Great. I'm looking forward to it. Thanks, Olivia."

Out of the corner of my eye, I see Parker pop his head around the corner, checking in on me. I turn my attention to him, and he mouths the words, *You okay?* I instantly feel my body tingle at the gesture. I nod and he disappears into the living room again, leaving my heart bursting. Parker's family has welcomed me with open arms. It feels so nice to be included by them, almost as if I were a part of the family.

"Dinner is ready, girls. Jules, can you let the men know? And Olivia, do you want to help me bring the food to the table?"

"I'd be happy to."

I help Mrs. Bennett carry the dishes to the table. There is a platter of perfectly grilled flank steak and a bowl of parmesan white wine risotto. A fresh caprese salad and warm buns are already waiting on the table and a platter of roasted asparagus completes the menu. She has cooked enough for an army. It all looks delicious and is plated beautifully, and the smell is out of this world.

I find Parker waiting for me at the table and he pulls out the chair beside his. I am seated between Parker and Liam, with Mr. Bennett at the head of the table, Mrs. Bennett at the foot and Jules, Alex and Miles across from me. Parker rests his palm on my knee under the table. I can feel the warmth from his hand though the denim of my jeans and it feels good. I rest my hand on top of his and he laces our fingers together.

He whispers in my ear. "I'm so happy you are here with me, babe."

I look at him and whisper back, "Me too. Thank you for asking me."

I feel like I'm in a dream, right where I've always wanted to be. The way Parker looks at me with love in his eyes, the way he keeps me close to him likes he's afraid to lose me or can't stand to be apart. It feels like the pieces of a puzzle are finally falling into place. I feel warm all over; I can't remember being this happy in a long time.

"Help yourself everyone, but first, Michael do you want to propose a toast?"

"Sure, honey. To making your mother and I incredibly happy by all being here together tonight. We also want to welcome Olivia back to our home. It's good to have you here. Now let's eat." I feel the room shift their gazes towards me. Parker's grip on my hand tightens and I take a deep breath. We all raise our glasses, clinking them together with whomever we can reach and I'm relieved when platters begin to be passed around, taking the attention off of me.

"Mom, this looks amazing. Your cooking is what I miss most when I'm on set," Miles says, scooping a heaping spoonful of risotto onto his plate.

"More than your mother?"

"Not possible, Mom, but you know how I love my food."

"And ass-kissing apparently," Liam grunts in between mouthfuls.

Mr. Bennett raises a warning eyebrow at Liam, a gesture he appears to have perfected with his children over the years.

I find myself imagining what it would be like sharing Christmas dinners together around this table, bonfires and clam bakes at the beach house, even the sound of little feet pattering around us. I stop myself. I can't let my mind drift too far into the future. There are no guarantees. I should know that better than anyone.

Dinner passes quickly and the jokes and banter continue into dessert. I can't help but think how long it has been since I enjoyed a family dinner. My life before Parker all of a sudden feels lonely and incomplete. In such a short amount of time, Parker has managed to change my perspective completely, and I realise now that I want someone to love, to share the good and the bad with.

We all chip in clearing the table and doing the dishes. I help Mrs. Bennett pour the coffees and after dinner drinks while the rest of the family gather outside around the fire pit. I can see Parker and his brothers from the kitchen window and my heart swells. He lights up around them. I love seeing this side of him.

"My three boys have always been close," Mrs. Bennett says, interrupting my thoughts. "We raised them exactly the same, but they are each so different. Parker has always been the boy I've worried the least about. He's always worn his heart on his sleeve, which made it easier to know when he needed me. He's steady and grounded and has always stood up for the people he cares about. I still remember the time I received a call from his principal. He was eleven years old and he'd punched a classmate right in the nose. At first, I was shocked when they told me, because he had never been a violent kid. When I met him in the principal's office, he was still angry. The story went that the kid he punched was making fun of a new child who was wearing thrift store clothing. The boy taunted this poor kid in front of a handful of other children and Parker told him to stop. It turns out the boy was almost a head taller than Parker, but that didn't stop my son. The bully knocked the kid to the floor and that was all it took. Parker clocked him right in the nose. Instead of reprimanding him, I took him straight out for ice cream."

"I couldn't imagine the Parker I know hitting anyone, but that kid had it coming," I told her. "You raised an incredible man. You must be so proud."

"I really am. I'm proud of all of my kids. Olivia, I know relationships can be complicated and they require a lot of work but trust me when I say, he's worth it. Just be patient with him. He's going to make mistakes. Give him time and he will always make things right."

"Thank you for your advice. I know he's worth it and I can be patient." Mrs. Bennett places her hand on top of mine and gives it a squeeze. Her warm eyes soften in an understanding way. It feels a little like I just received her blessing to date her son.

Mrs. Bennett lifts the tray of drinks and heads for the patio doors. I'm relieved I didn't have to answer any questions about my dad. I follow her out but realize I left my sweater inside. I run back into the house to grab it, throw it on and reapply my lip gloss.

"There you are."

I turn around to see Parker with a silly grin plastered on his face. He looks so happy and I can't help but feel responsible for some of that happiness. Tonight has gone so smoothly.

Parker's strong arms wrap around my neck and he nuzzles his nose by my ear. "My family loves you, you know. You've made quite the impression. Not that I'm surprised."

"The feeling is mutual. I've loved my time here with them tonight. Your family is just as wonderful as I remember."

He pulls back, finding my eyes with his. *Those eyes* that do crazy things to me. "You're staying with me tonight at the beach house." It's not a question but a command. The answer would have been yes, of course. I couldn't say no if I tried.

"Did you have something in mind for us when we get there?"

"I have a long list and I intend to spend all night getting through it."

"All night? Are we forgoing sleep?"

"We might have to. Any objections?" Parker runs his thumb over the edge of my jaw. My skin heats under his touch.

"Not one."

"That's my girl. And for the record, in case there was any doubt, I'm not with you for all the incredible sex we have. Trust me, I'm loving every second of it, but I'm with you because you're *you*. You put everyone before yourself, you challenge me and put me in my place and your kisses drive me out of my mind. I can't go a day without seeing you. I'm lost in you, Livy."

"I'm lost in you too, Parker." I go up on my toes and kiss him. His lips part and we deepen the kiss. His tongue seeks mine and the kiss turns breathless. I don't want to stop but this is not the time or place. I'm about to break it when I hear Miles' voice interrupt us.

"Jesus you two. You haven't been able to keep your hands off each other all night. I'm not blaming you, Parker. If I had a girl that looked like Olivia, I'd have my hands all over her too."

Parker side-eyes his brother and laughs, quickly rearranging himself behind me to hide the obvious swell in his pants. He then quickly pulls me in close to hide my embarrassment from his brother.

"We are on our way outside. Give us a minute."

"Don't stop on my account," Miles jokes, heading back outside.

We spend the rest of the night cuddled up under a blanket on a loveseat by the fire table, listening to stories about Parker and his siblings. It's been a really long time since I've laughed so hard. Tonight is everything I could have hoped for and more, surrounded by a family who fiercely love and protect each other.

It's just after ten when Parker announces that we need to be going and we give each of his family members a kiss and a hug. His parents walk us to the door. "We love having you home Parker," his dad says before we leave. "And it was also our pleasure to spend time with you, Olivia. Hope to see you both soon."

"Thanks. Love you both." Parker side hugs his dad and kisses his mother on her cheek.

"Love you too, son, beyond the moon. I hope to see you soon, Olivia. Good night, you two." Mrs. Bennett stands in the doorway watching us walk down the driveway.

We make our way to the car and settle in. The engine revs to life and Parker leans in close and whispers in my ear, "We still have that list we need to get to."

This anticipation is almost too much. This perfect night is about to get even better.

FOURTEEN

Olivia

I PULL MY HOODIE OVER MY HEAD AND SIT BACK ON MY MAT beside the rest of the girls. Jules and I arrived together at Breathe Yoga, meeting Kate and Ellie here. They both greeted Jules just as I expected, like they had known her a lifetime.

I look forward to these weekly get togethers and I'm excited to include Jules in our girls' night. We usually go for dinner and a glass of wine afterwards and get caught up on each other's weeks. It crossed my mind to cancel tonight to be with Parker considering he will have to leave soon to go back to the city. But so much of my life is changing at the moment, it felt important to keep up this part of my routine and my commitments to my friends.

"Did you get any sleep at all last night? I bet you and your hot boyfriend had a steamy sex marathon."

"Geez Ellie, did you forget she is Parker's little sister? I am not talking about this in front of her. No offense, Jules."

Could it really be that obvious? I woke up this morning in Parker's arms feeling like I was on cloud nine. I barely made it to work on time and had to rush through a shower. Parker couldn't keep his hands off me this morning, complaining that he wouldn't get to see me all day and then tonight due to my yoga class. Two orgasms later, I was finally out the door on my way to work. He made me promise I would stay with him tonight and of course I said yes. I've become insatiable when it comes to him, which is a new feeling for me. I've always enjoyed being intimate but never needed it the way I crave it with Parker. It feels like I can never get enough of him and there is a part of me that worries about that. We have yet to figure out where our relationship is going and how we are going to ever make this work.

"As cringy as it is to think about my brother in bed with a woman, I'm just happy it's you."

"Thank you. I think." We all laugh and start to stretch before class starts.

"Did Olivia tell you about the special delivery she received at work today from your stud brother?" Ellie asks.

"No, she did not. Geez, Olivia, I've never seen him act like this before. He is head over heels for you. What did he send?"

I release my arm I'm stretching across my chest. "He had the prettiest petite chocolate cake from my favorite bakery delivered to me. He knows chocolate is my weakness."

"Is that not the absolute cutest? How do I find a guy like him?" Ellie groans.

"I know! There are *two* more Bennett boys that I believe are single. One for each of us, Ells. I'll even let you have first choice. I'll just take the other one. I'm a giver like that," Kate jokes.

"Ew, these are my brothers you are talking about," Jules squeals, covering her ears with her hands. "I can't with this convo. Besides, those two are a long way off from committing to anyone for more than one night."

"They just haven't met the right girl. Look at Parker. There's hope. He seems to have done a complete 180 since meeting Olivia," Kate says, stretching her legs in front of her, reaching for her toes.

"It's true and we are all happy you two have found your way back to each other. My mother is ready to start planning your wedding which is a little frustrating since she has never been excited to plan one for me."

"What do you mean?" I ask.

"Well, I've been with Alex now for over a year and she's never mentioned an engagement, never mind a wedding. I know she likes him; she just doesn't show much interest in our relationship."

"Do you think Alex is the one? The one you'll spend the rest of your life with?" I ask carefully, curious but not wanting to pry.

"I think so. He makes me happy. He's not super affectionate but I don't think most guys are. Med school keeps him busy too, so I try to give him his space."

"How's your sex life? I mean is he hot and steamy in the bedroom? Is he McSteamy or McDreamy? You must role play doctor-patient all the time." We all cringe at Ellie. Jules is never going to want to hang out with us again.

"It's fine."

"It's *fine*? What do you mean it's fine?" Ellie chirps back, looking dumbfounded.

"He's tired a lot from studying so we don't see each other much unless it's the weekend."

"Okay, but when you do, how's the sex? Do you make up for lost time?"

"It's nice," Jules replies quietly, then gulps from her water bottle.

"Nice?! Jules, *nice* doesn't cut it. Are there fireworks? Mind-blowing orgasms? You shouldn't be able to keep your hands off each other."

"Ellie, stop. Ease up on the psychoanalysis. It's her relationship. It's not for any of us to judge. She's happy. I met Alex last night, he's a really great guy."

Thankfully our instructor starts the class, putting an end to the uncomfortable conversation. Jules didn't seem too bothered by it and we all have a great class. I leave feeling relaxed and centered, but I know the feeling won't last long. I've been putting off talking to my mom, but I know I need to do it soon. I decide that I also need to talk to Parker about it all, to let him in. He deserves honesty from me if we are going to have a chance at making this relationship work.

We end the night with dinner and drinks at one of our favorite Mexican restaurants. I drop Jules off at her house and almost immediately my phones buzzes with a message. I laugh, thinking how in tune Parker is with me. He knows the minute my evening out has ended and I'm sure he's excited for our night to begin.

I check my phone and am disappointed. It's a text from my mom and as soon as I see it a pit forms in my stomach. I pull up the text and it's her confirmation of my father's release date, this Monday. She's written it like it's something we should all be celebrating. Like it's an invitation to a party. I feel sick to my stomach. I drop the phone into my purse, unable to respond. My hands start to shake. I take three deep breaths and try to clear my head. I know I should be relieved that he's finally being released; I guess a part of me is. However, I've worked really hard to rise from the ashes he left behind, and to take back control of my life. I've moved past the shame and the hurt and have found a way to carry on. I'm scared of starting our relationship over. I'm also scared to watch my mother take him back with open arms after all these years without asking for what she deserves. An apology, at the very least.

After several minutes, I start my drive to the beach house. I pull into the driveway in a fog, not even knowing how I got there.

Parker is waiting for me, leaning his shoulder into the doorframe with a gorgeous, smoldering smile. He looks so handsome in a faded grey t-shirt stretched across his muscular chest and black athletic shorts. I should be ecstatic to see him, but not even this beautiful man standing in front of me is enough to calm my nerves.

I get out of my car and walk towards him, closing the distance between us. It must be written all over my face because I watch his face drop as I get closer. He pulls me to him, and his strong arms feel like a blanket wrapped around me. I feel a tear roll down my cheek and try to hold myself together, swallowing the lump in my throat.

"Baby, are you okay? You look sad. Did something happen with the girls?" Parker wipes the tear away with the tips of his fingers.

"No, our night was great. It's not that."

"Well then what is it? You know you can talk to me, Livy. Let me try to fix it."

I lay my cheek on his warm chest and he kisses the top of my head. I feel safe in his arms and protected from the world outside this house. He continues to run his hands up and down my back.

"Come here, babe. Let's go inside."

He guides me into the living room and lowers himself to the couch bringing me into his lap. He has one arm behind my back, his other hand on my legs that are draped across his thigh.

"Talk to me, Livy. What's going on?" Parker brushes the edge of my jaw with the back of his hand, his tone warm and caring, and it makes me want to melt into his arms.

"My mom just texted me with my dad's release date. He's coming home Monday. I know we haven't talked about any of this, but I think we need to now."

"I agree. I've wanted to bring it up but didn't want to push you. You haven't seemed ready to talk about it and the last thing I wanted to do was make you feel uncomfortable." Parker's warm hand grips my thigh gently. "I'm here for you and I want to help you through this."

"It's not something I like to talk about. I don't even bring it up with my mom or my sister. I carry so much shame over it and wish it would just go away. It all makes me so angry. It's confusing. My mom lives in some crazy dream world. She pretends like he's off on some vacation and will return to us like nothing ever happened. Doesn't she see what he did to us? He ruined all of our lives."

I feel so vulnerable in this moment with Parker, and that feeling is foreign to me. I have become so much stronger over the years. I've gotten used to not needing anyone. Until now.

"I'm so sorry, Livy. I wish I could take all of your pain away. Do you visit him?"

"I have, but not often. I go with my mom on holidays and special occasions and when I do, I feel like I'm just going through the motions. It's awkward and I doubt our relationship will ever be the same. I don't know if I will ever forgive him for the suffering and embarrassment he has caused us."

"I think you need to talk to him. You need to hear him out and get his side of story. It's not always black and white. Give him the opportunity. You will never know until you try." Parker takes my hand in his and kisses the back of my knuckles. "You can't live like this forever. You're so tense, your whole body is rigid. It's not healthy."

"Parker, you saw what it did to our family. We lost everything because of him, and our name was dredged through the mud. It wasn't fair to us. He should have thought about us before he did what he did. And don't even get me started on that hoe he was doing behind my mother's back. She was eight flipping years older than me. Eight!"

"I know. It was awful and my heart broke for you. Correction, it was awful and revolting. But he's your dad. People make mistakes and deserve second chances. Forgiving your father doesn't mean you are okay with his actions. It means you will no longer allow those actions to hurt your heart. Let me go with you on Monday. We can face it together."

"I haven't even decided if I want to see him on Monday." I close my eyes, holding back the tears that are threatening to spill down my cheeks.

"Whatever you decide, I'm here for you. Take some time to think it over and when you're ready let me know. It's your decision, Livy, and you need to do what feels right." Parker places his finger under my chin and tilts my head, so his eyes meet mine. "Okay?"

"Okay. Thank you, Parker." I press a gentle kiss to his mouth. I am starting to realize that I need him more than I have been willing to admit.

"As much as I like your body on mine, let me make you some tea and run you a warm bath. Maybe we could take a walk on the beach afterwards? How does that sound?"

"Perfect. I would like that a lot." I wrap my arms around his neck and kiss his cheek, his forehead and his jaw, followed with a kiss to his lips, showing Parker how much I appreciate him.

I follow him down the hall to the bathroom, and watch him run the water, filling the tub. He adds a handful of Epsom salts. Together we lift my workout top over my head and then I remove the rest of my clothes.

"Hop in, baby, I'll go turn the kettle on."

"Parker?"

"Yeah Livy? Is it too hot?" He spins around in the doorway before heading to the kitchen.

"No, it's perfect. Thank you for this."

"I want to take care of you."

"I know," I whisper. "You are. You make me really happy, Parker. One more thing, after our walk, will you take me to bed?"

I don't need him to respond. The heated look in his eyes is all the answer I need.

Parker

I end my call with Nelson and roll my neck to relieve the tension in my stiff muscles. Although plans were approved on the Cape May project, our architect is suggesting a change to our commercial space, which means more work and more headaches for me.

I'm also worried about Livy. Last night was a breakthrough. We needed to have that talk. I'm relieved her walls finally came down. I want her to feel like she can talk to me and really let me in. It's a sign that she trusts me. I want to do everything I can to be there for her, to show her how much she means to me. I know now that a weekend away, just the two of us, is exactly what she needs. It's what we both need. The next few days are going to be hard on her emotionally, so a distraction and an escape will help her to get her mind off of what's coming.

I put in a call to James to see if his vacation home in Seaside is available for this weekend. Our dads are brothers and we have always been extremely close. We grew up living within miles of each other, spending weekends, holidays and vacations together. James lost his mother five years ago in a car accident and it crushed us all. It's still hard to think about, but that loss was a painful reminder of how important family is and we've stayed very close and fiercely loyal to my uncle and cousins.

Thankfully his home is available this weekend, and James said he's more than happy to allow us to stay there. It's a beautiful spot overlooking the ocean and I can't wait to take Livy there. The idea of spending a few days alone, with no interruptions, makes me feel happier than I've felt in a long time.

I make one more call to Ellie and run my plan past her, making sure she can handle the store without Livy for the weekend. I want to pull this surprise getaway off without Livy knowing a thing. Ellie loves my idea and thinks it's perfect timing to get Livy away. She has no problem covering the shop with Leah's help.

I walk into my father's office with only one more thing on my to-do list. I need to clear my schedule for Friday afternoon. He's seated behind his mahogany desk combing through a file. The sun pours into his office through the large window behind him.

"Hi son. How's my boy?" He looks up from his paperwork, removing his glasses.

"I'm great, Dad. How's your day?" I take a seat in one of the leather armchairs across from his desk.

"Better now that you squared away the retail space issue with Nelson. I still think you might need to take a trip out there to make sure it was the best decision. It's smart that you go over the new plans in person."

"I agree, I can make that happen next week."

"That would be great. Wasn't last night nice? Your mother and I had a great time getting to know Olivia again. She's a wonderful woman and you seem to be really taken with her."

"I am. That's actually the reason I'm here. I was hoping it would be okay to take tomorrow afternoon off. I called James and his place in Seaside is free this weekend, so I am hoping to take Livy away. She has had a rough week finding out that her dad is being released from prison on Monday. I would really like to do something special for her to take her mind off of things."

"Parker, I'm really proud of you. Your heart is in the right place. It's definitely going to be a difficult time for her and she's going to need you." My dad removes his glasses, setting them on his desk, and leans back in his chair. His arms cross over his chest. "Things seem to be moving quite quickly with the two of you. Your mother thinks that she is the one for you. Is there a chance she could be right?"

"I think she could be. I love her, Dad. I don't know if I ever stopped." It's the first time I've said those three words out loud and the admission pumps adrenaline through my veins.

"You have our blessing, son. Your mother and I think she is perfect for you. You picked a good one and we are really excited for your future together."

"Thanks Dad. It means a lot." I look at the blue skies outside, feeling hopeful.

I know what Livy and I have is real. I've never felt like this with anyone but her. I decide I'm going to tell her that I love her this weekend. I only hope she feels the same.

FIFTEEN

Parker squeezes my hand and weaves his fingers through mine. His other hand grips the steering wheel, driving us to a secret location. My window down, the sun warms my skin. I rest my head back against the seat and gaze out the window. I watch the Cypress trees roll by as the city fades away behind us and I think I might just be the happiest I've ever been in my entire life.

"You good, babe?"

"I'm better than good. I feel like I'm in a dream. But I'm dying to find out where you are taking me. It's killing me." I turn my head to face him, the breeze from the window blowing loose strands of my hair across my face. He grins, his eyes hidden behind his Ray-Bans which make him look even hotter than he usually does. I'm not sure how that's even possible.

Parker had arrived at Bloom in the late afternoon, stealing me from work, and surprising me with a weekend away. I'm still shocked that he would go to the trouble of planning this for us. Ellie was even in on the surprise, which made me feel so good. We left Bloom and went straight to my apartment, packed my bag and hit the road. His bags were already packed in the trunk along with some road trip snacks and a box of my favorite caramel apple croissants. He never seems to forget a thing.

As we drive along the highway, I can't help but feel excited about spending time alone with Parker without work or distractions. *Is that how I'm now referring to my father returning home from prison? A distraction?* Why can't I manage my feelings about this? Why can't I better understand why I'm feeling this way? I wish I could feel happy to have my father back again. Instead, it just feels like re-opening old wounds. I've built a wall around my heart to protect it from the scrutiny, the disappointment and the shame. I decide to focus on the weekend with Parker, trying to ignore the sinking feeling in my gut.

Just under three hours into our drive, I spot a sign for the town of Seaside and Parker veers off the highway to the exit. I straighten my back, sitting up in my chair, and Parker notices the excitement in my face.

A few miles up the road, we pull into a quaint little town with Victorian buildings and red brick cobblestone streets. There is a charming B&B on the corner, painted in a shade of butter yellow, with a porch lined with rocking chairs. A small coffee shop and a restaurant called the Lobster Shop are anchored beside it. There are children riding scooters and couples strolling the streets hand-in-hand. I can't wait to get out and explore with my man.

I steal another glance at Parker, trying to read his eyes for clues of exactly where he is taking me. He catches me staring at him and the corners of his lips turn up.

"Are you going to tell me where we're going yet?"

Parker turns to me with a wry smile. "Nope! What kind of surprise would it be if I told you before we got there? Patience, my sexy girl. You are just going to have to wait and see. But first we need to make a quick pit stop for groceries."

He flips on his turn signal and makes a right into a parking lot.

We go into the grocery store and purchase enough food and essentials to hold us over for the weekend. Whatever I eye or touch seems to make its way into our shopping cart thanks to Parker. He pulls me into his hard body every chance he gets, covering me in kisses in practically every aisle of the store. With each kiss and embrace, the stress that seems to have taken root in my body eases. I'm starting to feel more in the moment with him. I want to make the most of each and every second of this weekend together. He deserves that. We deserve that.

The sun is still shining brightly in the sky when Parker turns his Audi down a paved driveway. It leads down to a stunning home on the edge of the ocean. Parker tells me it's his cousin's cabin and it's all ours for the weekend. The home is so large that calling it a cabin seems ridiculous. It has a pillared front porch entrance and is covered in wood shingles the color of driftwood, with a painted white trim.

The manicured lawn in the front of the house gives way to sand dunes edging the back. I'm in awe.

"Parker, this is gorgeous. It's really all ours for the weekend?"

"All ours, babe." He flashes me a sexy smile and I swear my heart stops for a split second.

He parks the car and steps out, jogging around to my side. He helps me from my seat and slips his hand in mine as we walk to the front doors.

I feel his hand rest at the curve of my back guiding me through the front doors. Impossibly, the inside of the house is even more impressive than the outside. It has a warm, lived-in feel with an open floor concept and exposed beams in the vaulted ceilings. There are water views from almost every window at the back of the home. The living room boasts a large wood-burning fireplace and a pair of leather recliners. I envision the two us cuddled together in front of the fireplace with a glass of wine and my heart warms.

We move through the house to the gourmet kitchen at the back of the home, where French doors lead to an outdoor dining area. I can see a dock at the foot of the beach with a large boat house and wonder what floats inside of it.

"Do you think it will do, Liv?"

"I think I'd be crazy if it didn't do. It's just beautiful. I can see the ocean from every angle. Thank you for bringing me here, Parker."

"I'm happy you like it. I sort of knew you would." Parker winks. "There's still one part of the tour left. Let me show you the master bedroom upstairs and then I'll bring in our bags from the car. Follow me." He takes my hand, tugging me behind him.

Parker leads me up a set of wood stairs to a long hallway with four bedrooms. The master bedroom is on the left with a king size four poster bed covered in white linens and a mass of accent pillows. We move inside towards the French doors leading out to a balcony overlooking the ocean. My hand glides over the gauzy curtains and I take in the view. I feel Parker behind me. He wraps his arms around my waist and nestles his face into my neck. I exhale. He breathes me in and my skin tingles all over. I run my hand up the side of his face and rest it behind his ear. My fingers play with the short strands of hair at the base of his neck and I drink in his scent. That scent. I swear I'm going to figure out how to bottle it one of these days.

"There's a boat in that house that I thought we could take out tomorrow." He says, pointing toward the dock. "I was thinking we could pack a lunch and head out for a few hours. What do you think?"

"Yes!" I practically squeal and turn in his arms to face him. "I might never leave here. Can we stay forever?"

I grew up on my dad's boat. We spent most of our summers exploring different bays and eclectic marinas, sleeping in the small cabin down below. We would kayak in the ocean and fish off the bow. We barbequed whatever we managed to catch in the evening and played board games, listening to the classics because those were my dad's favorites. They are my fondest memories with him, before he was gone.

Parker is beaming as I clasp my hands around his neck. His hands join at the arch of my back.

"I could never say no to you, Livy. The answer will always be yes with you. If you like it here that much, we will buy a place."

"We will? Parker, I don't have that kind of money." I clear my throat. "I didn't mean for it to sound the way that it did."

"I know that." He tips his face down towards me and places his lips on my forehead. "But I do have the money and what's mine is yours when we get married one day."

"Married? Don't you think you are moving a little fast?"

"Honestly, I don't think we are moving fast enough. Livy, if I thought you would say yes, I would have already moved you into the beach house with me permanently. I hate the thought of going to bed without you and waking up alone in the morning. I want more of you. This is it for me. It's only you. It's always been you."

I feel my knees go weak and I'm thankful I have Parker's embrace to hold me up.

Did he really just say we'd be married one day?

He feels the same way about me as I do about him. He has to. He wouldn't see marriage in our future if he didn't love me. I want to tell him how I feel but I'm confused how he could be ready for a commitment so soon? This is Parker Bennett standing in front of me. Gorgeous, successful, sexy as sin with a history of serial dating. My head is still spinning when he pulls me from my thoughts.

"Livy, what's wrong? Where did you just go?" His eyes narrow as he looks at me.

I bite my bottom lip and pause.

"Livy, talk to me. Don't shut me out."

"You are saying all the right things, Parker. It's everything I want to hear, so please don't take this the wrong way. It's just, it was only a few weeks ago you couldn't commit to more than one night with a woman and now you are talking about a lifetime with me. How can I be sure that you really want this?"

"Because none of those women were you. There's a reason why I never let myself get close to anyone else. My heart belonged to you. It still does. You wrecked me the day you broke up with me. I couldn't function for months."

I flinch knowing I have never given him the truth. The real reason I broke up with him.

"I didn't want a relationship with any of them because they weren't you. Funny thing is most of them were brunettes. I don't even fucking like brunettes. I think I subconsciously sabotaged things with those women before they even began."

"Great, now I'm left with this image of you and some hot brunette with her hands all over you. I'm going to need to bleach my eyes out." His laugh makes my heart so full that I feel myself smiling.

"Do you feel better?"

My mind is still spinning at his admission and I need to remind myself to breathe.

"Listen to me, I need you to believe me when I say I am ready for this. It's important to me that you know that." He locks his gaze on mine.

"Yes Parker, I do feel better and I do believe you." I go up on my toes and kiss his mouth, his nose, the tip of his chin and the center of his neck. "But right now, I'm going to a scary place," I say in mock seriousness. "I am super hungry, and you are about to see my hangry side. I'm warning you it's not pretty."

"That's my cue! Why don't you go sit outside with a blanket and enjoy the view while I unpack the car? And don't argue with me. Then, I'll make you something to eat."

"Fine, if you insist."

I sink into a chair on the patio while Parker runs to and from the car, unloading our things. I breathe in the salty scent of the ocean and it immediately eases the tension in my body. My mind replays our conversation in the bedroom. The complexity of our situation keeps making my mind whirl.

He eventually brings me a glass of wine and some cheese and crackers to snack on. We decide to stay in and make dinner. Parker grills us two steaks and I put together a salad and baked potatoes. It feels good to work together in the kitchen, a glimpse of what life could feel like one day in the future.

We eat dinner on the patio, enjoying the cool breeze off the ocean, and make plans for tomorrow. We clean up the kitchen and I let Parker know I'm going to run upstairs to the bedroom and grab my sweater.

By the time I return, Parker has started a wood fire in the living room and cleared the coffee table away, replacing it with a bed of blankets and pillows. He's opened a second bottle of wine and there are two glasses waiting for us on the hearth. He motions for me to sit down and I lower myself on to a cushion beside him.

"This is so cozy. I feel spoiled." It's been a long time since anyone has gone out of their way to care for me and make me a priority. And I have to admit I like it. I never would have imagined a year ago that I would enjoy sharing so much of my life with another person. My quiet and lonely apartment has felt normal to me for such a long time.

"I like spoiling you. It's my job." Parker shifts to his knees to stoke the fire. He sits back down and I hand him his glass of wine.

He takes a sip and sets his glass back on the hearth and I can feel a shift in his energy. He clearly has something on his mind, his jaw is clenched, and I can't help it, I start to panic. My neck feels warm all of a sudden.

"Livy, can I ask you something?"

"Of course." I fiddle with the hem of my sweater, not sure where he is going with this. From the hitch in his voice, it doesn't sound good.

"Why did you break up with me? When we were kids. I know what you told me, but what was the real reason?"

Shit. Is this really happening right now? I could lie but I know Parker deserves the truth, and I need to give it to him if we are going to take the next steps in our relationship. I'd known I would have to tell him soon, but I don't feel prepared to have this conversation right now.

He moves a little closer to me, removing my fingers from my sweater and intertwining them with his. I fix my stare on our hands as I start to explain as best as I can.

"I lied."

"I know. I just never could figure out why."

"You were so sweet to me and I loved you. That never changed. Ever."

"Then what happened, Liv?" he asks. "I want to know."

My hand is still in his, and I'm sure he can feel my pulse racing. I inhale a deep breath and continue. "My dad had just been charged and sent to prison to serve his sentence. It was all over the news. It was a struggle for me to even function. I heard the whispers in the hallways. I saw the stares. I was humiliated and ashamed and in so much pain."

"I remember. It was awful. I did everything I could to protect you."

"Yes, you did."

"So, what happened Liv?"

"You brought me to Hunter's end-of-year party at his house. Do you remember?" Parker nods. "I didn't want to go but you thought it was important that I get out and carry on with life. You said I needed to surround myself with my friends. So, I went." I swallow the lump in my throat and exhale.

"I remember the night going better than I expected and I actually managed to have fun. I forgot for a few hours about all the heartache I was dealing with at home. You hadn't left my side for most of the night, making sure I was okay until I finally convinced you I was fine and that you should go talk with your friends. You were at the bar in the living room with the guys and I watched you from across the room throwing your head back in hysterics at whatever it was they were saying. It made me happy to see you happy." I can still to this day see that image in my mind, likes it's imprinted there forever.

"Hunter approached me, seeing me watch you laugh with your friends." I pause. The words that will fall from my mouth next will have repercussions. They are words that have been taking up space in my head for a long time. The fear of telling him gets to me and I blank for a second.

Parker scratches his head; his mouth opens, then shuts again. He's choosing his words carefully. "Did he say something to you?"

"He... he said..."

"What did he say Livy? What did he say to you?" his voice raises in frustration and he's looking at me with a pointed stare.

"He said I would be crazy to ever think I belonged with a guy like you. He said something about your pedigree and how your family would never allow you to embarrass them by dating the daughter of a convicted felon. He said my time was up and that I should do you a favor and break up with you because you were too nice of a guy to do it yourself."

Parker blinks at me and I see the rage in his eyes.

"I will fucking destroy him."

"Parker, please. Take a breath."

"Why would you believe that bullshit? I never once gave you reason to think I would leave you after your dad went to jail.

Not once, Livy." I watch as he releases my hand. His eyes darken two shades and his mouth presses into a thin line.

"I was confused. Hunter was practically the closest person to you. He was like family to you and I knew he cared about you, so I considered what he said. I figured he knew something I didn't. It wasn't hard for me to convince myself he was right; I was already so ashamed and embarrassed about what my family was going through. I knew after graduation you would have the whole world at your feet. The sky was the limit for a guy like you. You didn't need me holding you back or ruining your good name. I kept watching you with your friends. You were so happy. I was the exact opposite. I started to feel like I would never be able to bring you that same happiness and it wasn't fair to you."

"Jesus Livy. That was not your decision to make. It was mine. You took it upon yourself to decide what was best for me without even considering how I felt. You had no right." Parker gets up suddenly and starts to pace the room.

"Fucking Hunter. That prick." His voice is sharp. Then he mumbles something I can't make out.

"Parker, I'm sorry. I thought at the time I was doing the right thing. I never wanted to hurt you. You have to believe me. It was never my intention. Breaking up with you nearly destroyed me. I've never felt pain like that. Everything inside me was screaming in pain for months. It's my biggest regret."

"I wish you would have just told me what happened. You made an assumption about what I wanted for my life without even asking me. You should have known me better than that. I've never been an asshole to you."

"I was in such a terrible place. I was insecure, my whole life had drastically changed. I wasn't thinking straight, and I was just so young. I know I hurt you but at the time I thought I was doing what was right for you. I thought if I let you go then you could have the life you deserved."

Parker shakes his head and squeezes his eyes shut. He stops pacing and his gaze finds mine.

"Livy, this cost us eight years. Eight years apart that we will never be able to get back."

"Parker, who's to say we would have stayed together? We can't change the past, we can only move forward from here. And I *want* to move forward with you."

His jaw tightens and his fists clench. My heart hammers in my chest and it feels hard to breathe. I give in to my emotions, feeling the sting of my tears pooling my eyes.

"Talk to me. Parker, please. Come sit with me. I'm scared."

"Why are you scared? Livy, please don't cry. I can't stand to see you cry." He moves closer and slowly lowers himself in front of the fire again with me.

"I don't want to lose you."

"I'm not going anywhere, Livy. I just need time to process this. I want to knock Hunter the fuck out."

"I don't blame you."

"He's lucky I'm not in Reed Point right now. I'm going to kill him for the way he made you feel. You didn't deserve that."

"I'm sorry I never told you, Parker."

He runs his fingers over his temples and his jaw muscles flex. The pressure building from deep down inside me is too much and the tears that were stinging my eyes began to spill. They roll down my cheeks, my hands swiping them away. I feel desperate for Parker to touch me.

"Come here Livy, I've got you."

Parker gathers me into his chest. I feel his chin rest on the top of my head and his hands roam my back.

"I've got you. Don't cry, Livy. Please don't cry." His arms wrap around my body a little tighter.

"I hate that I upset you. Can you forgive me?" I ask in a soft voice, my cheek pressed firmly against his chest.

"You, I forgive. Hunter, not ever."

"You two will need to talk."

"Talk? I'm not interested in talking to him."

"Parker, you don't mean that."

"Like hell I don't. How could I be friends with a guy like that? How could I ever forgive him for what he said to you.? I'm done talking about him."

His jaw is a little less clenched and the warmth in his eyes is back. So, I gather my courage and ask, "Are we okay, Parker? Do you want to go back to the city? I will understand if you do."

"No Livy. I want to stay right here with you. I'm not mad at you. I understand why you did what you did. I don't like it but you're right, what's done is done. Let's finally just put the past where it belongs."

"I'd like that. I would probably feel better if you kissed me."

"I'd like to do a hell of a lot more than just kiss you right now." He smirks and takes my hips in his hands.

I stare into those deep brown eyes that have the power to destroy me. He pulls me closer to him, so I straddle his lap. His eyes turn dark and drop down to my mouth. He covers my mouth with a kiss and my lips part giving his tongue all the access it needs to find mine. He kisses me breathlessly. I tip my head back as he drags his mouth down the sensitive skin of my neck.

"Parker." I moan his name.

"I've got you, baby."

"I know you do. You always have."

SIXTEEN

Parker

"You did all this while I slept? What time did you get up this morning?" Livy's eyes are on the cooler I'm packing in the kitchen for our day out. "This all looks so good. I can't wait to get out on the water."

"Morning beautiful. How did you sleep?" I take the few steps between us, wrapping my hand around the curve of her hip and squeezing her into my chest. I dip my face into her neck and kiss the smooth skin behind her ear. My hand moves up the curve of her ass underneath my t-shirt that she has made her own. I like it. A lot.

"I had the best sleep. That bed is a dream."

"Good, I'm glad because I have a big day planned for us. We should get ready and head out. We can have breakfast on the boat. I packed croissants and fruit and I can make us coffee to go." Her skin feels soft and smooth and the sight of her long tan legs under my t-shirt is making me hard. "If I stay here any longer looking at you in that shirt, I won't be able to control myself."

"Is that so?" Livy teases, looking up at me through her long, dark lashes.

"It's definitely so."

"Well, maybe you should help me take it off then?"

"Livy, you can't say things like that to me and expect me to behave." I give her a playful look, squeezing one globe of her ass in my hand.

"Who said I want you to?"

We spend the next twenty minutes in the shower together, then get dressed and pack our bags with our swimsuits, sunblock and a change of clothes. I watch Livy buzz around the room, singing along to a country song she has playing from her cell phone. She amazes me. Not only is she breath-taking, but she is also kind and compassionate and honest. The best part of all is that I can be myself around her. The fact that I'm a Bennett isn't a big deal to her. She's never wanted me for my money, unlike other women who look at me with dollar signs in their eyes.

"I'm ready," she says, catching me watching her. "You too?"

"I'm always ready."

"You're insatiable, Parker."

"Maybe, but just admit it: you can't get enough of me." This gets a laugh out of her as we head to the doorway to grab our things.

We head to the dock. The sun is already shining and there isn't a cloud in the light blue sky.

My mind wanders momentarily to last night. Livy fell asleep with her head on my chest long before I finally succumbed to sleep, my thoughts consumed with Hunter. It all makes sense now. I finally know the real reason Livy broke up with me. It feels like I've been sucker punched, knowing my best friend was the cause of all that heartbreak. It's no secret Hunter can be an ass when he wants to be, but what he said to Livy is on another level of low. It's vile. I'm not sure I will ever be able to move past this with him. I shake my head, needing to forget about that bullshit and enjoy the day with my girl.

I focus on the ocean, so calm that the peninsula is like a sheet of glass. There is the faintest breeze in the air. I inhale the ocean air and admire the view from the dock.

We load up the boat. Livy effortlessly unties the lines and pushes us away from the dock. She climbs in as I guide us away from our slip. It's sexy as hell watching her navigate her way around the boat in her cut off shorts and bare feet. I don't have to ask her for help. She takes control, removing the buoys and ropes once we've cleared the boat house. She knows where to be and what to do. I set up the stereo and turn on a country music station for Livy. She hands me my coffee and I flip my ball cap backwards so I can steal a quick kiss.

"Where are we heading to? Do you know your way around here?"

"I do. You won't have to worry about getting lost at sea. Scout's honour!" I say, raising a hand.

Livy laughs. "If you are trying to make me believe you were ever a Boy Scout, I'm not buying it."

"You wound me. I am a good, Catholic momma's boy. I was made for that shit."

"Um, good Boy Scouts don't have gutter mouths."

"I didn't hear you complain about my mouth last night when I..."

"Parker, you are impossible!" Livy swats me on my shoulder and her cheeks brighten three shades pinker.

"I'm going to take us to a bay about twenty-five minutes from here where we can anchor and go for a swim."

"Sounds perfect."

We glide into the calm waters of the bay and Livy takes the wheel so I can check the anchor. It's a sunny day, the air hot and humid. There are other ski boats and sail boats anchored, boaters lounging on floaties and sunbathing on their decks. Once I'm happy with the anchor, we decide to have breakfast before taking a dip. We change into our swimsuits and lay on the sun bed that covers the bow of the boat. Livy is killing me in a pale blue bikini, her face tipped to the sun and her hair splayed out all around her.

"You're going to be the death of me in that suit, you know."

"Would you rather I take it off?" She side-eyes me with a smirk. *This girl is really going to kill me.*

"I plan on taking it off you myself at some point today."

"I hope you are a man of your word, Mr. Bennett." A coy smile pulls at her lips and I reach for her hip, pulling her into my side.

"That I can guarantee, Miss Madden." Hooking my finger under her chin, I tip her face to mine and kiss her, deep and slow, hoping she knows from this one kiss what I really want to say to her.

Livy sits up and wraps her hair in a bun on top of her head with an elastic she has around her wrist. "I have an idea!"

"Should I be scared?"

"No silly. There's so much more I want to know about you. We have years and years of catching up we need to do. Let's play a game! 21 Questions. I used to play it in college, it's a great way to get to know people. It will be fun, I promise. Game?"

She looks so damn cute I can't say no. I'm not sure how it happened so fast, but I'm absolutely in love with her. She's the type of girl you take home to your parents, the girl you want to take on expensive vacations just to see her face light up, to bring flowers every week just to see her smile. With a woman like Livy, you spend the rest of your life making sure she knows how much you love her. And maybe have a handful of babies along the way.

"Game! You go first, babe."

"Okay, question number one. Snow or sun on a vacation and where?"

"Sun, always. I love Hawaii."

"Me too. I hate being cold. I've always wanted to go to Hawaii but never been. Now it's your turn to ask me a question."

I make a mental note to take her to Hawaii once Cape May is operating smoothly. "Okay, biggest pet peeve? I can't stand it when people talk through a movie. They should all be banned from movie theaters and sent to live on their own island."

"Wow, you really mean that. Ha! For me it's line drifters." I draw my eyebrows together, having no clue what she's talking about. "You know," she continues. "Those people who drift into line while you're not paying attention and then pretend they were there the whole time. They think they got away with it, but you know the truth. They're awful."

I laugh because that just might be the cutest thing she's ever said. It's one of the things I love most about her. She's genuine, always herself.

"Okay, it's my turn. What's one goal you hope to accomplish in the future? It's kind of a tough question."

"No, it's not, it's easy. I want to be a dad someday." Livy's eyes go wide. "What about you, Liv, do you want kids one day?"

"I do."

"That's good."

"It is?" Her brow arches.

"Of course it is. We are on the same page. In the same book." It's a question I've wanted to know the answer to, but I haven't wanted to scare her. It wouldn't have been a deal breaker, but I was really hoping she wanted to have a family one day too. The thought of Livy pregnant with our child makes my heart feel like it's about to explode right out of my chest.

We play 21 questions for the next half an hour and I learn that she's afraid of sharks, never been on a nude beach (which I thank God for because yes, I'm turning into that jealous guy), her celebrity crush is Chris Hemsworth, and her longest relationship was with me. I admit that last answer makes me feel like I'm winning at life at the moment.

Final question and it's my turn to ask. I can't pass up this opportunity to go for it. So, I do.

"Okay Livy, last one before we take a swim. Are you ready?"

"Ready." She looks like a kid on Christmas morning and adrenaline pumps through my veins.

"Tell me a secret that you've never told anyone else."

"That's a tough question. My goodness. I have to really think about this. I don't have many secrets. I'm kind of boring, I guess. You go first so I have time to think."

"Okay." I move onto my knees in front of her and take her face in my hands. I pin my eyes on hers and kiss her softly. I pull back to find her eyes again. "I love you, Livy."

Her eyes go wide. She reaches for me and wraps both hands behind my neck, pulling my body into hers. I need to feel her hands on me, and it feels too good when she drags her soft fingers down the front of my chest. She kisses me, the kiss demanding.

It's lust. It's heat. It's passion. All in one kiss.

"Parker." She says my name in barely a whisper.

"Sshh. You don't have to say a thing." I press a chaste kiss to her lips. I don't want her to feel like she needs to say it back to me if she's not ready.

"But Parker. I need to tell you my secret. Don't you want to know what it is?"

I pull away from her, sitting back on my knees and nod. She searches my eyes, and her lips curve up towards the sky.

"I love you too, Parker. I don't think I ever stopped."

Just like that, I'm the happiest guy on the planet.

In the universe.

I feel like I'm freefalling from one thousand feet. A rush courses through my body that I don't ever want to stop.

I scoop her into my arms and bring her into my lap. I have everything I'll ever need in my arms and nothing else matters. I kiss her like it's the first time, forgetting everything else.

"You really mean it, Livy? You love me?"

"I do. I absolutely do without a doubt. I love you." Her smile radiates through me.

"I love you too. So damn much."

We spend the next twenty minutes in the ocean. The water is cold, so Livy spends most of that time with her legs wrapped around my waist and her arms around my neck while I tread water. I'm not complaining.

Afterwards, we dry off on the sun bed, both nodding off for a nap and then wake up to eat. After a charcuterie lunch, I can't take it any longer. I've been tormented for too God damn long at the site of Livy in her bikini. I want her now. I can't wait another second. With my pulse racing, I take Livy's hand and lead her down the three small steps into the cabin. Finally, I get to remove the swimsuit from Livy's body. I plan on wasting no time showing her exactly how much I love her.

I turn to face her when I reach the bottom of the stairs and grab her by her waist. She is still standing on the bottom step, I'm that impatient, needing her that bad. Needing to get my hands all over her. Needing her like my last breath.

My mouth finds the smooth skin at the center of her torso, kissing her, watching her skin pebble under my touch. I trail kisses down her flat stomach to her belly button, lost in that vanilla scent that intoxicates me. I savor every kiss as I run my fingers up both sides of her ribcage around to her back, pulling the string of her bikini top. I pull the second string that is fastened around her neck and watch as the pale blue fabric falls to the floor. My eyes run over the length of her body, taking every inch of this gorgeous woman in.

My hands fall to her thighs and I lift her into me, her legs circling my waist. Our eyes lock and I pull her in, kissing her deeply and earning a moan from her lips. Her fingers run through my hair, gripping strands, heat pulsing up my spine with her touch.

"Parker..."

I carry her to the bed and lay her down, her golden eyes peering up at me. Her bottom lip is trapped between her teeth. Her damp hair splays across the blankets. Her breath is ragged, her bare chest rising and falling.

My God.

"You are so fucking sexy," I say in a low voice as I strip my swim shorts to the ground, not wanting to wait another second to feel her skin on mine. Her eyes go to my arousal, shamelessly fixed on it. I take my length in my hand and give it a stroke for good measure.

I crawl over her body until my mouth reaches hers, claiming her. My kiss full of need, intensity and lust. Her back arches and her hands find my neck, pulling me closer. Needing me as much as I need her in this moment, she erases any space between us. I lower my body down to hers, deepening the kiss. Our hands are everywhere, her body flush with mine. She breaks the kiss and tips her neck back.

"Parker, you make me feel so good."

Giving her what she wants, I kiss her jaw, her neck and her collarbone and run my hand up the side of her body to her breast. I cover it with my mouth, sucking and teasing. Her body shuddering beneath me. I pay the same attention to the other one, teasing, nipping and circling it with my tongue. I move lower down her body, pressing a kiss to her ribcage, tracing her hip with my fingers. I take my time, exploring every delicious inch of her. I run a finger beneath the fabric of her swimsuit bottoms reaching the corner where it's tied with a string. I pull the string, then pull the other on the opposite hip, drawing the bottoms from her skin.

Livy sits up and moves into my lap, and her legs straddle my center. Our mouths crash together, her hands on my neck, my dick pressing against her stomach. Her hands move from my shoulders down the muscles of my back, digging her fingernails into my skin. It's frantic. It's primal. My pulse quickens, loving the way she touches me.

"Parker," she whispers.

"Tell me what you want, Livy."

"You Parker, I want you. Always only you." She pants and pushes me backwards onto the bed, straddling my hips. "Do you have any idea what your body does to me?"

My lips part and I reach for her breasts, cupping them in my hands.

Her eyes narrow. "No Parker, it's my turn." She shimmies down my legs running her hands along my abs, tracing each line, every groove, followed by her mouth. Her tongue sweeping the plains of my body, taking each nipple in her mouth. She kisses my neck, my jaw and then my mouth, sweeping her tongue against mine. She takes what she wants and I fucking love that about her.

"I want to feel all of you. I need you now, Parker."

She shifts forward, rising up on her knees. I feel like the luckiest son of a bitch on the planet. I grip her waist and position my hips, easing her down onto me. Joining our bodies. Our hearts. Our souls. Her soft eyes never leaving mine. I couldn't take my eyes off her if I tried.

She rocks up and down, harder and deeper, our bodies finding that perfect rhythm. My abs flexing with every thrust.

"Fuck Livy, nothing has ever felt so good." We move faster. Breathless. Giving and taking. "Kiss me. I love your mouth, Livy."

Her eyes fall with lust to my mouth, her body dips forward, and our mouths collide. I turn us over so I'm now in control, never breaking our connection. I know I'm not going to last much longer so I need to set the pace.

I slow us down and kiss her again until I've gained some control. I plunge my hands into the mattress on either side of her shoulders and begin to move back and forth inside of her again. I can't wait another second. She grips my waist and I rock faster, thrusting into her. Back and forth.

Livy moans my name and that's all it takes as I follow her right over the edge.

Down, down, down.

It's heaven on earth. Our bodies shudder together as the aftershocks roll through us.

I nestle my face in her neck, kissing her, trying to catch my breath. My body melts into hers, my heart in her hands.

"That was..."

"Fucking amazing." I finish her sentence for her.

"Yes, fucking amazing." She manages to get the words out through deep breaths. I can't help but smile, Livy rarely ever curses.

"We are magic together, Livy. I love you so much."

"I love you too."

We both catch our breath. We've never been able to hold back with each other. It's always been this way with us. It's finally feeling like this could really last forever.

SEVENTEEN

Parker

It's late afternoon and Livy and I are strolling the picturesque streets of Seaside. The beach town is bustling with people on bikes and tourists window-shopping, lined with stores and restaurants.

We showered and changed on the boat, then docked at the marina in town to do some exploring and have dinner. Livy's wet hair is pulled back into a bun and she's changed into a flowy sundress. Her skin is sun-kissed from our day on the water. She's oblivious to the stares she gets from other men and it still surprises me how some guy didn't find her and make her his before I had the chance. She's so fucking beautiful. Once again, I'm thanking my lucky stars.

Livy pulls me into one of the larger shops along the street, which carries home décor and candles among other things. I follow her through the knick-knacks and watch her browse the store. There's an area in the corner with jewelry that catches my eye, so I wander over there and leave her to what she's looking at.

I'm browsing the earrings and necklaces for something that catches my eye and reminds me of Livy, when she finds me. She arches a brow, and the corner of her lips tip up.

"So many pretty things," she muses. "It's hard to know where to look."

"You find anything you like, Liv?"

"The whole store is beautiful, but I don't need anything, I just like to look. We can go now, maybe get some ice cream?"

"Not yet, you haven't looked in this section. Tell me what catches your eye." I reach for her hand and pull her towards the jewelry case.

"Parker, I don't need anything more from you. This weekend is a gift in itself. The best gift ever. If only it didn't have to end."

I am right there with her on that. I wish we could stay here in Seaside forever, just the two of us.

"Just take a peek and then I will take you for ice-cream."

"No can do. I know you and you can't help yourself. If I asked you to buy me the entire case of jewelry, you would. How about I let you buy me an ice-cream cone instead. I'll even make it a double scoop." I can't hide the smile on my face. She is right. I would buy her every damn piece of jewelry in the store if it made her happy.

"I promise I won't spend a cent here today, I'm just curious what you like. How about this red gem? I think it's a ruby."

"It's beautiful, but red has never been my color." Livy peers into the cases, admiring the different pieces, and stops in front of a dainty white gold chain with a tiny diamond star pendant. I watch her eyes widen as she admires it.

"Do you like that one, Livy? The necklace with the diamond star?"

"It's so pretty. It reminds me of you."

"Of me? How so?"

"It reminds me of that night we snuck away. You brought me to the viewpoint, and we laid together in the back of your pickup truck. The night we spent wishing on stars and... well, you know." Livy's cheeks flush.

I did know. How could I ever forget it? I made love to Livy in the back of the truck bed. It was her first time and I wanted it to feel special for her under a blanket of stars. I told her that night we were written in the stars and I meant it. I have missed out on more memories with her than I want to admit, but her first time will always be mine. That moment will always belong to me.

"I do know. I've never forgotten, Livy." I slip my arms around her from behind and smother her with kisses, overcome with the love I feel for her. "Now, how do you expect me *not* to buy this necklace for you?"

"A deal is a deal and you agreed. A gentleman never goes back on his promises."

"You don't play fair, Olivia Madden."

"You just don't like my terms. Now come on, I believe you owe me a double scoop ice-cream cone and I would like to collect on it now."

I give in, begrudgingly leaving the store without the necklace that belongs around Livy's neck, and I make good on my promise.

The afternoon flies by in a flash. After hours of walking, we stop for coffee and decide on a trolley ride so Livy can see more of this small town that has already won her heart. I pay close attention to her, hoping the distractions of the weekend away are enough to help her momentarily forget what's waiting for her on Monday. I've promised to go with her and support her if she decides that's what she wants. There is nothing I wouldn't do for this girl. Nothing.

We hop off the trolley at the stop closest to The Wharf, where we have reservations for dinner. It's a casual spot, people come here as much for the scene as they do for the food. The white painted patio dotted with blue and white striped umbrellas overlooks the pier. It's best known for its fried clams, lobster rolls and oysters. James and I would make a point of coming here each time we visit.

After giving the hostess my name, we are seated on the patio in a private corner. A live band playing '90s music is situated at the far end of the patio with a small dance floor overlooking the pier. Our waiter appears, taking our drink orders. I order myself a scotch neat and Livy orders a glass of wine. I glance at Livy. She sighs, turning her gaze to the ocean.

"How are you doing, my Livy girl?" The sun is shining directly over her and she looks like she's glowing. She's breathtaking. Her hair has dried from the hours spent in the sun and she has taken it down from the knot on top of her head, it flows over her shoulder in beachy waves.

"So good. I love it here. Do you think we could come back here again this summer? I mean, if you aren't too busy with Cape May."

"We definitely can. And we will."

The waitress interrupts us, arriving with our drinks, and has just taken our order when my phone vibrates in my pocket. I dig it out and read the screen.

Shit. It's Nelson. I continue to read the text, my face falling as my jaw tightens. He needs me in Cape May first thing Monday morning. The project can't move forward without me signing off on the changes to the site plans. There's no way around this. I have to be there. Livy notices my disappointment. Her lips press into a straight line, concern on her face.

"What's wrong Parker? Is everything okay?"

I drag my hands through my hair. This couldn't be worse timing for a whole bunch of reasons. I don't want to cut this weekend short with Livy and I really wanted to be there for her when she faces her dad. I feel gutted having to break this news to her.

"Livy, it's work. I'm so sorry. They need me in Cape May on Monday morning. If there was any way I could get out of going, I would. I swear."

I watch her face, see the happiness fade from it and the sparkle leave her eyes. *Fuck,* I feel like such a jerk.

"It's fine. It's not your fault. I completely understand."

"I feel awful, Livy," I stumble. "I wanted to be there for you on Monday. This isn't how this was supposed to go."

"It's fine, Parker. Honestly. I need to do it on my own anyway. I had already decided. I just hadn't told you yet because I knew you were going to fight me on it."

Fine. Does she mean that? Is it ever really fine when people say it's fine? The need to protect her tugs at me. I reach for her hand and hold it tight. I want to get out of my chair and pull her into me. I wish I could take her pain away, carry it myself so she no longer has to.

"Livy, are you sure?" In an instant, I decide, fuck it. My voice is clear when I tell her, "You know what, forget it. I don't give a shit about the hotel. You are more important to me than anything else in this world. I'm not going."

"Parker, no! You need to go, and I need to face this together with my family. I need to be there for my sister. She's going to need me, and I want to be there for her. I want you to go. I need you to go. You do what you do best, and I'll be in Reed Point waiting for you when you return."

I search her eyes, needing to know she is okay with her decision. "But then who will be there for you? Livy, I know you are strong. I'm not doubting that for a minute, but you shouldn't have to face this alone."

"The three of us will do this together. My mom, myself and Kate. I promise I'll be okay. I can call you as soon as I leave them if it will make you feel better. Let me do this so I can give you everything. All of me. I want to finally put this in the past so we can move forward together."

Our eyes meet. I lean in closer. My mouth opens, wanting to tell her she isn't alone. That she never will be again. Instead, I lower my mouth to hers and kiss her. This girl has quickly become everything to me. My whole world. I pull back and reach for her hand.

"Dance with me?"

"I would love to." She places her small hand in mine, and I guide her to the dance floor. I pull her in to me, happy to have my arms wrapped around her body. Her cheek against my chest. We sway to the music sharing the dance floor with three or four other couples. I'm not much of a dancer but I can get by.

"Remember the last time we danced together, Parker?"

"Senior party. I stepped all over your toes. I was a mess."

"You looked better than you danced. You were so handsome all dressed up in your suit. I think every girl in the room must have hated me that night, watching us together."

"I doubt that. They just felt sorry for you and your sore feet that I was trampling all over. I felt like the lucky one. I still do."

"Look at us now. We've come a long way. We could give Fred Astaire and Ginger Rogers a run for their money." I laugh and inhale her, kissing her temple. I notice the sun is setting, leaving ribbons of red and purple across the horizon in its place. I never want this night to end. I want to burn it in my mind, to never forget a single second.

The song ends and we make our way back to our table. The waiter brings us our entrees. I ordered the sablefish and Livy ordered the scallops. We finish our dinner and split a chocolate chip skillet cookie with vanilla ice cream for dessert.

I pay the bill and we head back to the boat to cruise home under the stars. The sky is jet black and blanketed with stars that appear to go on forever. We both seem to have moved on from our conversation at dinner, wanting to make the most of our time together in Seaside before I have to leave her.

We hop onto the boat and I grab her a blanket and a glass of wine. We slowly cruise back to the house, eyeing the homes that sit on the ocean's edge. We play the game of choosing our dream home. Turns out we both like gigantic homes with pools overlooking the bluffs. *Go figure.*

It's been the perfect weekend with Livy, but it's killing me that I have to leave her on the one day she needs me the most. It's also killing me that I'm going to have to leave her when I move to Cape May. There's no way I will be able to live that far away from her.

There has to be another way.

I can't be without her.

EIGHTEEN

Olivia

I pack the last of my things in my bag and take one last look at the view of the ocean from the bedroom windows. This weekend was a dream, and I will never forget a second of it. I'm full of hope for a future with Parker. I am finally ready for us.

Then I remember that we're leaving. I'm trying my best to hide my disappointment that we have to return to Reed Point earlier than planned. It's not Parker's fault and I understand that, but that doesn't make it any easier. The peace I felt over the last two days is already starting to subside, knowing the reality I will face tomorrow. It's actually just as well that we are leaving early. As much as I don't want to step out of this fairy tale, I should get home and call my mom and Kate and figure out the details for tomorrow. I feel my body tensing, not knowing what to expect. *How will my dad react to us? Will he think he can just walk back into our lives like nothing has ever happened? And will my mom erect a welcome home banner? Throw a party? Good Lord, help me.*

Parker walks through the door and I plaster a smile on my face as best I can. I don't need him feeling any worse than he already is about leaving.

"Hey baby, all ready?"

"Yes. All packed."

He wraps his strong arms around me from behind and kisses my forehead. I lean into his embrace.

"I'm sorry we have to go. I wish we could stay here longer."

"I do too. Parker, please don't feel bad. I know this wasn't your choice." I rest my head against his shoulder. "How long will you be gone?"

"I should only be gone for a few days. Don't worry Livy, you won't even have time to miss me. I will be filling up your phone with messages and calling you every chance I can get. You are going to be so sick of me, you won't want me to come back."

"Never."

Parker takes my bags, loads the car and we head back to reality. The drive home is quiet, both of us dreading the next few days for so many different reasons.

Parker pulls to a stop in front of my apartment and we both hesitate, not wanting this weekend to officially be over. The silence gets the better of me, I reach for him over the console, kissing his cheek, and then ask him to walk me to the door. We meet on the sidewalk. Parker has my bags, and we walk the short distance to my door. Every step feels like agony knowing that Parker is leaving. I open the door to my apartment and Parker places my bags inside.

“I wish I could stay, Livy, but I really have to go.”

“I know, Parker. Thank you for an amazing weekend.”

“I miss you already. I’ll call you as soon as I get there.”

We hug each other for a long time, neither of us wanting to let go. When we finally do, Parker promises to call me when he arrives in Cape May tonight, check in with me a minimum of one hundred and fifty times tomorrow and Facetime chat before bed. Then he’s gone and I’m left wondering how it’s possible to miss someone so much after only five minutes. And I know this is just the beginning of long goodbyes. I know the day is coming when Parker has to go back to the city, and I need to stay and run Bloom. If this is any indication of what those goodbyes are going to feel like, I won’t make it through.

I’m trying to take one day at a time, but the thought is always there lingering in the corner of my mind. I haven’t for the life of me figured out how we can make things work between us and it terrifies me. Reed Point is where my heart is, where my life is. I’ve worked hard build to my business here and I’m not ready to walk away from Bloom. I’m proud of the success I’ve achieved and there is still so much more I would like to accomplish. I can’t just walk away from the company I’ve grown from the ground up, and I don’t expect Parker to walk away from his life either. But I can’t think about any of this right now, because I need to deal with my dad.

I make myself a cup of tea and curl up on the couch with my phone, needing to call my mom and my sister. I call Kate first, biding time before I talk to my mom. She picks up on the second ring.

"Hey Olivia, I wasn't expecting to hear from you until tomorrow morning. Are you still away in Seaside?"

"No, unfortunately I'm home. We had to leave Seaside early. Parker has an emergency meeting tomorrow morning which meant we needed to end our vacation early."

"Aw, I'm sorry. I hope you still had a great weekend despite calling it short. Did you like Seaside?"

"We did Kate, it was such a great weekend. Parker is honestly the best boyfriend." I know I sound like a school-girl with a crush, but I can't help it. And honestly, I don't even care.

"He planned everything so perfectly, and Seaside is the cutest beach town. I can't wait to go back." I fill her in on the rest of our trip, from the gorgeous house we stayed in, to our boat day and stroll through the little town.

"I'm happy for you. You deserve it all, Liv. He really is a great guy and you two are going to have the most beautiful babies."

"Ha! Don't get ahead of yourself. How can we make babies if we can't even figure out how to live in the same zip code?" I set my tea on the side table and flop back onto the sofa, hugging my knees into my chest.

"It will all get worked out. If you two love each other, you will find a way. That I know for sure."

"I hope you're right. But the real reason I called is to talk about the giant cloud looming over our heads - tomorrow and dad's release. Have you heard what time he's getting out?"

"A tentative time. Mom talked to his lawyer and it looks like sometime around four o'clock. So, I was planning on being at mom's house for two. I can pick you up along the way if that will work for you?"

"That would be great. Thanks Kate. Can you swing by Bloom? I should work in the morning considering I've been a little MIA lately."

"Ellie understands. Don't worry for a second. She is just as happy as I am for you and Parker. But yes, I can pick you up at Bloom. Where are you at with all of this? How are you feeling about seeing Dad tomorrow?"

I watch the steam rising from my mug and reply, "God Kate, I just don't want to see him. Does that make me a bad person? I am really nervous how my reaction will be when I do see him. How are you feeling about it?"

"I'm nervous too, but I'm looking forward to putting this all behind us. Mom is happy and although you and I have mixed emotions about that, it's her life and she's a grown woman. If she can put it all behind her and move forward, then we have to support her."

"You are probably right, but I just don't get it. I know how happy mom is, but I can't get past what he did to her. The man cheated on her for over a year and destroyed our family in the process." I know Kate is right but unlike her, I just can't leave it in the past. I could never forgive my husband for sleeping with another woman half her age, let alone the illegal shit he was doing behind our backs.

"Olivia, I am struggling with it, too. I don't expect to have a perfect relationship with Dad right away, but we have to try and piece together some kind of relationship with him for Mom's sake. You don't have to forgive him. Let's just see what he has to say."

"Oh, don't worry, I'm not forgiving him. I'm nowhere near forgiveness."

"I can appreciate that. You don't have to forgive him today, tomorrow or even next year, but you do have to find a way to move past it. For your sake. You need to put this to rest so you can move on with your life and truly be happy."

Over the years, I'd wondered if it would ever be possible. I've been so bitter and angry that forgiveness has seemed impossible. But I've found happiness now and being happy can put things into perspective. I don't want to hold a grudge forever and it would be nice to have my family back together. I know I'll never be able to forget what he did, but could it be possible to find forgiveness?

"I know you are right. I'll try to keep an open mind tomorrow. I better run, I need to call mom and I should probably down an entire bottle of wine before I do that. I can already hear her now. How excited is she? Like a forty on a scale of one to ten?"

"Let's just say you'll want to make it a quick call. And yes, I recommend the wine."

"Tell me she didn't order a slew of pink flamingos for the front lawn?"

Kate chuckles. "Close. But even she's not that crazy."

"Let's hope. Okay, I guess I'll get this over with. See you tomorrow, Katie-Kat."

"See you tomorrow, Olivia."

I take my mug to the kitchen and swap it for a glass of wine. I'm definitely going to need something stronger for my next call.

My mom is in an annoyingly fantastic mood when she answers the phone. She is clearly excited that the big day has finally come. I bite my lip, not wanting to steal her joy, but it's hard. So hard.

"Hi angel, did you hear? Your dad will be released at four tomorrow. Isn't that just the best news? You are able to make it, right? He'll be so happy to see you."

"Yes Mom, I'll be there. I already talked to Kate and we will be by your place just after two to pick you up."

"I know it's going to be tough, but your dad really wants to make amends with you and your sister. He just feels awful for what he's done to you both. I hope one day you can find it in your heart to forgive him."

It's not worth getting into it with my mom. We have never seen eye-to-eye on this subject and that isn't going to change anytime soon. It's easier if I just tell her what she wants to hear.

"I'll get there, Mom. I just need some time." I flick on the television as a distraction.

"Olivia, try not to focus on the bad. There was plenty of good, too. Your dad was a wonderful father to you. Remember all those summers on the boat? He taught you how to fish and you two would sit on the back of the boat for hours waiting for a bite. He never missed one of your school theater productions and he would treat you and your friends to ice cream after every performance. There was nothing he wouldn't do for you."

I sigh, trying to keep the frustration from my voice. "I wish I could forgive as easily as you, Mom. I really do."

"It will come, baby. Go into it with an open heart. That's all I ask. Speaking of an open heart, will you be bringing Parker?"

"Unfortunately not, Mom. He was called to a hotel he is overseeing in Cape May at the last minute, so he left today. He should be gone only a few days."

"That's too bad, Olivia. Hopefully he will be able to visit with us soon. I would love to see him. It's been so long. I always liked him. He was sweet to you," she continues, clearly in the mood to chat. "How are things going with him anyways? You've been seeing an awful lot of each other lately."

"Things are great between the two of us. They couldn't be better. I know he would love to see you too. I'll bring him by the house soon."

"I would love that, honey. Okay, I need to run. I'm getting my hair done at the salon, so I look my best tomorrow. I love you."

"Love you too, Mom. See you tomorrow."

I hang up the phone and exhale. Although my mom drives me crazy at times, she is one of the most loving and giving mothers a girl could wish for. It was hard for her after Dad left, but even then, I knew she was trying her best to make Kate and I feel loved. Some days her broken heart just won out.

I say a silent prayer that tomorrow goes well. I think about going to the beach and watching the waves, but I'm too tired from the weekend and lack of sleep. I decide instead to change into my pajamas and hop onto my bed to write. I pick up my journal from my bedside table and try to pour my thoughts onto paper, hoping it will help me gain perspective. The silence in the apartment is almost eery after having Parker around for the last few weeks.

Three hours later, I'm woken to the sound of my cell phone. It takes me a minute to figure out where I am and that I fell asleep while writing. It's a Facetime call from Parker and I pick it up immediately, hoping he's calling to let me know he arrived safely.

The screen lights up with his gorgeous face and I'm immediately regretting that I didn't at least put a brush through my hair before I picked up.

"Hey baby. There's my beautiful girl. You are in bed, is everything alright?"

"Everything is fine, babe, I fell asleep writing in my journal. I guess the weekend must have caught up with me. I'm happy to see that you arrived safely in Cape May. How was the drive?"

Parker is shirtless and he's leaning against the headboard of his bed in his hotel room. His hair is messy and his five o'clock shadow is just the right amount of stubble. He is insanely attractive without even trying. I still can't get over how good looking he is.

"The drive was good. It was lonely without you, though."

"I miss you, and seeing you looking the way you do right now isn't helping."

"Looking the way I do? What does that mean?"

"You know, your bare chest, your tousled hair, looking all sexy."

"Sexy, huh? You think I'm sexy?"

"Yes, sexy." Parker has always been able to bring out my playful side and I love how that feels. I love our banter back and forth. "On a far less enticing note, I talked to my mom and Kate. My dad should be getting released tomorrow around four. Kate is going to pick me up at work and then we will pick up my mom and make the drive."

"Are you okay?"

"I'm fine. I promise."

"I'm worried about you, Liv. I fucking hate that I can't be there with you." His eyes reveal a pained expression as he runs his hand down his jaw.

"I know. Please stop worrying about me. Okay, subject change. How's Cape May? Do you think you'll be happy living there?"

"It's definitely not New York. It's actually a lot like Seaside, just bigger. The streets are wider, the beaches are larger, but still clean and beautiful, and it has most of the stores that I'm sure you like to shop in. You will love it here. There are a lot of other towns nearby too, so there's plenty to see and do. Maybe you could come with me the next time I have to go for work?"

"That sounds great. But won't the next time be when you move there permanently?" *Without me.*

That's all I can think of when he talks about Cape May, the fact that he will be moving there without me. I look anywhere but at him, hiding the sadness reflected in my eyes.

"Not necessarily. I'm going to put off the move as long as I can. And once I do move to Cape May, I will drive back for weekends so we can see each other."

"Parker, that seems like a lot of driving. I can't ask you to do that. It wouldn't be fair to you to spend hours every week in a car. Or safe, for that matter."

"I know Reed Point is where your heart is, I would never expect you to leave. I know Bloom is like your baby and I completely understand that you don't want to walk away from it. I will do what I have to do to make our relationship work. And if that means I come back to Reed Point on week-ends and any other chance I get, then so be it. Remember Livy, living in Cape May is a temporary move for me. It won't be forever."

I can't help but wonder if we will ever be able to live in the same city together. Right now, it feels like that is impossible. Could I really live this way for the next couple of years, waiting for weekends to see my boyfriend? I guess I don't have much of a choice. If I want to be with Parker, and I do more than anything, I'm going to have to suck it up and be patient.

"We'll find a way, Parker. One day at a time. Together."

"That's my girl. I love you and you love me and together we will make this work." Parker yawns and stretches his arm to the sky.

"I'll let you go. I know you must be exhausted. It's been a long day for you. Go get some rest."

"Okay babe. I'll give you a call in the morning. Good luck tomorrow, Livy. I love you."

"I love you, too. Night."

We end the call and I roll over onto my side, waves of apprehension fluttering through me. My life has never been better and never been more stressful, all at the same time.

NINETEEN

Olivia

"THANKS FOR HOLDING DOWN THE FORT THIS WEEKEND." Ellie glances up from the stem she is shearing with her floral clippers and shrugs.

"I was more than happy to. It was totally fine, Olivia. Leah and I had it under control. No problemo. You know, Leah wants to work more, and we should be taking advantage of that. We can't always be here, and we know we can trust her."

"You're right, I know. It's just been the two of us for so long, it's hard sometimes to make changes."

"Well, get used to it. I assume now that you are Parker's love slave, he will be wanting to whisk you away more often."

"God Ells, you make my relationship sound super sexy." I shake my head and continue reviewing the orders that need to be completed for the day.

"Are you ready for today? What's the plan once your dad is released?"

"We are going back to my mom's for dinner. I don't expect to stay too long. Seeing as he is moving back in with her after all these years, I think they will need some time to feel comfortable around each other. They have a lot they need to sort out, and that's an understatement."

"I think you are right about that. I also think it's best that you ease in to being a part of your dad's life again." Ellie moves around the large table to grab floral foam for the arrangement she is working on. "Kate seems to be handling it well. Did you hear that she went to another speed dating event again this past weekend? I swear that girl will never learn. She said one of the guys brought his mom with him – she had a binder and was taking notes the entire time. She had an actual notebook with colored tabs to keep track of all the women. But that wasn't even the worst part! He still lives with his mom in a two-bedroom apartment. Kate said he is in his late thirties! Are you fucking kidding me?"

"Stop it! I can't take it. She'd be better off trying to find her future husband at a gay bar," I tease at my sister's expense.

"I'll spare you the details about the guy who came after him who smelt like brie cheese. We need to save her, Liv. We can no longer stand by and watch this train wreck."

Ellie and I spend the rest of the morning filling orders and helping walk-in clients choose the perfect gift. My phone vibrates in my pocket and I expect it to be Parker, considering he'd already texted and called me more times than I can count.

I check the text and am surprised to see that it's not from Parker. It's from Jules and she would like to meet for lunch. Something tells me Parker has put his sister up to this considering the timing. It's his way of being there for me even though he's hundreds of miles away. It's thoughtful of him and I'm touched by the gesture. I send her a quick text back and let her know I can meet for a quick one. She replies with an offer to come my way to make it easier for me. We decide to meet at the coffee shop right down the street from Bloom at noon.

It's five after twelve when I rush through the door of the café and find Jules already seated at a table by the window. She stands and greets me with a hug.

"Thank you for having lunch with me, Olivia. I was looking forward to seeing you on Wednesday for yoga but I'm really happy I get to see you a little sooner."

"Me too, Jules. Thanks for inviting me. I don't often get out for a real lunch, so this is a treat. How have you been?"

"I've been great. Busy with work, nothing exciting. Alex was away at a conference all weekend, so I spent some time with Miles. He's leaving soon for his vacation before he starts filming so it was nice to get some extra time with him."

"I love your relationship with your brothers, the love you have for one another." I unfold my napkin, laying it across my lap.

"I'm a lucky girl. Not always, though. Dating in high school was pretty much impossible with three older brothers."

"I can only imagine."

The waitress takes our orders, but only after going on and on about Jules being related to *the* Miles Bennett. I think she might be the head of his fan club. I think she might also have his face tattooed on her back. Maybe a shrine to him in her living room? Just a guess.

"Does that happen often? She was intense."

"It does. Reed Point is a pretty small town, especially when your brother is a celebrity. I'm used to it."

"He has definitely made a name for himself. His face is everywhere. I really need to watch one of his movies."

"You mean you haven't seen one of Miles' movies? He's made so many, how have you managed to avoid them?" She scrunches her face together in shock.

I sigh. "I haven't, I'm embarrassed to say. I tried for many years to push Parker from my mind. Watching one of Miles' movies wouldn't have helped with that."

"Gah, Olivia, I'm so happy you two have found your way back to each other. It really is a love story. I've never seen him so happy. He's crazy about you. He's also really worried about you. I know today is a tough one for you."

"So, my suspicions were right. Parker asked you to check on me today, didn't he?"

Jules clears her throat and shifts in her seat. "He did. He called me this morning and asked if I could check on you, but I was happy he did. He filled me in on your dad coming home today. I hope you don't mind me knowing."

"I don't mind. It's okay and I appreciate you being there for both myself and your brother. I'm lucky to have you both in my life."

"Of course. We are friends now, Olivia. You're stuck with me. I'm hoping for life, by the way. And it doesn't end with me. My whole family would like to be here for you and support you in any way we can."

My eyes well with unshed tears. I bite my lip, trying to keep them from spilling down my cheeks. Not only do I have this amazingly supportive man, but I have his equally caring and loving family who have always made me feel like I belong.

"Oh no, I'm sorry Olivia. I didn't mean to make you cry."

"No, no. It's okay, Jules." I dab my eyes with my napkin. I feel like such a fool. "I just feel so lucky to be loved by your family. It means more to me than you'll ever know."

We finish lunch, hug goodbye and make plans for yoga and drinks with Ellie and Kate on Wednesday. By the time I get back to Bloom I feel like I just might be able to get through this day. My visit with Jules gave me a renewed sense of faith that everything will be okay. No matter what happens today, I have Parker, a man who loves me and who will always have my back. I am overcome with the feeling that I'm where I'm supposed to be, that I deserve happiness after everything I've been through.

"A special delivery for Olivia Madden." Ellie grins as a delivery guy walks though Bloom's doors. I take the package from him and politely thank him. I can't find a sender's name on it anywhere, so I unwrap it and find a small royal blue box tied with a white ribbon. There's a note in the package as well.

Always my star. I love you. Parker.

"Let me guess. Judging by the look on your face, it's from Parker?"

"Yes." I open the little box and my eyes go wide. I cover my mouth with my hand. It's the star necklace I eyed in Seaside. My heart nearly bursts through my chest. *When did he purchase this?*

Just when I thought I couldn't love him more.

Ellie is smiling. "Can I help you put it on?"

I hold my hair up so Ellie can slip the chain around my neck and fasten it. It's the nicest gift I have ever received. I rub the diamond star between my fingers, wishing Parker was here to see me wearing it, to see the happiness he brings me. Six months ago, I never would have believed that my life could be this good.

"I THINK THAT'S HIM." KATE POINTS TO THE PRISON GATES. There is a lump in my throat. I fight to swallow it down.

My father walks towards us, accompanied by his lawyer. He's wearing grey slacks and a navy sweater. His hair is trimmed very short, almost buzzed. With each step he takes I'm closer to the man responsible for so much of my pain. I notice the changes in his appearance. He looks pale and thin, he's aged.

He approaches us with hesitation. He doesn't look like the powerful, confidant man he once was. My chest tightens. For the first time in years my father is within reach.

"My girls, thank you for coming today. You have no idea how good it is to see the three of you. I've waited for this day a long time."

"It's good to see you too, Dad. You look good." Kate moves towards him and hugs his narrow frame.

I stand to the side, avoiding eye contact. It is difficult seeing him like this, a weaker version of himself. My mother pulls him in, immediately bombarding him with our plan for the evening as though he's just arrived home from a business trip or something. My dad seems to be going along with her craziness for the moment.

I'm saved for last because it's no secret that I have struggled the most with this. I can see the nervous tension in his eyes and feel the apprehension thick in the air between us. My pulse is racing.

"Hi my sunshine. It's good to see you. Thank you for coming. It means a lot to me, Olivia." I look up, making eye contact, but don't move. *Sunshine*. Hearing him use the old nickname sparks something in me that I wasn't expecting to feel. It brings me back to a time when we were all happy. I wonder if it's possible to get back there again.

We are interrupted by his lawyer, who runs through the conditions of his parole. He will have to check in with his parole officer bi-weekly starting with his first meeting in person tomorrow. Travelling outside the United States will be off the table for the next five years. His lawyer pats him on the shoulder, tells him to go be with his family and that they'll talk tomorrow.

We thank him for what he has done for my father and head to the car. Kate offers my dad the passenger seat while she drives. We drive to my mom's house, an uncomfortable tension between us.

Kate awkwardly attempts to make conversation but reverts to silence when it falls flat. My mother, on the other hand, is talking a mile a minute like a toddler on a sugar high. It's a lot. If Kate would just slow down the car just a little bit, I'd consider throwing myself from it. My hand floats up to the pendant around my neck, my fingers rubbing the small star. I think about Parker. He has given me the strength to get through today without even knowing it.

Kate pulls into the driveway and my seatbelt is off and I have one foot out the door before she has time to put it in park. We make our way to the front steps, my dad eyeing the house my mother now lives in, one he has never even stepped foot in. I wonder what he thinks of it. It's a far cry from the four thousand square feet we lived in before we lost it all.

"The gardens look beautiful honey. You always had a good eye for flowers. It's where Olivia gets it from." My dad turns to me with a sheepish grin on his face. "I would love to see Bloom one day soon. Do you think it would be okay if I stopped by for a visit?"

"That would be fine, Dad. I would be happy to show you around."

"Thanks kiddo." I'm reminded it has been that long since I have had him in my life. I was a kid when he left, and he still thinks of me that way.

"Let's get you inside and get you fed. I bet you are dying for a home-cooked meal. I'll get dinner ready while you three catch up. Maybe you girls can show your Dad around." My mom opens the door and we follow her inside.

"We can do that."

The tour takes all of five minutes. The house is small with just a family room and kitchen on the left side of the entrance and three bedrooms and two bathrooms on the right. It's dated, but in good condition. My mother has always made sure the home is well taken care of and does her best to fill it with love.

We sit down for dinner at the small round table, there is just enough room for the four of us. It feels so different. The last time we ate a meal together, we sat in a large dining room under an oversized crystal chandelier and ate off of fine china. I notice my dad shift in his seat and wonder how he's feeling, seeing all of these changes that he is responsible for.

"This really looks delicious. Thank you for this meal and for being here tonight with me. I know this hasn't been easy on all of you and I'm fully aware I'm to blame. I hope we can start to rebuild what we lost, and you can find it in your hearts to forgive me."

"Of course we can, honey. We are a family. Right girls?"

I quickly fill my mouth with a fork full of food, thinking that's the easiest way to avoid answering the question. I nod my head to smooth things over.

"What's your plan now, Dad?" Kate asks.

"Good question. I'm going to start by apologizing to all the people I hurt. It's going to take some time, but I hope I can undo the wrongs I inflicted. I want to move forward with my life after that." My dad rakes his hand through his short hair and lifts his gaze to Kate and me.

"I'm not sure what the future will hold for me, honestly. I've had eight years to think about this. My priority is becoming a good husband and father and making up for the time we lost. I need to start by apologizing to my family first. Kate and Olivia, I hope you know how sorry I am for the pain I caused you both. You lost everything because of my actions. That was never my intention. I don't want to make any excuses for my actions but please know I never wanted to hurt you."

If there's anything I've learnt from the last two weeks with Parker, it's that second chances can be worth the risk. Letting go of the past is the only way to move forward. I've spent too long being angry and I need to let it go. Being with Parker has changed my point of view. It won't be easy, but I need to give my dad a chance.

"We'll get there, Dad. It's just going to take a little time. But I'd like to try."

TWENTY

Parker

He's already sitting at the bar when I walk into the pub. I can't even look at him. The son of a bitch is lucky I've had four days to calm down. I take the seat beside him. My teeth are grinding in my mouth, my jaw ticking.

"Hey man." Hunter looks up at me from his stool. I don't waste any time because I can't. I feel like a ticking time bomb ready to explode.

"How could you?"

"What the hell are you talking about?"

"Livy told me what you said to her. You are the fucking reason she broke up with me back then. It was you. My supposed best friend." My eyes narrow on this prick beside me who I thought I knew.

Hunter sits in silence, staring into his pint of beer. I am prepared to sit here all night if I have to in order to hear whatever bullshit excuse he has for me. The bartender takes my drink order and brings me a scotch neat. I think I might need this drink to take the edge off. Every part of me wants to kill him.

"How dare you say that crap to her? Who the fuck did you think you were to belittle her like that? What kind of an asshole are you?"

"I was a dick," Hunter says, shaking his head. "It was a total dick thing to do."

"Why did you do it? Why the hell would you say that shit to her?"

He takes a long pull of his beer, his knuckles turning white from gripping the tall glass.

"I don't know man. It was a stupid thing to do."

"You're going to have to do better than that Hunter. You owe me an explanation after what you did," I sneer, my teeth clenched. My molars most likely disintegrating as we speak.

He runs his palms down his face and drops his head to his glass. "I guess I just got tired of always watching you get what you wanted. You got the car, the trophies, the good grades, the girls, and it grated on me. I wanted Olivia. I used to walk home from school with her and I thought she liked me too. But she wanted you. It was one more thing you had that I wanted."

"So, you thought cutting her down and breaking her heart was the way to get back at me?" My head is spinning. "I thought I knew you, but apparently I never have."

"I'm sorry, Parker. I can't believe I did that to you."

"I can't believe it either."

"I'm sorry, Parker," he says again.

"Fuck you, Hunter."

I down the rest of my scotch and stand up, my fists cracking at my sides. Hunter turns his face towards me, and I can tell he's not sure if I'm going to leave or knock him out. I don't make him wait long for the answer. I draw my right hand back and land a punch to the center of his face. He takes it like a man, I'll give him that much. The asshole had it coming.

"WHAT HAPPENED TO YOUR HAND, PARKER?" I GRIMACE AS Livy inspects my battered knuckles. She moves towards the freezer, fumbling through its contents. She finds the bag of peas that she's looking for and motions to the kitchen table for me to take a seat. She searches though the drawers for something else.

"Hunter's face," I blurt out.

She glances over her shoulder at me and her eyes go wide.

"Shit Parker, what happened?"

She finally pulls a tea towel from a drawer and wraps it around the bag of frozen vegetables. She sits in a chair across from me and reaches for my throbbing hand, resting the cold peas across my knuckles. Her brown eyes travel from my hand up to my eyes, her brows knit with worry.

"I let him know what an asshole he is."

"Oh God Parker, I'm sorry it came down to that."

"Don't be. I'm not. I don't want to talk about it. I haven't seen you since Sunday. Can we take this bag of peas to the patio with a couple of glasses of wine?"

"We can," she says without judgement in her eyes. She gives me a quick kiss and I push up from my chair and kiss her again.

"I missed your mouth. Fuck, I love your mouth." My chest tightens as she turns towards the kitchen. I watch her perfect, toned ass as she walks away from me to fetch a bottle of red and two glasses. My girl has no idea what she does to me. My mind wanders to the all the different ways I could make her scream my name right now. I'll save that thought for tonight.

For the next couple of hours, we sit together on the porch of the beach house watching the sunset. I drove home last night and asked Livy to meet me here with enough clothes for the next two weeks. I like having her around me as much as possible. It's not the same when we are apart. She humored me, arriving with a small suitcase of her belongings. Not even remotely enough if you ask me, but I'll take what I can get.

We spend the next two weeks in our usual routine, working during the day and spending evenings together at the beach house.

We met Miles, Kate and Ellie for dinner at Catch 21 on a Saturday night and on the following Sunday we had dinner at her parents' house. The last and only time I met a girlfriend's parents it was the Maddens, and that was way back in high school. Livy's parents were more than welcoming and any tension I was expecting was nonexistent. For the most part, Livy was very much herself and her dad seemed like he was readjusting as well as possible. It was good to see the weight of everything lift from Livy's shoulders.

We trade flirty texts during the day, and nights always end with the two of us racing home to tear each other's clothes off. We have made the beach house our home together and there's nowhere I'd rather be. I can't imagine going back to my old ways, living in a hotel on my own with a different girl every weekend. That whole life feels foreign to me now. Livy is it for me. She's the one I've wanted my entire life and now I have her. I just need to figure out how we are going to make this work long-term.

I have an official move date now on the calendar. In five days, I will settle into a hotel near the Cape May property we are building. Then shortly after that, my rental home will be ready for me.

The thought of only seeing Livy on weekends is killing me, but for now, it's our only option until we can work something out. On that front, there is something Livy doesn't know, something I need to tell her. I found the perfect spot in Cape May for a new Bloom location. It's a bright and airy retail space in a heritage building on one of the busiest shopping streets in Cape May, and it's up for lease. It is smack in the middle of a row of popular cafes and boutique shops and it wouldn't take much to get it up and running. When I saw it, all I could think about was Livy. I could practically see her in the window doing what she loves and smiling back at me. I have no idea if she will love the idea and consider moving there to be closer to me, or if she might hate me for even suggesting it.

Tonight, we've invited my brothers, Jules and Alex and Kate and Ellie over for a cook-out at the beach house. It feels like we are all going in different directions soon, so we wanted to get everyone together while we still can.

Livy raced around all day shopping for groceries and cleaning the house. She has fresh flowers in every room and candles covering the patio. She's made some sort of tropical drinks that smell like rum and pineapple and are going down way too easy. A playlist of her favorite country music plays in the background. She's the perfect host.

Jules and Alex are the last two to arrive. Livy hands them each one of her special fruity concoctions before they can even get through the door. We join everyone else outside on the patio where Livy has a table full of appies laid out.

Ellie rushes over to Jules, who is standing next to me. "Jules! I'm so happy to see you. This must be Alex." She hugs the two of them, exchanges a few pleasantries, then pulls Jules by the arm to where Kate and Livy are. The four of them wrap their arms around each other and giggle. I love how Livy has embraced a relationship with my sister, but I'm not surprised. Livy has a way with people. People gravitate towards her because she's real and has a heart as big as the ocean.

"How's my brother? I haven't seen you all week. Is that what happens when you drink the Kool-Aid and fall in love?" Liam busts my balls.

"Seen me? I don't even recognize you. What's with the new hair, Liam?"

"Yeah Liam. Don't tell me you paid for that? Did you ask for the 'I've got a massive stick lodged up my ass' look?" Miles pipes up with a grin.

"Leave me alone, it was the girl's first day. I probably should've bolted when she told me that. Judging from *you* assholes, it's as bad as I thought," Liam snaps back and takes a long pull of his beer.

"It's not that bad if you were going for a 90s cheesy soap opera star."

"Dammit."

"I wouldn't worry about it. You have no one to impress but your computer screen and your four-legged friend Murphy. You know, Liam, I think he might be the only one for you," I add with a laugh.

"Thanks boys. You two are great for my ego."

"Anytime. Hey, have you talked to Hunter since you clocked him?" Miles questions me, sliding into his best boxer stance, his hands balled into fists.

"Nope, and I'd be happy if I never saw him again. That guy is a total douchebag."

"That's not news. Hunter has always been a bit of a dick. But do you really think your friendship is dead? Our families are close. There's no question you will have to see him from time to time."

"I'm nowhere near getting over what he did. Now can we change the subject? I invited you guys here for a good time and talking about that fuck nut is killing my mood." I knock back the rest of my beer and look over to where the girls are.

The girls are huddled together on the patio loungers and I wander over to see if I can get anyone a drink. I hear Jules say in total disgust. "I want zero part of this. I'm out with this conversation."

"What's going on over here ladies? Why does my sister look completely horrified?"

"Parker, sit. We need to run this past you." Livy taps the cushion beside her, and I lower myself down, stretching my arm around her shoulder.

My eyes take in her big brown eyes and long dark lashes. She's wearing a pale pink fitted tank top and a pair of her jean shorts that drive me crazy. Her hair is pulled over to one side, floating down her shoulder in golden waves. Her new diamond star pendant glimmers around her neck. I notice she likes to run her fingers over it when she is nervous or deep in thought, along with biting her bottom lip. She's fucking cute.

I lean in because I assume that's what I'm supposed to be doing since the four of them are crouched together whisper-talking.

"Olivia and I think that Liam and Ellie would make a cute couple. What do you think?" Kate asks, her eyebrow arched.

"Seriously? Even with that haircut?" I gesture to Liam, who is on his phone with a serious look on his face. Always working. *When will he figure out there's more to life?*

"Yeah, what the hell happened there? He didn't actually pay for that hack job, did he?" Jules laughs.

"Don't worry. We've been giving him the gears about it all night."

"Enough about of his hair. He's nice, smart and hot. Smoking hot, actually, and look at those muscles," Kate continues. "I can totally see the two of them together. How cool would it be if it worked out? Olivia and Ellie could be sisters-in-laws! It's perfect, like something you'd read in a romance novel. We have to set this up."

"Have you guys thought this through? Ellie would be bored to death. Liam's idea of fun is talking about... court things." I shrug my shoulders and pull Livy in a little closer to me.

"Court things? Are you drunk? What the hell are court things?" Jules asks.

"I don't know! That's the point. It's too boring for me to even think about what he does all day in his office." I laugh because it's true.

Livy grabs my face and pulls me in for a kiss and says, "It's a good thing you're pretty, Parker."

We all decide another round of Livy's drinks are needed. I also need to start up the barbecue. If we don't eat soon, this party is going sideways fast with the amount of alcohol we are all knocking back.

Everyone is having a great time. The girls have turned up the music, creating a makeshift dance floor on the sand below the deck. They are barefoot and singing at the top of their lungs, spinning and twirling each other around and around.

I watch the girls dance to a few songs together before I make my way to the sand and wrap my arms around Livy's waist from behind. I pull her back into my chest and sway to the music before pushing her out and around for a spin. I pull her into my chest, one arm on her lower back and the other behind her neck. Her citrus shampoo and vanilla scent are intoxicating as we sway, swept up in the cool ocean breeze.

"You're a good dancer, my Livy girl." I tell her, my mouth in her hair above her ear.

Livy pulls back, lifting her eyes to me. I put my hand on her cheek and lower to kiss her. She tastes like pineapple and salt. "I love tonight, Parker. I'm so happy we did this. I think everyone is having a good time too."

"Including those two. Look to your right Liv."

Livy turns her head, with a complete lack of subtlety. Her eyes grow large watching Ellie in Liam's arms, dancing to the music.

"Oh gosh, I *love* love. Look at them! Do you think it's possible? I can see them together. Oh my gosh, we could double date." Livy's eyes fall to the floor and her pretty smile is replaced with sadness.

"Babe, what's wrong?" I have a feeling it's because I'm leaving soon and it's killing her as much as it's killing me. There isn't a fragment of me that wants to leave her here in Reed Point without me. Everything in me screams that it's wrong for us to be apart, but I can't ask her to give up her life for me. I lift her chin with my fingers, forcing her to look at me.

"No, it's nothing. I'm fine, Parker."

"Livy, it's going to be okay. We will figure it out." I kiss the top of her head and wish I could do something to make her laugh. That turns out to be incredibly easy when I look back to my brother and Ellie.

"I'm not sure Liv, but match-making might just be another one of your secret powers." I shift our bodies, so Livy has a better view of Ellie and Liam.

Liam has his two feet planted in the sand, his arms crossed over his body, seemingly captivated by the display that is going on in front of him. Ellie is lip syncing to "I Wanna Dance with Somebody," her hips shimmying left to right, one arm in the air and the other mimicking a microphone. A cocky smile crosses Liam's mouth, his eyes never leaving Ellie. He's into it.

Livy gasps and quickly covers her open mouth with her hand.

"As different as the two of them are, Ellie is just what your brother needs. Someone to loosen him up and get him away from his office. I mean, just look at him - he's loving every second."

It's been a long time since I've seen my brother with a woman, and I'd be surprised if this went any farther than tonight. My brother is addicted to his work. Everything else is a distant second. He doesn't like distractions, so he sticks to one-night stands and no strings attached. Ellie is strong enough to handle him, though. I make a mental note to push him in her direction. Livy is right, a girl like Ellie is just what Liam needs.

"I'm thinking your tropical drinks might get the credit for what's happening between them," I laugh. "It looks like Ellie has had her fair share."

I take Livy's hand and spin her around, dipping her towards the sand. I kiss her soft lips and she smiles. She tilts her head back, so I move in and kiss the sensitive skin of her neck. She squeals and I pull her up to standing. Livy reaches her hands up to my shoulders and wraps her hands behind my neck. I kiss her again, this time with a little tongue.

"Get a room, you two," Miles hollers from the deck. "The barbecue is ready, and these steaks aren't going to cook themselves."

A few minutes later, the boys and I are grilling the steaks while drinking beers and when they're ready we all find a spot on the patio to eat. The sun is setting as we finish dinner, and the party continues under the glittering expanse of stars. The flicker of the candles Livy placed around the patio provide just the right amount of light.

Livy is on the patio talking to Miles and Alex. She must feel my eyes on her because she turns to face me, and our eyes hold. There's an electricity that pulses through the air between us. It feels like we are the only two people on the patio. Her eyes sparkle and lock on mine and there's lust in her eyes. It's the sexiest form of foreplay. My dick twitches in my pants thinking about finally getting her alone tonight.

I shoot her a wink and in four long strides I'm standing beside her. I clasp my hand in hers and lace our fingers together. I press a kiss to her temple.

"Hey you. Miles was just pointing out that Liam and Ellie have been missing for a while. Any idea where they are and if they are together?"

"No." I shrug. "I know nothing, but I'm definitely curious."

"Let's find them!" Kate grabs Livy's arm and they rush into the house.

"Poor Liam, those two won't quit until they find them," Alex sighs, and I nod because I know he's right.

"I'll be back. I'll bring beer." I walk inside towards the bathroom and find Livy and Kate peeking into the bedroom doors. They are tiptoeing. Olivia has her pointer finger touching her lips, shushing Kate. They look ridiculous and I can't stop myself from smiling.

"Really, you two? Get a life. Let them have their fun."

"We have to know if they're doing what we hope they're doing. Then we will leave them to it. Go away, Parker, you are a heat score."

I roll my eyes and reach for the handle to the washroom. Before my hand can properly grasp the metal, the door opens a smidge and Ellie slips out with a little less lipstick than usual and her cheeks flushed. Her hair tousled, there's a guilty look in her eyes. She looks freshly fucked. My eyebrow arches, a smirk covers my lips.

She closes the door behind her and uses her body like a shield across the wood door, her arms at her sides and her palms pressed firmly against the door.

I cock my eyebrow and smirk. "Hi."

"Hi," Ellie answers nervously.

"Um, can I use the washroom?" I motion to the door, wondering what her next move will be and how she plans on getting out of this awkward situation.

Her neck starts to turn a deeper shade of pink and I actually feel bad for her. She is clearly dying of embarrassment and I'm not making the situation easier on her. It gets worse.

Kate and Livy arrive at my side and I'm pretty sure they will not go as easy on Ellie as me.

"I knew it!" Kate bellows. "Liam is in there isn't he? You guys just did it in the washroom."

Ellie is now the color of a tomato. Stammering, she says, "I plead the fifth."

"Of course you do. You just fucked a lawyer."

"Okay girls, the jig is up. Why don't you two get back to the party," I say through a laugh, motioning in the direction of the patio.

I'm interrupted by a sound from behind the washroom door, something hitting the ground and that's all the confirmation the girls need to know that Liam and Ellie were in there together. The girls grab Ellie and pull her down the hall for what I imagine will be a gruelling interrogation.

I definitely don't want to be standing here when Liam makes his exit. The master bathroom seems like the better alternative. I rap my knuckles on the door twice to let Liam know the coast is clear while making my way down the hall to the ensuite.

The party eventually winds down, with Liam and Ellie the last ones to leave. Liam offers to share his Uber with Ellie and we watch as Liam holds the door open for her. He sets his hand on the curve of her back, guiding her into the backseat.

"That was definitely unexpected." I follow Livy inside, shutting and locking the door behind me.

"Who would have ever expected Liam and Ellie to hook up? They are complete opposites, but I love it."

Livy walks to the kitchen and opens the cupboard under the sink, bending lower to remove a trash bag. She begins to move around the beach house tossing empty bottles into the bag.

"So, it went down in the bathroom?"

"I'll never tell. I'm the keeper of all her secrets. What kind of best friend would I be if I snitched? Snitches get stitches, Parker." She moves outside to the patio with the large bag, continuing to clean up the empties. I follow her onto the porch, checking the candles to make sure they've been snuffed.

"I had no idea my girlfriend is so badass."

"Oh, you have no idea."

"I'd like to find out then." She's got my attention, whether she intended to or not. The thought of Livy playing the bad girl puts me right over the edge.

"Parker, you have that look in your eyes. I know exactly what's going through your mind right now."

Livy stops what she's doing, and she drops the trash bag to the floor.

"If you want me, Parker, come get me."

Dammit, this girl is my weakness. I'm standing in front of her before she can blink. Her eyes narrow as she reaches for my neck, grasping the base of my neck. She pulls me down for a kiss. It's heated and full of need. I've waited all night to get my hands on her and I'm not wasting another second.

I break the kiss because I have other plans, scooping her up and throwing her over my shoulder fireman style. "Parker," she giggles and playfully slaps my ass.

I carry her inside, stopping to lock the patio door with my free hand, knowing I have no intention of leaving the bedroom until morning. And even then, I might just decide to stay there until dinner.

I carry her through the living area and down the hall to the bedroom, ignoring the mess from the party.

That can wait until tomorrow. Right now, I need to feel Livy's body underneath me and watch her lose control.

TWENTY-ONE

Olivia

I HANG IN DOWNWARD DOG AND SEE KATE'S FACE STARING back at me from between my legs. She sticks her tongue out at me and we both start laughing. We get shushed by our instructor followed by a dirty look from the yogi beside us, but we could care less. We can't help but act like silly kids when we are together. We should probably reconsider yoga and try Zumba for our fitness regime. Ellie is doing her best to hold it together but failing miserably. She flops out of her downward dog and onto the mat. It isn't graceful. It also isn't quiet. I try to keep myself together. It's probably for the best that Jules had a prior commitment tonight, having to ask for a rain check on our girls' night. We all seem to be in a mood tonight, acting a whole lot extra than usual.

We bow our heads in namaste to end the class and head to the changing room, receiving glares from an older woman who I'm guessing is pissed that we ruined her class.

"That was all your fault in there, Kate. I doubt we will be welcomed back."

"Whatever Olivia, you need to loosen up. You've been a total grump since Parker left two weeks ago."

"Kate is right, you know. I have the pleasure of working all day, every day with you and you have been acting like a rotten three-year-old who's been told no. I can't take much more. You need to get your ass to Cape May and get laid."

The same woman who gave us the evil eye earlier is now eavesdropping on our conversation from the bench. She looks appalled.

"I thought it was bad when you were all love and unicorns shitting rainbows, but sad and mopey Olivia is way worse."

Although Ellie is hardly eloquent with her choice of words, she does have a point. I haven't been myself. It was ten days ago that I had to watch Parker pack his things and walk out the door. It was one of the hardest days of my life and it hasn't gotten easier. I knew being away from Parker was going to be difficult, but I didn't expect this constant ache in my chest that never seems to go away. Parker and I have been texting and Facetiming multiple times a day but it's just not the same. I need to touch him, to fall asleep in his arms and wake up to his gorgeous face in the morning.

I'm not up for dealing with this judgemental woman who looks like her head is going to pop off at any second. I grab my change of clothes and head behind a curtained changing room. I know Ellie is right. I can barely stand to be around myself in my sad state. I need to figure out how to deal with this.

"When are you two seeing each other again?" Ellie's voice sweeps over the curtain beside me.

"Not for another week."

"Another week? Oh, hell no! I can't take your shitty attitude for seven more days. I will never survive. Why not this weekend?"

"I can't. We have two big events this weekend. I have too much work to do." I fling my sweat top over my head and adjust my ponytail.

"And Parker is not coming here?"

"He has a meeting scheduled for Saturday morning and with the two events I have on Saturday and Sunday, I told him I would be too busy to see him."

"Olivia Madden, you know we have Leah and she and I can handle the shop without you. We can also handle the events this weekend. You are going to see Parker. I have everything under control."

"That's only two days away. I can't leave on such short notice."

"What exactly do you need to do? Pack a bag and go. What do you really need to pack anyways? I'm sure you'll spend the entire time naked in Parker's hotel room. I doubt you two will even stop boning to eat."

"You should surprise him," Kate says, adding her two cents to the conversation. "You can knock on his door and do the whole naked under a trench coat thing. Just spare us the details." I stuff my gym clothes into my backpack and throw open the cotton drape. I sit on a bench to lace up my sneakers. Thankfully, the woman with the judgy eyes has left.

"Seriously, Olivia. Kate is right. He won't expect it and he will love it. You need to listen to your little sister on this."

"Okay, I'll do it. You sure it's okay, Ells, that I leave you this weekend?"

"Positive. I will smash you if you don't go." Ellie emerges from her changing room dressed and ready to go.

"Eek! I'm going to see Parker in two days!"

"And just like that, she's back to her unicorn shitting rainbows self again. That was easy." Ellie throws her arm in the air and turns, opening the changing room door, waiting for us to follow.

The next two days are a blur. I help Ellie and Leah prepare the flowers for this weekend's events. The first is a gender reveal party, the second a baptism. We've done enough of these events that we have it down to a science. I'm not really sure why I was afraid to leave Ellie and Leah. It definitely won't be an issue. I've done as much as I can today to make sure they aren't overwhelmed, which means it's time for me to hit the road.

"Have a great weekend, Olivia, and drive safe. Text me when you arrive so I know you've made it. Love you."

I head to my car with my suitcase, taking a minute to call my mom. I'm sure she won't miss me now that she has my dad to fawn over, but a call to let her know I'm heading out of town is only polite. She sounds happy and it makes my good mood even better. As much as her excitement over my dad annoyed me at first, I have come to accept it. She was lonely for so long and had to sacrifice a hell of a lot. She gave up everything she had the day my father was arrested, so I have come to understand that she deserves to be happy today, in whatever form that takes.

I chat quickly with my dad too, and listen to his spiel about not doing anything he wouldn't do. I think he forgets I'm twenty-six and not the teenager I was when he left us. I roll my eyes and go with it. He adds in a few dad jokes before we hang up. I actually think it is kind of cute. What's also cute is that my dad and Parker talk frequently. Parker has been so helpful at advising him on new industry trends and has been a sounding board to bounce ideas off of.

The drive to Cape May feels like an eternity. I pass the time listening to my favorite country music playlist, thinking up ways to surprise Parker. I drive straight there without stopping, my body humming with excitement.

It's just after eight o'clock when I pull off the highway and turn into the hotel Parker is staying at. I park my car and flip down the visor, checking my appearance in the tiny mirror. With a fresh coat of lip gloss, I head inside the lobby of the boutique hotel, leaving my bag in the trunk. I can come back for it after I pull off the surprise.

Check-in is to my right as I enter the upscale lobby. The walls are painted jet black, accented with white moldings and colorful abstract paintings with a large cream-colored light in the ceiling that resembles a sea urchin. Black leather armchairs and tall green tropical plants fill the lobby. The sound of live music filters in from a large arched entryway leading to a dimly lit lounge. Round tables with dark green leather bucket chairs mark the center of the room. A white marble bar with backlit mirrored liquor shelves stretches across the crowded room to the left of the entry way.

As I run my fingers across the soft velvet of one of the couches, my eyes suddenly narrow on a beautiful woman sitting on the edge of a bar stool wearing a form-fitted black cocktail dress, her nude-colored four-inch heels teetering on the foot rail of the stool. Her long legs cross at the knee, and she oozes temptation and sin.

My gaze follows her seductive smile to the dark-haired man sitting in the stool in front of her. His back is to me but I don't need to see his face. I would know that man anywhere because he is mine. I am intimately aware of every inch of his body. A wave so strong it causes tremors ripples through my body. What I already know is confirmed when he turns his attention to the bartender, flashing his credit card between his thumb and two fingers. His profile hits me like a punch to my gut. It's Parker. My eyes blink and my knees go weak. A landslide of emotions hits me with full force. *This can't be really happening.*

This must be a misunderstanding. Parker just told me he loves me. He meant it. There's no doubt in my mind he meant it. Memories of his body tangled in mine at the beach house flood my mind. Parker calling me Livy girl, his strong arms wrapped around me as we danced together in the sand. I reach for the star pendant around my neck, rubbing it back and forth between my fingertips, and decide there is nothing going on between the two of them. There can't be. Parker would never betray me. I will give him the opportunity to explain.

I walk towards him, never taking my eyes off the woman who I can now see clearly. She is beautiful. A sickness rolls in my stomach.

Her legs uncross and she shimmies from her seat. She stands in front of him, their bodies so close her knees must be touching his. She leans forward and her hand reaches for him, clutching his thigh. I stop dead in my tracks and my breath hitches. My legs feel weak again and my heart plunges in my chest. She's confident and aggressive and nothing like me. She's looking at Parker like she wants to devour him. My Parker. I want to smack her and knock her classless body across the room.

Her other hand moves behind his neck in one quick motion and her lips are on his.

My vision blurs, the sick feeling in my belly creeping up my throat. I can't take one more second of this. I whirl around, stumbling on weak legs, grabbing hold of the velvet couch in front of me to steady myself. My eyes burn, welling with tears. There's a knot in my throat. It's increasingly harder to breathe.

An older gentleman with concerned eyes is now at my side, his hand on my forearm, but I don't hear a word he's saying. I just know I need to get out of here. I race towards the door, leaving my heart in pieces on the floor of the lobby.

I drive away, sobs bursting from my lungs. There is an ache in my throat and my chest feels as though it's trapped in a vice. I wipe the tears from my eyes and realize I have no clue where I am driving. It doesn't matter as long as it's far away from the one person I trusted the most. The one person who I thought would never betray me.

I need to catch my breath. I need to figure out where to go. I consider calling Kate or Ellie but the shame cuts too deep. I want to be alone. I need to go home to Reed Point. The tears continue falling down my cheeks. *Pull yourself together.*

I drive along the coast, tears blurring the lines on the road. I pull my Prius into a parking lot. There's a pier and a handful of cars, the lot full of teenage kids tailgating and having a good time. The windows on the Mustang beside me are fogged. I don't want to imagine what is happening in there.

I put my car in park and force myself out the door on two shaky legs towards the pier. The ocean is calling to me like it always does when I need to think. I fill my aching lungs with the cool air, the breeze covering my skin in goosebumps. They also could be blanketing my skin from the shock of what's just happened. I pull my sweater tight around me, walking further towards the setting sun.

I stand at the head of the pier, tears stinging my eyes. I will my knees not to give out on me. The pain is almost too much to bear. I feel like such a fool, a complete and total idiot to think that Parker could have changed. I have no one to blame but myself. I put myself in this position. I let my guard down. A leopard never changes its spots, isn't that what they say?

I hate myself for believing he could have been happy without all the other women. How could I be so stupid to think I could have ever been enough?

I stay at the pier for half an hour, feeling defeated and lonely, before making the decision to drive back home. If I leave now, I'll be home before midnight. I can't be in this town with Parker. I want my home and my bed. I want to hide away from the rest of the world.

I return to my car, my head heavy from crying. My phone rests in the cup holder, flashing with an incoming message. I pick it up and check the screen. I have several missed calls that all went to voicemail. I delete them all without listening, shift my car into drive and make the long drive home in silence.

By the time I arrive home, I am all out of tears. My heart is shattered, a gaping hole in its place. I drop my bag at the door. There are memories of Parker everywhere I look. The coffee table where we ate Thai food the night I decided to let him back into my life. The kitchen counter where we undressed each other. My bedroom where we made love over and over in my sheets, until the sun came up and we needed to finally rest. The pain in my chest tightens. It's relentless and I wonder if it will ever go away.

I walk into my bathroom and strip my clothes to the floor. I turn the lever on the shower and wait for the temperature to rise. I step into the hot shower and let the nearly scalding water rain down over my skin. I tilt my face up to the spray hoping it will ease the strain in my eyes, and the throb in my head. I wash my body and my hand finds the diamond star around my neck. As much as I hate Parker right now, I can't bring myself to take it off. I remember how I felt opening the small box. My eyes squeeze shut. I'm so confused. I could've sworn what we had was real. *Who am I kidding?* It took all of two weeks living in a different city for Parker to find someone new.

I wrap a towel around my body and run a brush through my wet hair. I throw on a tank and my sleep shorts and crawl into bed. The scent of Parker suffocates me. My sheets smell like his soap, like fresh rain and cedar. I pull my knees into my chest and I close my eyes. I pray for sleep.

TWENTY-TWO

Olivia

THEY ARE BOTH NAKED, COMPLETE STRANGERS AND A STORM IS threatening the shitty shelter they have constructed to protect them from hypothermia, and bears that are apparently a predatory threat. *What the effing of all effs is this show*?

I shovel another mouthful of Ben & Jerry's Chocolate Explosion in my mouth and wipe the drip that falls onto my tank top with my finger. I get back to my show because I'm invested, with a strange need to know if they can last the twenty-one days.

There's a knock at my door and my heart sinks. I don't move because I can't. I feel frozen in place, and for a split second I wonder if it might be him.

"Olivia, it's me. Open up, I'm worried about you," Ellie hollers through my front door.

I'm not sure why she is worried about me. It's Saturday night and as far as she knows I'm in total bliss in Cape May with Parker. *Little does she know.* I couldn't bring myself to call anyone and explain why I'm home.

I answer the door and my best friend takes me in. Her eyes sweep my body from head to toe. I know I look bad. I haven't changed out of the tank and sleep shorts I went to bed in last night and I'm pretty positive my eyes are still swollen and puffy after hours of crying. I have a pizza stain on one side of my sleep shirt from today's lunch and a chocolate stain from the ice cream I've been binging on my left boob.

As strong as I try to be, I can't stop myself from falling to pieces in the doorway. Tears roll down my cheeks. She pulls me in for a hug.

"Oh Olivia, what happened? I was so worried about you when I couldn't get a hold of you." Ellie closes the door behind us and takes my hand leading me to the couch. She flops down beside me, tucking her leg underneath her. Her focus moves to the television and the reality show I am watching.

"Is this Naked and Afraid? Oh, I love that show. Sorry, Olivia - squirrel! You know me." She shrugs and it makes me laugh for the first time in hours. Focus is not one of Ellie's best attributes.

"How did you know I was here? I didn't tell anyone I came home." Ellie hands me a tissue from one of the three boxes I have in rotation around my apartment.

"I didn't. It's just the first place I looked when you didn't answer your cell or return my texts. Parker is really worried about you. He called me this morning and asked if I knew where you were. He said you haven't returned any of his messages or calls since last night." Ellie says carefully, "He asked me to check on you and have you call him. I don't get it. What's wrong, Olivia?"

I realize I haven't looked at my phone since getting home last night. I'm not even sure where it is in this mess of an apartment.

My eyes are clouded with tears that are threatening once again to spill over. Embarrassment and shame, I'm sure, are written all over my face.

"It's okay, Olivia. Whatever it is, I am here for you. We will get through it together like we always do. Promise."

I take a deep breath and tell her everything. Thankfully, she kept my surprise visit to Cape May from Parker, not sure if I would want him to know.

"I don't believe it. I've seen the way that man looks at you. Sparks fly when you two are in a room together. You had to have been mistaken."

"Ells, I know what I saw. They kissed. The slut bag had her hands on his body. Is it really that hard to believe? He doesn't do commitments. He likes his freedom. He hasn't been in a relationship since high school."

"Yes, since you. He only does relationships with *you* because he loves you. None of this makes sense."

I focus on the almost empty carton of ice cream on the coffee table, hoping it will distract me from my thoughts. I exhale, wrapping my arms around my knees, pulling them into my chest.

"You need to talk to him, Olivia. Hear him out. There are two sides to every story."

"I'm not talking to him."

Ellie sighs, pushing up from the couch to standing, clearing the dirty dishes from my coffee table.

"What are you doing?"

"I'm cleaning up your mess, and then I'm putting you in the shower and getting you out of those clothes. I love you, Olivia, but you smell, and your hair looks like you styled it with mayonnaise."

I can't argue. She's right. I shower and change into joggers and a loose fit t-shirt. When I'm done, I find Ellie in my newly cleaned living room shuffling through Netflix. There are two cups of hot tea on the coffee table.

"Have I ever told you there's no one better than you, Ells?" I lower myself to the couch beside her, and she wraps one arm around my shoulder.

"You are *very* lucky to have me. I am pretty amazing. I know a bunch of people who would agree."

I chuckle and lean forward, reaching for my tea and taking a sip, letting the hot liquid soothe the knot in my throat. It warms my chest, lulling the ache that consumes my body. It feels good going down, but I wonder if a tumbler of something stronger to numb the pain might have been the smarter choice.

"Should we watch a movie, or do you want to talk?"

I think about it for a second. "I don't know. What is there to say? He broke my heart. I thought he was it for me. I could have sworn he was the one. I saw a future together. I saw babies. Now I just feel like an idiot."

"I'm sorry, Olivia. I thought he was the one too." Ellie runs her hand down my ponytail. "I have to text him and let him know you are alive. He asked me to check on you. He's worried sick and it's not fair for him to think that something bad happened to you."

"That's fine. What will you say? Not that it matters anyway, he obviously couldn't care less about me."

"I will tell him that you are safe at home and that he's a giant asshole."

"All true," I grumble. My chest tightens thinking of him. The image of the woman's lips on his replays over and over in my mind and I can't make it stop. I set my mug down on the coffee table and rub my eyes with my palms. I fall back into the couch and pull my legs into my chest.

"It hurts so bad, Ells. I feel like I can barely breath." I feel the warmth of my best friend's arms wrap around my trembling body. She smooths my hair from my face and tells me to cry it out. It's going to take endless tears and an entire lifetime to get over Parker Bennett, and even that might not be enough.

A RAY OF SUNSHINE CUTS A STRAIGHT LINE ACROSS MY bedroom. My eyes adjust to the morning light as I roll over, looking for Ellie. We fell asleep last night on the couch watching a movie. Ellie nudged me at some point, waking me from my sleep and we relocated to my bed. I fell back asleep in a little spoon position with Ellie's arms around my center.

I rub my eyes and stumble out of bed and into the kitchen. She's left a note beside an empty mug on the counter. My phone that I haven't seen since Friday night is plugged into the wall and charging. The note reads...

***Morning! Off to work, wanted to let you sleep. I'll see you tonight. I'm taking you out for dinner. Get out of the house today and stay far away from chocolate ice cream, I promise you'll feel better. Love you*, Ells**

I pop a coffee puck into the machine and slide two pieces of bread into the toaster. My apartment is ridiculously quiet as I sit at the breakfast bar and turn on my phone. The screen lights up, alerting me I have more messages from Parker. I lock my phone and throw it back to the counter without opening any of his messages. I have nothing to say to him so what's the point?

I finish my toast and coffee and get back in my preferred position on my couch. I catch myself staring out the window. The sun is pouring in, taunting me to get my ass off of the couch and get some fresh air. I decide to take Ellie's advice. I need to run. I need to feel the sun on my face. I'm done thinking about Parker. I'm done feeling sorry for myself.

I dress in my sports bra and running shorts, lace up my sneakers and head out my door. The warmth of the sun feels like a heavy blanket wrapped around me. My feet pound the pavement, my heartbeat hammering in my chest. It's my escape. An escape I needed today more than ever.

I travel my usual route along the boardwalk. Closing my eyes, I inhale the fresh ocean breeze and then exhale a full breath back out. I can breathe again. The sounds of the waves crashing into shore calm my frayed nerves. I typically have my ear buds in, music high, motivating me to run faster, but today I left my phone at home. Parker hasn't stopped sending me messages. I'm too angry to respond, but instead let that anger fuel me to a personal best. I run seven miles before losing steam. My heartbeat feels like it's bursting through my rib cage as I bend over, my hands on my knees, breathing fast.

Ellie was right. I needed to get out. Clear my mind. Erase the images of Parker and that night from my memory. I need to move on without him and find happiness again. Sitting at home watching shitty television and crying into a bowl of ice cream is not going to help.

I walk down Main Street, stopping at Bloom, not wanting to be alone in my apartment. I know I won't be able to stop thinking about him if I'm by myself. The memories won't stop. His dark brown eyes, the sexy smile he gives me when he catches me staring at him. I can still feel the grip of his hand on my hip when he pulls me into him. *Olivia, you need to stop this.*

I'm a sweaty mess, so I sneak through the back door in hopes of no one seeing me. I grab a bottle of water from the small fridge in the back room and crack the top, hearing Ellie as she speaks to a customer. I turn to sit at the desk and when I do, I trip over my own foot, sending a glass vase to the floor. It smashes into smithereens as it hits the hardwood. *You've got to be kidding me.*

I hear footsteps running towards me from the front of the store. I'm mortified, wishing I could find somewhere to hide. I bend to the floor to clean up the colossal mess my clumsiness made.

"Olivia! You scared the shit out of me. Are you okay?" Ellie stares down at me, watching me pick up the larger pieces of glass, stacking them in my hand. I'll need a broom and dustpan for the rest of the glass.

"I'm fine. Just bruised my ego tripping over my own two feet trying to be quiet. I didn't want to see anyone except for you." I can feel my face heat. Ellie's expression changes and I'm confused as to why she is looking at me with an apology in her eyes.

"Is everything okay back there?" I look up to see Hunter standing beside Ellie, a look of concern on his face. Now I understand why my best friend was looking at me the way she was. Of all people to see today, it had to be Hunter.

"What are you doing here, Hunter?" I ask sharply. This can't be happening. Who in this universe did I piss off so badly to deserve the last three days of hell? I must have stomped on a kitten in my previous lifetime to deserve this special kind of torture. I'm not sure how things could get worse but if I was a betting woman, I'd put money on it that they will.

"I came to see if we could talk, Olivia. I'll only take up a few minutes of your time."

Ellie watches me, waiting on my decision. I know she would have zero problem throwing his ass out into the street if I said the word. My eyes meet hers and I nod, letting her know I will talk to him.

"That's my cue. I'll be out front if you need me, Olivia." Ellie narrows her eyes at Hunter, her lips pressed together in a straight line, leaving the two of us alone. I inwardly laugh. My best friend is a pit bull.

"What do you want, Hunter?" I leave the pile of glass at my feet and throw the pieces I collected into the garbage can behind me.

"I want to apologize to you."

"Apologize for what?"

"For being such a jerk to you back in high school. I said some awful things to you that I never should've said. I'm not proud of myself and I know I screwed up. For what it's worth, I never meant what I said."

"It was a long time ago, Hunter. It's my fault for believing you."

"No, Olivia. It was completely my fault that you and Parker broke up. He loved you. He always has." I wince at his words. "I was just a jealous prick who wanted what he had."

I'm not sure what he means by that, but I'm too tired to care. None of it matters anymore. Parker and I are done, and there's little point in dredging up the past.

"It's fine, Hunter. It was a long time ago. We've all moved on. I'm not one to hold a grudge."

Hunter exhales a deep breath and the corners of his mouth rise just a little. It's a different side to Hunter. A softer, sweeter side than I remember from when we were kids. I guess even total asshats can change and mature.

"Parker is a lucky guy, Olivia. I'm really happy you found your way back to each other. You both deserve to be happy."

I feel my eyes sting, tears blurring my vision. I swallow hard, willing the tears away. I do not want to cry. Especially in front of Hunter. He must notice because the small smile he had on his face is replaced with worry.

"Are you okay, Olivia?"

"I will be." I pause uncomfortably. "Things didn't work out with Parker. I'm sure you are going to hear sooner or later."

Hunter looks genuinely confused. His fingers scratch the scruff of his jaw. I look away, pretending not to feel as uncomfortable in this moment as I do.

"I'm so sorry." Hunter's eyes soften. "I don't know what to say. I've never seen Parker happier. I'm shocked."

"Well, you and me both." I've already said too much, and I can feel the tears burning the rims of my eyes. I can't break down in front of Hunter. I need to get out of here. "Look Hunter, I appreciate the apology, but I really need to clean up this mess and go home. I hope you and Parker are able to mend fences. You've been friends too long not to. It would be a shame."

Hunter nods and smiles. It doesn't quite reach his eyes, but it's warm and thoughtful. It's the closest I've ever come to seeing a sympathetic side to him.

"I doubt a friendship with Parker is in the cards, but I will always only wish him the best. Take care of yourself, Olivia."

He says goodbye and leaves. I realize in that moment how much his apology means to me, how much I needed to know he never meant the hurtful things he said to me. That was the lowest point in my life. It was *his* words that made me feel shame for who I was. For who my family was. I feel one weight lifted from my shoulders. It's too bad I still feel like I'm carrying the weight of the world on me.

"Everything okay back here? Hunter just left." Ellie's eyes meet mine, her brows pulled together. I know she is dying to hear what he had to say.

"It's fine."

"What did he want?"

"To apologize, believe it or not."

"Wow, the dick bag has a heart after all. What did you say?" Ellie pushes the tall garbage bin closer to me. I sweep the small pieces from the dustpan into the bin.

"I forgave him, of course. My mother always told me that when you hold a grudge, your hands aren't free to catch blessings. And I believe that."

"Well, you are a better woman than me, Olivia. I would take that grudge to my grave."

Amused by Ellie, I can't help but smile. I put the broom away and take a long drink of my water.

"Go home and get ready. I'll clean up the rest. I am taking you out tonight and we are going to have some fun."

"Ellie, I don't know. I think I'm more in the mood for ice cream, playlists full of sad songs and drinking alcohol like it's my full-time job." I grumble like the pathetic, broken, sad excuse for a human that I am.

"Not on my watch. And besides, you can still drink your brains out while wearing a cute outfit in a fun restaurant. I'll pick you up at seven."

I love so many things about Ellie, but right now her tenacity is not high on that list.

TWENTY-THREE

Parker

It's been three days since I've talked to Livy. Almost three weeks since I've seen her or held her in my arms. I slam my phone down on my office desk. She hasn't responded to a single call or text. I just want to hear her voice. Ellie messaged me to say Olivia is okay and to leave her alone. *What the fuck does that mean?* What am I supposed to do with that?

The last time I spoke to her we were planning our next weekend together. How can it go from that to total silence? I replay our last conversation over and over in my mind, looking for a reason for her to disappear on me. My mind is blank.

Rolling the sleeves of my dress shirt up my arms, I lean back into my leather chair, crossing my ankle over my knee. I rest the back of my head against the cool leather and squeeze my eyes shut. The muscle in my jaw clenches. The dull ache in my head has been relentless all weekend and I'm running on zero sleep.

I straighten in my chair at the sound of a light knock on my office door, pretending what's happening to me right now doesn't hurt like hell. Carmen stands in the doorway with the files I requested. I have a video call in ten minutes with Liam that I need to be prepared for. Somehow, I'm going to have to get some work done today. To do this, I'm going to need a miracle.

"Sorry to interrupt you. I have the budget update you asked for." Carmen motions towards my desk, her heels clicking across the shiny hardwood floor. She drops the folder on my desk in front of me. "I made notes in the margin for you to review. I emailed you the link to your video chat as well. Let me know if you have any issues."

Carmen is my new assistant. She has long brown hair with bright green eyes and is a few years younger than I am. I've known her for the two years she's worked at our Reed Point office under my father. She was happy to make the move to Cape May, needing a change of scenery. She's undeniably beautiful, but more importantly she's good at her job and performs well under pressure. Miles has had a thing for Carmen for years, never able to be discreet about it. It's obvious why, she's the total package. But since finding Livy again, she does nothing for me.

"Thanks, Carmen. I'll look at it now." I take the file and open it. I raise my elbows to my desk and press my fingers into my temples.

"Are you feeling okay? I'm sorry, I didn't mean to overstep. You just look like something is bothering you."

"I'm fine," I answer back, forcing a swallow. "I just have a headache I can't seem to shake. Thanks for asking."

"Can I get you a bottle of water or Advil? I get headaches often and I know how awful they can be."

"Actually, that would be helpful. I would appreciate that." Carmen spins around and walks out of my office.

I pick up my phone to text Ellie quickly before my meeting. I'm hoping when I glance at the screen there will a text from Livy. Nothing. I need answers and I need them now. I can't eat, I can't sleep and I'm sucking balls at my job right now.

ME: Hey Ellie. I'm going out of my mind. I really need to talk to Livy. What can I do to get her to talk to me?

Bouncing dots appear telling me she's typing. Fuck, I hope she has something for me.

ELLIE: I'm sorry Parker. This is between the two of you. Give her space and when she's ready, I'm sure she will talk to you. Give her a few days.

Dammit! My anger bubbles to the surface. I feel like slamming my fist through a wall.

I stand and pace my office, adrenaline coursing through my veins, I feel like I'm losing control. Life has come full circle. I feel exactly like I did when I was eighteen and heartbroken, left without an explanation. History is repeating itself. Livy gets scared and she quits. The thought of never seeing her again burns in my chest. *How can this be happening?*

I swore what we had was real. I choke back the lump in my throat, walking towards the window. I unclench my fists, trying to release the tension, to ease the panic taking up space in my chest. She has always been my weakness.

"HAVE YOU HEARD A THING I JUST SAID? WHAT IS IT WITH YOU today?" Liam's face is staring back at me through the computer screen, tense and annoyed. We've been on this video call for over an hour and I'm trying my best just to follow along.

"I'm listening."

"Yah, prove it. What did I just recommend you do with the cap-x budget?"

I have zero clue what he's referring to. I guess I really wasn't hearing a word he was saying.

"I'm sorry, man. Can we go over it again?"

"Parker, what's going on with you? You can't focus and you're edgy as hell."

"It's that obvious?" My shoulders sag, he's looking at me like I just grew a second head.

"It is. You're a fucking mess. I'm guessing this has something to do with Olivia?"

Carmen pokes her head in my office, and I motion for her to come in. She hands me a bottle of water and two Advil. I nod my thanks and then wave her off. I pop the two pills in my mouth, chasing them back with a mouthful of water.

"It's that bad that you have to self-medicate?" Liam raises his brows, sitting back in his chair while spinning a pen through his fingers.

"I wish I knew how bad it really is. Livy has been avoiding me all weekend and I have no idea why."

"How can you not know why? You obviously screwed up in a big way if she won't talk to you."

"Fuck if I know. I don't get it. I don't know how relationships work, Liam." I drop my head into my hands. "What do I do?"

Liam groans and leans forward, his face filling the space in my screen. I realize asking Liam for relationship advice is ridiculous but desperate times call for desperate measures.

"Let me ask you a question."

I nod.

"Do you love her?"

"More than anything," I admit.

"So that means you want to fix this?"

"Of course, I do. I just don't know how." I close my eyes and drag my fingers through my hair.

"Go to Reed Point, you idiot. You have to talk to her. If she won't answer your calls, you need to go see her. You're not going to just sit back and watch her walk away, are you?"

"She won't even answer my text messages. Who's to say she will answer her door to me?"

"So, you are just going to give up? You're a Bennett, we fight for what we want. You need to fight for her." Liam looks at me with a pointed stare.

It sounds simple enough and suddenly I see it's the obvious solution. I need to get to Reed Point as soon as possible.

"Hang tight, I need to pull up my calendar to see how soon I'm able to go." Tuesday is full of meetings, but my Wednesday looks clear. I ping Carmen and ask her to block off my Wednesday and Thursday.

"Done, I'm leaving Wednesday."

"Great, so what's your plan?" Liam asks, like I might actually know the answer to that question.

"I'm going to find her and talk to her?"

"And say what? You can't just show up without a plan." Liam's right. I need to think this through.

I drop my chin to my chest. I recognize this feeling. This is heartbreak. The feeling of drowning when you aren't even in water. The sting of the pain in your lungs because there isn't enough oxygen in the room to fill them. It's a pain I've now felt twice in my life, and I wouldn't wish it on anyone.

"Parker!" Liam snaps me back to our conversation. "Get your head in the game. Focus. What are you going to say to her?"

"I've got tonight and tomorrow to figure it out." Wednesday seems like forever away but I know it will come soon.

"You better figure this out if you don't want to lose her. You need to do something so it's clear how you feel about her."

"Yeah," I mumble. "Thanks, Liam."

There isn't anything I won't do to fix this. I know what I want, and what I want is Livy.

Now the real question is... how am I going to get my girl back?

My Audi glides to a stop in front of Livy's apartment. I'm immediately racing up the steps two at a time to get to her door. My mind is jumbled with all the things I want to say to her, questions I need answers to spinning through my mind.

"Livy?" I knock on her door, "Please answer the door if you are in there. We need to talk." I pound on the door again. "Livy please, talk to me."

I wait for the door to swing open, for her to answer so we can fix this. I kick myself, wishing that I had asked her for her entry code so I could go in and force her to talk to me. I know if we could just talk, I could make her see we belong together. I could fix whatever the hell it is that is upsetting her.

My palms press firmly on the door and I rest my forehead against the cool wood surface, listening for sounds that she's there. Silence. I wait a few minutes, then call her name again through the door one last time. Nothing. I'm not giving up. I walk away, looking over my shoulder one last time at her door, then run down the stairs exiting her building. I will find her. I have to. I'm not losing Livy again.

Later that night, I'm standing in front of Breathe Yoga, waiting for Livy to finish her usual Wednesday night class.

I'm taking a chance that she's in there with the girls like she is every week. I tried Bloom after I left her apartment and neither Livy nor Ellie was there. I talked to Leah hoping for a clue where I could find her, but I came up short.

A group of people begin to filter out and I spot Ellie stepping out onto the sidewalk, her yoga mat under her arm, a duffle bag over her shoulder. She's by herself. *Shit! Where's Livy?*

I wait a second longer, hoping she appears somewhere in the small crowd of people behind Ellie. My heart sinks. There is no sign of her anywhere. Out of options, I approach Ellie, hoping she will talk to me. She spots me and her eyes narrow. She looks pissed. She is not going to make this easy on me from the looks of it.

She crosses her arms over her body and thankfully stops to talk to me.

"If you came to see Olivia, she's not here."

"Where is she, Ellie? I've been looking everywhere for her. I need to talk to her."

"She's not ready to talk to you, obviously. I told you to give her space."

"This is ridiculous. I have no idea why she isn't talking to me. How can I fix this if no one will tell me what the hell I did wrong? How is this fair?"

"Are you kidding me right now? What you did to her is so freaking far from fair. Seriously, Parker. You're supposed to be a smart guy, do you really need me to tell you what you did?"

"Yes, I do." The tone in my voice is one of pure frustration. This is going nowhere.

"I am so disappointed in you. I was always on your side, pushing for the two of you to be together. Team Parkey, remember? I can't believe I had you so wrong," Ellie snaps, digging through her bag to find her car keys. She rushes past me towards her car that is parked along the street.

"What are you talking about?" My head is spinning, I feel sick to my stomach. Why can't someone tell me what the hell is going on? "I would never do anything to hurt her." I turn to follow her down the sidewalk.

Ellie whips open her car door to her back seat, tossing her duffle bag and mat across the seat. She slams the car door and moves towards the driver's door, opening it.

"You really are impossible, Parker. Do I need to spell it out for you?"

"Clearly you do, Ellie, because I have absolutely no clue what's going on here. I dropped everything to drive here. I've been all over Reed Point looking for her. She won't talk to me. I'm clearly getting nowhere with you. I'm trying here, but I don't know what more I can do?"

"Well, how about for starters you stop kissing women in hotel lobbies." With that, Ellie climbs into her car, slamming the door behind her. The engine roars to life and her cars pulls away from the curb into traffic.

I'm left standing on the street on shaky legs with no time to respond. For a minute, her words don't register. What is Ellie talking about? I would never betray Livy. And then it hits me. Friday night in the hotel lobby bar, the woman who sat down next to me who wouldn't take no for an answer. I tried to be polite at first when she introduced herself and made small talk but then realized she mistook my kindness for a come on.

My admission that I was already in a relationship did nothing to stop that woman. She knew what she wanted.

Me. On her bed in her hotel room. She basically told me as much.

Asking the bartender to settle my tab, I knew I needed to get away from her. Unfortunately, she pounced on me before I had the chance to leave, catching me completely off guard when she forced her mouth on mine.

Was Livy there that night? Could she have seen that crazy woman assault my mouth? That must be it. It was Friday night when she started to avoid me. Fuck. I can only imagine what that must have looked like, the conclusions she must have jumped to. No wonder she won't talk to me, I wouldn't talk to me either.

I walk to my car, gathering my thoughts. The good news - I now know why Livy is avoiding me and I know I can fix this. It's too late to drive back to Cape May so I drive to the beach house where I'll stay the night and figure out how to get my girl back.

I need Livy to understand that she's the only one for me. I'm sure she must think I've gone back to my old ways but that couldn't be further from the truth. The days of going out to bars to meet girls are long gone and there's nothing about casual hook ups that I miss. I only want a life with her. I want late night walks on the beach together. I want Livy in the chair beside me at family dinners. I will never be able to see a star in the sky and not think of her wearing my necklace. I need to make her see this. I need to show Livy with actions and not just words that I want to spend the rest of my life with her.

I lay in bed with my phone in my hand thinking of her, thinking of ways I can really show her she's my whole world. I flip through the pictures of Livy I have saved on my phone, smiling when I get to the photos of her in my arms in bed with me at the beach house. I can still feel her hands all over me, her long golden hair tickling my chest. I fell in love with her that weekend. I miss her so fucking much. I can't wait to get her back in my arms where she belongs. And I know just how I'm going to do it. I close my eyes, hoping to dream of Livy and praying I can pull this off.

I wake up the next morning with a plan. It's a plan I want to set in motion right away, but I can't do it alone. I pick up my phone and dial her number, hoping together we can pull this off.

"Hello?"

"Ellie, it's me Parker. Please don't hang up." The desperation in my voice is real. I'm not too proud to get on my hands and knees if I have to.

"Fine. You have two minutes. What do you want?" Ellie sasses me back while I say a silent prayer.

"Look, the whole situation Livy saw at the hotel bar was not what she thinks it was. Seriously, she has the world's worst timing but that's beside the point. I love her, Ellie. I can't be without her. I need your help."

I tell her everything about that night. She confirms to me Livy was there and witnessed everything. My heart sinks, knowing Livy had to see that and think for even a second that I could ever hurt her like that.

“Okay Parker, I’m listening. But if you hurt my best friend, I’ll have no problem killing you and hiding your body. Got it?”

“Loud and clear.”

TWENTY-FOUR

Olivia

After five days of hiding away in my apartment, I have zero tears left to cry and I'm ready to go back to work. *You just need time.* This is the advice I've been given from multiple people, Kate and my mom included when I poured my broken heart out to them. I will just have to trust that whoever it was that said time is a broken heart's best friend was probably right. I'm assuming they know this after having also had their hearts stomped on by an ex-boyfriend.

Ellie and Leah have been so patient with me, but I've wallowed long enough. It's time to ditch the sweatpants and filthy hair and get my ass off the couch - if it's not permanently stuck there at this point. I've been down this road before and I will survive another breakup with Parker. I have no other choice.

I may have stopped crying, but that doesn't mean this is easy. Figuring out a way to stop loving Parker feels impossible. I haven't been able to go more than five minutes without thinking about him. A rotation of memories plays on a loop through my mind. I wonder where he is or what he's doing, if he is thinking about me as much as I'm thinking about him? Or has he already moved on with that bimbo?

I'm standing at the wooden worktable carefully trimming an order of ice blue lacecap hydrangeas. Their scent fills the air and brings me a little happiness. This is the most beautiful time of year at Bloom, when all of my favorite flowers are in season, marigolds, dahlias, peonies. I love them all, but peonies are particularly gorgeous. Especially the pale pink and white ones. They remind me of our garden growing up and I feel a pang of nostalgia each year when they are back in season.

Ellie and Leah are working across from me, trimming bunches of dusty millers and leatherleaf ferns, filler stems for the prearranged bouquets we sell. They are also doing their best to make me smile. This morning they brought me my favorite caramel apple croissant and a coffee for breakfast and switched out our playlist at the shop from Michael Bublé hits to country top 40.

Leah steps away to answer an incoming call, giving Ellie the opportunity to thoughtfully check in with me.

"You okay, Liv?"

"Yeah. I'm okay. One day at a time, I keep telling myself. I know it will get easier."

"Good girl. I'm really proud of you. Kate told me you guys had a great dinner last night at your mom's. She said it's starting to feel a little like it used to. I'm really happy you are getting your family back. That's one good thing, right?" Ellie's eyes are full of warmth and I'm reminded that my life isn't all bad. I have supportive friends who would do anything for me, a successful business that makes my work a joy and my family is back together. On the last front, the adjustment to my dad's return has been better than I ever expected. It's a reminder that even without Parker, I am not alone.

"Thanks, Ells Bells. It really was actually... nice. You will be able to see my dad tomorrow when he visits Bloom. He's coming by for a visit to see the shop and then taking me out for lunch."

"Wow, Olivia, big steps. That's great."

We both turn our attention to Leah who seems to be frustrated with whoever she is talking to on the other end of the call. She eventually puts the person on hold, rolls her eyes to the ceiling and sighs, turning to the two of us.

"This woman is obnoxious. She's inquiring about a massive order of all white flowers that I'm not sure we can accommodate."

"Like how many are we talking?" I ask.

"700! It's a fancy clam bake at White Harbor Beach. I don't even think Caroline Kennedy had that many flowers at her wedding. Who do these people think they are? She also seems very particular and nauseatingly high maintenance, like she expects us to just drop everything else."

"When is the event?" Ellie asks with curiosity, putting down the stems in her hand and wiping her hands down her work apron.

"Friday. Can we do it? What should I tell her?"

Ellie looks at me and then we both look back at Leah. It's like watching a tennis match, our heads turning from right to left.

"What do you think, Liv? Can we find that many stems in time? I'm free Friday to do the set up."

"I think we can pull it off if we have all hands on deck," I answer her. It will be a lot of work, but honestly, I could use the distraction heading into the weekend. Leah gives us a thumbs up letting us know she is available this week to help. If this event goes through, we are going to need her.

"Take down her info and tell her we will call her back this afternoon with a quote. We'll need a fifty percent deposit if we are going to bring in an order that size."

"On it." Leah nods and returns her attention back to the phone call.

I dig my cell phone out of my pocket and call Mabel, hoping she can supply such a ridiculous amount of perfectly matched white blooms in time for Friday. She answers on the third ring and lets me know that she should have enough. She will confirm with me in one hour.

She also requests that I have my "hottie" assistant at Bloom with me when she does the delivery. Immediately my mind wanders to Parker, all six-foot-two of him, thinking back to how carefree and confident he was that day, when we visited Meadow Flowers. I'm reminded of how good it felt to have his muscular arms around me, and how I will never get to feel that way again. *I wish, Mabel. You have no idea how much I wish.*

Three hours later, Mabel calls to confirm the order. She promises seven hundred of her best white peonies will be delivered to us on Thursday morning. That will give us almost two days to arrange them exactly how our client would like.

I make the call to Bianca, the customer who is hosting this insanely posh clam bake, to let her know we can do it. The bill is astronomical and frankly kind of ridiculous for a clam bake, but apparently Bianca has money to burn. Fine by me. She insists on paying the invoice in full upfront, adamant the flowers are to be delivered to the beach by five o'clock Friday evening. I assure her this won't be a problem and graciously thank her for her business, ending the call. I shake my head. Some people in this town have more money than they know what to do with.

The next few days are spent working nonstop on Bianca's order. Our uber-rich and rather demanding client has called several more times with added requests. I've got to hand it to her, she knows what she wants. Between her lavish order, dinner at my parents' and an after-work shopping and dinner date with Kate, this week has fortunately turned out to be not half bad. It's nowhere near great either, but it's a start.

I'm still kept up at night with thoughts of Parker. I try writing my thoughts in my journal, but it doesn't help. My mind is too jumbled to write more than a few words. Instead, I stare at my phone, part of me wishing he would call, and the other part not knowing if I would talk to him even if he did. I'm still so angry with him. I just want to be happy again. Most nights I give up, wrapping my arms around my pillow and fighting off thoughts of Parker until I finally drift off to sleep.

It's half past four on Friday and we just carefully shut the back door of our Bloom van. We were able to fit the largest order we have ever received in it. The van is bursting with the most gorgeous soft white peonies arranged in elaborate bouquets, centerpieces and garlands. Their sweet and rosy scent is enough to intoxicate you.

Working on this order has been the rainbow in my dark and stormy week, the reprieve I so desperately needed to take my mind off of Parker. This order has possibly been my favorite project we have ever worked on and I'm proud of how it turned out. I can't help but think how proud Parker would be too, if he could see it.

Ellie jumps into the driver's seat and I take shotgun. We leave Leah at Bloom to run the store while we head to the location to meet Bianca. I'm secretly curious to meet this woman whose floral décor budget seemingly exceeds my annual mortgage payment. I soon realize that my assumptions about her were one hundred percent off track.

We are met by a smiling Bianca, who is wearing a pale blue and white striped off-the-shoulder sundress, her long hair swept up in a wavy high ponytail. She's around my age and not pretentious in the slightest. She's sweet, kind and eager to meet the two of us. Not at all the affected socialite I was expecting.

She greets Ellie and I with a warm hello and motions to the section of the beach where she would like the flowers to be set up. It's secluded and private, tucked away from the crowds, and it looks like we are the first vendor to arrive.

I can't help but notice she's flustered, apparently waiting on the long tables and chairs to arrive, along with the rest of the décor she ordered. She tells us they're stuck in traffic, looking more than a little concerned.

It takes Ellie and I a solid hour to unload each and every arrangement, carting the flowers back and forth over the cool sand. When we finish, we are a sweaty mess, exhausted and in need of a good calf massage and a shower. Unfortunately, that will have to wait.

We're also disappointed that we won't be able to see the finished look. Thankfully, Bianca has agreed to take Instagram-worthy photos and share them with us.

After thanking her for trusting us with her vision, we exchange hugs and head back to the van. I hop into the passenger seat and twist my hair, damp from sweating under the hot sun, up into a messy bun. Ellie takes a long drink from her water bottle then turns the engine to life, heading back to Bloom.

"That couldn't have gone better. It's funny, we had Bianca all wrong. She's actually really cool."

"I know, right? I don't know what I was expecting but that wasn't it." Ellie holds her right hand in the hair, palm facing me, "Go team!" I high five her.

"I'm just bummed we won't get to see our largest order ever all set up in its glory."

"I know, but it's going to be gorgeous. I'm proud of us." Ellie beams from the driver's seat, her window rolled down, the breeze whirling through her hair.

"Me too."

We park the van behind Bloom and quickly head inside to grab our car keys so we can make our way home. Leah has locked up the store and gone home for the day, so our job here today is done. I follow Ellie out through the front door, and after she locks it, we both head towards our cars parked along the street. We agree that a hot shower and a quiet night in alone is all we can handle after the week we've both had.

"I'll see you tomorrow, Ells. Have a good night."

"See you tomorrow, baby cakes," Ellie winks, before sliding into her car.

Forty-five minutes later, I'm showered and full from a plate of leftover pasta from my fridge. I'm cozy on my couch with a blanket and a mug of peppermint tea. With the business of the day finally done, my mind immediately drifts to Parker. I find myself wanting to call right now, to tell him about the order and how well it all went. I want to tell him about Bianca and her completely over-the-top clam bake. I want to tell him about the largest order we've ever received and then watch his face beam with pride for me. I want him to run a hot bath for me because that's exactly what he would do if I told him my legs were sore from walking the beach back and forth all afternoon. Then I would ask him to join me in the tub. We'd share a bottle of wine and swap stories from our week.

I pull the blanket up to my chin, wishing I could go a day, an hour, even a minute without thinking about him. Fat chance.

I flip through shows on Netflix, finding nothing that holds my interest. I'm in no shape for a rom-com and I'm sure my mind is too scattered for a drama. I sip my tea, finding myself staring into the steamy hot liquid a minute or two later. My gaze is broken when my phone lights up on the coffee table in front of me. My heart immediately leaps in my chest, wondering if it's Parker. It's not. It's a phone call from Ellie.

"Hey, Ells."

"Hey, Olivia. Shit," she says, talking fast. "Bianca just called in a panic. She said she's missing the table runner of peonies and her guests are arriving in thirty minutes. How did we miss that?"

"I don't know, but that's not good."

"No, it's not. I'm putting on my shoes and I'm heading to work. Can you meet me there?"

"You bet. I'll be ten minutes behind you. I just need to change out of my pajamas and I'm on my way."

"Great, see you soon." I end the call disappointed in myself.

I get changed out of my pajamas as swiftly as possible, throwing on a sundress and a pair of strappy sandals. I take my hair down from its top knot and run a brush through it, in hopes of looking somewhat presentable for Bianca. I shake out my hair and it falls into loose, beach waves, making me thankful for the natural curls I used to curse when I was a kid. There's not enough time for makeup but I manage to coat my lips in a thin layer of lip gloss and run a little blush over my cheeks.

Grabbing my keys, purse and cell phone, I'm out the door and on my way to Bloom to fix our blunder and make sure Bianca is happy with how we quickly remedy the situation. We've worked too hard on this event to have an unhappy client or worse yet, a negative review.

Ellie is waiting for me when I arrive, the runner of peonies safely placed in the Bloom van before I even put my car in park. Ellie offers to drive, and I don't argue.

"So, should we be scared for our lives? How mad *was* Bianca when she called?" I ask Ellie.

"No, she was actually very reasonable. It's going to be fine."

"On the bright side, at least we will get to see the setup."

Ellie's eyes remain focused on the road, the corners of her lips turning up in a smile.

"Can I ask you something, Ells?"

"Of course, shoot."

"Anything happening with you and Liam? You two were so cute that night at our beach house party. You haven't said much since."

"Nope, nothing."

"Really? You two seemed like you hit it off. Have you heard from him at all?"

"Maybe once or twice." She smiles.

"And you kept this from me? Ellie..."

"I'm sorry. I didn't think you'd want to talk about a Bennett. You know I would've told you under any other circumstance."

"I know, but I'm fine. I'm a big girl and I can be happy for you even if my own love life is a wreck. So, tell me more." I shift in my seat. The sounds of a Friday night in Reed Point billow from the busy streets. I can't help scanning the crowds for Parker.

"There's not much to tell. We've traded texts a few times and he's asked me to go out with him. But I said no."

"No? Why would you do that?" My gaze whips around to face her.

"Well, because I'm not looking to start a relationship right now. The timing is off."

"Are you kidding me, Ells! There must be more to it than that. Don't ninety-eight percent me. That's the most ridiculous thing that has ever come out of your mouth, and that's really saying something."

Ellie earned the nickname in college because ninety-eight percent of what she says is exaggerated or made up to make her story more impressive. This is one of those times.

"You missed the turn, Ells. Make a U-turn right up here."

Ellie ignores me and continues to drive further past the area of the beach where we set up earlier today.

"Ellie! You need to turn around."

She grins but remains silent. It's pretty clear she is ignoring me. She shrugs and a smile creeps over her mouth.

"What are you doing? Where are you going?"

"I love you, Olivia, you know I do, but you can be so stubborn sometimes. I'm going to need you to trust me on this."

And then it hits me all at once when she makes the left turn towards the beach house. One more right turn and we will be directly in front of it. My pulse starts to race.

"Ellie, what's going on?"

A second later, Ellie is pulling our Bloom van into the driveway of the beach house. My eyes narrow on Parker standing in the doorway and I feel like the air is squeezed from my lungs. It all happens so fast that I'm not prepared for the thousand different emotions I'm hit with all at once. Seeing him for the first time in over three weeks sends chills over my skin. He's wearing jeans that fit him perfectly in all the right places and a short sleeve black t-shirt. His hand grips the door casing above his head. *Why does he have to be so sexy?*

And then comes the sinking feeling as I remember *why* I haven't seen him in weeks, and it hits me like a freight train. It all comes back to me, flooding my thoughts. I'm supposed to be mad at him. I *am* mad at him but it's like my heart hasn't quite caught up to what my brain is telling me. Ellie must see my body tense.

She reaches over the center console and squeezes my hand. "Hear him out, Olivia."

"Why the hell would I do that?"

"Could you live with yourself if you didn't and possibly miss out on something amazing?"

"Ells, you are supposed to be on my side."

"Let me ask you a question. Do you still love him?'

"You know I do. I'm the idiot who can't stop loving the man who chose to cheat on her." I say, trying not to cry.

"Then you owe it to yourself to hear him out. I promise. You can do this." She squeezes my hand in reassurance.

"I don't think I can, Ellie." I blow out a breath.

"I know you can. Trust me, you are going to want to hear what he has to say." She gives me the nudge I need to move my body from the passenger seat.

On shaky legs, I exit the car and walk slowly towards him. I stop inches away from him, my heart beating through my ribcage. We are face to face, only the breeze from the ocean between us. I can feel myself wanting to reach out and touch him, but I restrain myself. There's so much he needs to explain before I even consider allowing him to touch me.

"Hey." His voice is hesitant but sure, with the slightest hint of a smile. "Will you come inside with me? Can we talk?"

"We can talk here."

"Livy please. I only need ten minutes of your time. Please come in."

"This is a bad idea, Parker."

He considers this. "I promise you, Livy, ten minutes. That's all I ask."

I'm so nervous I'm shaking, but recalling Ellie's advice, I follow my instincts and nod. I can listen to what he has to say and then leave.

I follow him through the front doors of the beach house and freeze. It takes me a second to realize what he's done. I inhale sharply and my palm covers my mouth. I'm in shock.

"Parker...."

"Do you like it?"

Of course, I like it. I love it. The room is filled with Bianca's order. Every corner and every surface are blanketed with the white peonies that we delivered to her on the beach today. It's the most incredible thing I've ever seen. They scatter the countertops, the coffee table, spilling from the mantel and hearth, even the floor. The house is barely visible underneath the hundreds of flowers. It's breathtaking. But it doesn't change the fact that he cheated on me.

I can feel Parker's eyes on me, looking for my reaction. I want to tell him how beautiful the room is. I want to ask him how he did this, how he knew peonies were my favorite flower? *How did this happen?* But I can't. Not yet.

"It's okay, Livy. You don't need to answer me. All I ask is you hear me out." Parker steps further into the room and I follow hesitantly. His eyes find mine, a crease forming across his brow.

I look away because I have to, focusing on the explosion of peonies covering the coffee table.

"Shit, I had everything I wanted to say to you in my head but then I saw you and I've forgotten it all." He pauses, inhaling a deep breath.

My eyes find his again, my heart aching at the sight of him.

"Livy, I know now what you saw, or at least what you think you saw."

"Your mouth on some woman in a hotel lobby bar is exactly what I saw."

"You're right, you did see that, but I promise it's not what you think."

"Parker, I know what I saw. It was pretty clear." I press my lips together, trying to steady myself. He shakes his head, his gaze falling to the floor then back to me.

"Let me finish, Livy, I can explain. What you saw was a very aggressive woman that didn't want to take no for an answer. All I wanted that night was a quick drink at the bar before heading back to my suite to Facetime you. I definitely wasn't looking for company when she sat down on the stool beside me. I was trying to leave when she literally assaulted my mouth. It made my skin crawl, Livy."

I laugh a little. "You really expect me to-"

"Livy, why is that so hard to believe? When have I ever intentionally hurt you? When?" His voice is firm. My heart riots behind my ribcage. "I can answer that for you. The answer is never."

"Well, I guess there's a first for everything. Breaking hearts all over Manhattan wasn't enough for you, you had to come home and break mine too."

"Livy, you know that's not true." The air suddenly shifts in the room, the temperature in my body spiking to what feels like two hundred degrees. "Who picked you up from White Harbor when you called needing stitches in your knee? Who drove halfway across town to pick you up from that bar that you had no business being in when you were too drunk to drive yourself and thought you were dying? Who took you home from school in the middle of Spanish class the day the news hit that your dad had been arrested, so you wouldn't have to walk out to whispers? Who, Livy? It was me."

I blink twice, the memories flooding back one by one like a tsunami barreling at full force towards me.

"Me, Livy. How can you not see that I am the constant here? I have always been there for you. I would do anything for you. I always have. I've never hurt you and I never will. That hasn't changed."

Parker rubs a hand across the back of his neck as I realize what I've done. I feel dizzy, my mind is muddled. My knees go weak, and I reach for the armchair to latch on to.

"I swear on my life, Livy. I know what it must have looked like, but I wanted nothing to do with her. I would never do that to you. You have to believe me. I love you. I love you so much." Parker's voice is full of emotion.

One thing I know for sure, what I've always known, deep down: Parker would never lie to me. The truth hits me, and I realize that I if only stayed a few more minutes or given him the opportunity to explain himself, this could all have been avoided.

"Do you believe me? Say something. Please." His chest rising and falling waiting for me to say something. To say anything.

"I believe you." There's relief in his eyes and he's smiling when I look at him. "I'm sorry I never gave you the chance to explain. I shouldn't have ignored your messages. This is all my fault. I was just so scared when I saw you with another woman."

He reaches for me, his hand catching mine, "It's okay. It's all in the past. I just want to move forward with you, Livy. These last two weeks without you have been the worst days of my life. I don't want to spend another second of my life without you."

"I'm sorry, Parker. I'm just so sorry," I say.

"It's not your fault. I would've reacted the same way if I saw what you saw. Scratch that, I would have pummelled him on the spot. I'm not mad, Livy, I'm just happy I have you back."

He takes my cheek in his hand, his thumb brushing over my edge of my jaw. I feel every ounce of tension drain from my body.

"I do have you back, right, Liv?"

I can't hold back the smile that is tugging at my lips. "I'm yours. I always have been."

Parker pulls me in for a slow kiss and I wrap my arms around his neck. He holds me tighter against him, so tight I feel breathless. Nothing has ever felt so good. He breaks the kiss and pulls back to look me in the eye.

"I've been dying to kiss you since you stepped out of the van. You taste so good."

"I've missed this, Parker. I've missed us."

"Come with me, I want to show you something."

He slides his hand into mine and walks me in the direction of the patio. The doors are wide open, and my heart stops at the sight before me for the second time tonight. I stop in my tracks and gasp.

More of our white peonies cover the patio. It's hard to see anything but the white velvety blooms mixed in with tea light candles. Behind the patio and the ocean, the sun is setting leaving the sky in swirls of reds and oranges. It looks like a painting it's so beautiful. I shake my head, taking in the incredible sight before me. My heart feels like it grows larger, expanding through my chest. My eyes fill with tears.

"I can't believe you did this all for me." My tears are hot as they roll down my cheeks.

Parker takes my face in his hands, wiping the tears away with his thumbs.

"I'm happy you like it. Ellie helped me surprise you."

"She did?"

"From the start." I can't believe Ellie was able to keep this secret from me.

"And Bianca?"

"Bianca is a friend of my sister's. She loved my idea to win you back when Jules called her. She was all over helping me out."

"You're kidding, Parker." I shake my head. "What about the flowers? We delivered them to the beach."

"I now owe Liam and Miles a huge favour. The three of us hauled them from the beach to here. There were a few complaints, but they were happy to do it. For us."

I'm speechless. Never have I ever felt love like this. Not only do I have the person I love most back in my life, but I also have a space in his family too.

"Thank you, Parker. I will never forget this as long as I live."

"I'm glad you like it. I missed you so much, Livy."

"I missed you too, Parker. So much."

I smile watching him bring his hands to my face. He cups my cheeks and presses a slow kiss to my lips.

"Any ideas of what we should do now?" He flashes me a smile, lust in his eyes.

"Bedroom, Parker. Take me to the bedroom."

Parker laces his fingers through mine and lifts our joined hands to his mouth, pressing a kiss to my hand.

"There's nothing I want more. Follow me..."

TWENTY-FIVE

Parker

I wake up with Livy on my chest. She is back in my arms and I will never let her go. Lying here with her feels like heaven.

I'm lying on my back, her fingers tracing the grooves in my stomach and I breathe in her citrus and vanilla scent. She lifts her head, her eyes meeting mine. Those deep brown cocoa eyes that slay me every time.

I slide my hand behind her hair and draw her face closer. She brings her hand to my jaw and runs her tongue along her bottom lip.

Fuck. She is amazing.

Her soft lips cover mine and I kiss her slow and long. Her lips part and I slip my tongue inside to find hers. One kiss turns into two and then three and a sexy sound escapes her perfect mouth.

And I'm gone.

My fingers lazily roam down her jaw to the column of her neck over the fine chain resting along her collarbone. I ask her between kisses.

"You're still wearing the necklace I gave you?"

"I couldn't bring myself to take it off."

"I'm glad." She whimpers as I kiss my way down the column of her neck. Her eyes flutter closed. I bring my mouth back to hers and kiss her softly. Before I take this any further though, there's something I need to get off my chest.

"So, we need to talk."

"Right now?"

Her eyes meet mine, blinking hard. She's looking up at me and I can tell she is bracing herself for what I have to say.

"It's okay, babe, no more surprises. I was just going to tell you that I'm not going back to Cape May on Monday without you. There's no way I am letting you go. I am bringing you with me."

"Okay."

"Yeah?"

"Yeah, I'm on board. After the last three weeks, wherever you are is where I want to be. I don't want to be away from you either."

I'm surprised she doesn't fight me on this. I've always been careful not to push her when it comes to taking her away from work, but I've just got her back and it's too soon to leave her again.

She has changed my life, made it crystal clear what I want from it. A life with her. Sunrises and sunsets, making memories we'll never forget and laughing so hard together it hurts.

"You have no idea how happy that makes me, Livy. We will figure things out from there, I promise, but I don't plan on giving you up any time soon. Whether that means I discuss a transfer back to Reed Point with my dad or you stay in Cape May with me, we are figuring this out together. Okay?"

"Okay, deal. I love you, Parker Bennett." I'll never get tired of hearing her say those three words to me.

"Love you too." I can't resist her a second longer. I lift her on top of me and crash my mouth into hers. I plan on showing her just how much I love her with my hands and my mouth and my arousal that is pushing firmly against her center.

And when we're done, I plan on showing her all over again.

"This is honestly the best chocolate fudge brownie ice cream on the planet. How do they make it this good?" Livy's eyes light up as she takes another mouthful of her double scoop cone. It's the little things that make my girl happy. It always has been and it's one of the many things I love about her.

Livy and I have been in Cape May now for three days. After spending the weekend together at the beach house, she packed up her suitcase and we made the drive east. We made a few stops before leaving Reed Point, delivering the peonies to friends and family so they wouldn't go to waste. We packed a few with us too for my hotel room, not ready to let go of the memories of what Livy now calls my "grand gesture."

Livy is staying with me at the hotel and I'm scheming up ways in my spare time to get her to stay here with me permanently. We have come so far. Nothing has ever felt as good as having Livy in my bed every night and Livy to wake up to in the mornings. Waking up with her warm, naked body pressed into mine is a dream come true and I have zero plans of letting her go.

We are learning new things about each other every day. I could listen to her talk for hours. I can officially say I know how hot she likes her baths, I know she needs chocolate at some point every day, she likes her drinks loaded with ice and she can't wait to have babies. Three to be exact and I have no problem with that. The thought of Livy pregnant with our children is a thought that has crossed my mind more than once and knowing she wants them too makes me excited for our future.

On our walk to the beach tonight after dinner, we stopped for ice cream. This has become our nightly routine. Livy has been researching the best restaurants here in Cape May and every night after work, we try a new one. Then, I take her for dessert, and we walk the beach. I'm moving into my rental home next week, so until then we are enjoying eating our three meals a day in different local restaurants. One of the perks of living in a hotel.

"Be careful, Livy, it's going to drip on you." I scramble to find her a napkin and laugh to myself, watching her lick the sides of the cone as the chocolate streams down the side of her hand. I have to stop myself from imagining her licking parts of my body like that. Too late.

"I can spare a few," offers an older gentleman who reminds me of my grandpa. He is seated at a small iron table beside us on the sidewalk in front of the ice cream shop. He hands me a wad of napkins and I thank him, handing them to Livy.

"A girl after my own heart. My Dottie loved chocolate ice cream too. I could never get her to change her order to anything else." He is nicely dressed, with graying hair and the look of a well lived life in his eyes.

"See, I'm not the only one who knows what she likes and sticks to it," Livy says, nodding to the man who returns a chuckle in our direction. "My name is Olivia, and this is my boyfriend Parker. It's a pleasure to meet you."

"Pleasure is all mine, darling. My name is Walter. But you can call me Walt," He offers. "Are you two from around here?"

"Nope, we are both from Reed Point, about two and a half hours west of here. I am living here temporarily for business and Olivia is visiting. Are you from here, Walt?"

"Born and raised. It's always been my home. Eighty-three years if you can believe it and I'm finally retiring."

"No way. Good for you. What do you do for work?" Parker asks.

He sips his coffee, placing the mug back on the table with his wrinkled hand. He folds his arms across his middle and his chest heaves.

"I own my own business. An antique shop with my wife. You can see it from here, it's just past the blue awning." He points down the road, in the direction of the ocean, where real estate is prime, and the street is always busy with pedestrians. "But it's time to pack it in. It's just not the same without my Dottie, who I lost two years ago. My kids tell me I need to take it easy."

"I'm sorry for your loss," Livy says softly.

"Thank you. I sure do miss her. She kept me in line. I was a wild one before I met her."

"Sounds like someone I know," Livy teases me.

Walt affectionately tells us about his late wife and his eyes mist over. They were happily married for sixty years, shared three kids and worked alongside each other in their antique store for over fifty years. All here in Cape May.

"When will you officially start retirement?" I ask.

"Next month. I'll have an estate sale and then I'm closing the doors for good. It's hard to believe."

I ask him what he is doing with the building and he informs me his lease is up in ten months and until then he is planning on subleasing the space. It gets me thinking.

"Have you found someone to take over the lease?" I ask.

"Not yet, that's next on my list. Why? Do you know someone who could be interested?"

I eye Livy and she returns the look. If I'm reading her right, I think she's at the very least open to looking at it.

"I think I do. Walt, how would you feel about Olivia here, possibly opening up a flower shop in your space? I'm trying to get her to stay here with me and that could be my incentive."

"You mean, a guy as good looking as you needs an angle to get a girl to stay with him?"

I laugh. "I know! It's crazy but it's true."

Livy nudges my shoulder. I shoot a wink her way and she rolls her eyes.

"I think a good florist is exactly what this town needs. You two remind me of my wife and me when we were your age. Why don't I take you over now and show you the space? We can see if you like it. Then you can talk it over and give me a call."

I look Livy in the eye, trying to assure her we are just looking. Nothing more. We don't need to rush into anything, but secretly I'm hoping she loves the place. This could be the way I can get her to stay here with me. Walt just might be the answer to my prayers. My Hail Mary.

"We would love to take a look at it," Livy answers softly. I'm sensing by the hushed tone in her voice that she's not entirely sold, but maybe with any luck we can get her there.

When we reach the front doors of Walt's antique store, my eyes are on Livy. She takes in the exterior and the weathered board and batten siding that at one time was painted a bright white. She steps across the threshold into the small store and her gaze travels down to the worn pine wood floors that look original to the space. Sunshine pours through the two large rectangular windows on either side of the glass front door, casting a warm and welcoming feel. We move deeper into the open floor plan, admiring Walt's many treasures that seem to be displayed on top of each other over tables and shelves around the store.

"Well, this is it," Walt announces proudly. "There's a restroom in the back right corner and a back door that leads to access to the alley. There's plenty of parking back there too."

"It's really wonderful, Walt. I love what you and Dottie did with the place," Livy says, smiling, taking in the charm of the little shop.

"The bones are good. It just needs a little paint and some TLC, and you'd be up and running in no time. I'm sure you are well aware that it doesn't come better than this location here in Cape May. You'll have endless foot traffic all day," Walt says, proving himself to be quite the salesman.

"We are," I answer, moving around an old desk to extend my hand to our new friend. "Thank you, Walt, for your time. Can I give you a call to talk numbers and let you know what we decide?"

"That would be fine. I am happy to have met you both."

"The pleasure was all ours."

We say our goodbyes and Walt hands me his business card. It's been a while since I've seen one of these. We head for the beach, deciding to go for our walk along the shore like we planned. I'm hoping it will give Livy some time to let this new idea sink in and work through the details in her mind.

I take her hand in mine as we walk in silence for a few minutes, listening to the sounds of the waves crashing into shore.

After a little time has passed, I decide I can't wait another second to ask her.

"So, tell me what you're thinking, Livy girl." I'm trying to read her mind. There's a sparkle in her eye and I'm feeling cautiously optimistic. Hope fills my chest.

Shifting her gaze from the ocean to me, she lifts a hand to shield the sun from her eyes.

"I'm thinking it would be pretty perfect. I love the space. It felt like a lot of love has resided between those walls."

"Really?" I answer, feeling a little relief.

"Really. But there's a lot to consider. I need to talk it over with Ellie because she needs to have a say in this too."

"Of course. It's a big decision, one that will require some thought." *Say yes.*

"And it goes without saying, Livy, I'll do anything I can to help. I have construction contacts, designers, anything you need to get the shop up and running." *Please say yes.*

I can't contain my excitement, smiling like an idiot from ear to ear. How did we get so lucky, being in the right place at the right time tonight to meet Walt? I can't help but feel like this is all meant to be, like this could be the solution to our problem of how we can be together without giving up our dreams.

"I know, baby. Thank you. Now before I go discussing this with Ellie, are you sure you are okay with us moving in together?"

"Livy, there is no other option. I can't go a day without you." I unlace our fingers and palm the side of her cheek in my hand. She leans into my touch.

Livy's smile radiates back at me and it's all the assurance I need to feel like this is going to work out. I kiss her perfect lips and they taste like chocolate and salt and everything right in the world.

I love this woman, every single thing about her. I plan on never stopping.

It's been six weeks since Livy signed the lease agreement and started construction on Bloom's new Cape May location. Once Walt cleared out his treasures, we got to work bringing her vision to life. Livy refused a lot of my resources, wanting to do things herself and knowing how important that was to her, I bit my tongue and let her work. Over the last couple of weeks, on my days and nights off, I've been there helping her in any way she needed. If she asked, I did it, happy to feel like my independent girl needs me in some way. I'm so damn proud of her. The end result is nothing short of amazing.

"You ready, Liv?"

"Almost. Would you like to do the honors?" Livy walks towards where I am perched on the end of our bed in my

Armani suit, tying the laces of my dress shoes. She turns away from me, displaying the open back of her dress.

"Would I ever." I reach for the zipper at her waist, pulling it slowly up her delicate back. "Although, as much as I love this dress on you, I would rather be taking it off."

She turns to face me, and my hands reach for her waist, pulling her in between my thighs. She traces one finger down the center of my chest between my pecs and a heat pulses up my spine.

"You look fucking incredible." I nearly growl, reaching my palms around her to grab her ass. She's wearing a form-fitting white dress that rests just above her knees. *This girl is going to kill me.*

I release her, standing and offering her my hand. I can't have the guest of honor late for her own party.

"I'm so proud of you, Livy. Today is your day. You ready to do this?"

"As ready as I'll ever be." She flashes me a nervous smile and I squeeze her hand just a little bit tighter.

I help her into my Audi and drive us both to the new Bloom. We are meeting Ellie there, who has been here every chance she could, helping with the renovations and getting their second location up and running. This is just as much her grand opening as it is Livy's. Their dream of opening a second location coming to life. It's been no small feat.

It is nearing five o'clock and the grand opening begins in half an hour. I'm watching my girl race around the store with Ellie, making sure every last detail is in order. Servers are lining up flute glasses for champagne and the caterer is hard at work plating hors d'oeuvres on trays. He's going to have to work harder to keep up with Ellie, who is stuffing her face with them as she works.

"I can't eat another bite. Okay, maybe one more. Where did you find this caterer? You are going to have to roll me out of here," Ellie grumbles through a mouthful of food, rubbing her stomach with one hand.

"Jesus Ellie, stop eating all the food. I'm going to have nothing left to serve our guests if you keep up at that pace." Livy sasses back, swatting Ellie's hand away from the neatly placed finger foods.

"Damn Livy, have you seen how many people are waiting outside? There must be over a hundred people out there," I announce, peeking out the front window at the crowd that has formed. I spot my parents, Liam and Miles and my sister who are chatting with Livy's mom and dad and Kate. They were the first to arrive, securing a spot right in front of the yellow ribbon that crosses the front door that Livy will be cutting shortly. They are just as excited as I am and so damn proud of her too. I also spot Walt in the crowd, sitting along the perimeter in a chair we made sure to reserve just for him.

"Stop with the updates, Parker. I'm nervous enough as it is without you reminding me how many people will be staring at me. How am I going to get through my speech?"

This will be a lot of attention on her today and I know she is freaking out. She's managing to hide her anxiety from the people around us, but I know her better than anyone. Her bottom lip pulled under teeth and her hand rubbing the diamond star pendant around her neck is a dead giveaway.

"I'll be right there in the front row to support you. You've got this, Liv. I have no doubt. Just breathe baby." I kiss the top of her head.

I leave the girls to go over their speeches one last time and walk outside to check on the film crew. We should be ready to start in minutes if everything goes according to plan.

Glasses begin to be filled as guests wait patiently outside. Among our friends and family are neighboring business owners as well as the local TV channel, who will air the grand opening on their six o'clock news.

I walk back inside to Livy and Ellie after getting the go-ahead from the film crew. "Are you two ready? The news crew is set up and ready when you are. Just give me the thumbs up."

Livy inhales a deep breath and smooths her hands down the front of her dress, looking to Ellie who nods.

"We're ready."

I press a slow kiss to Livy's temple and give Ellie a quick hug. I escort the two of them out the front door and hand them the scissors they will be using to cut the ribbon before taking my spot in the front row with our family. I watch Livy take the microphone in her hand and welcome the crowd to Bloom. She connects with the audience, she's confident and her voice is smooth. She looks fucking gorgeous too.

She's crushing it.

God, she's unbelievable.

She hands Ellie the scissors and together they cut the ribbon, watching it split in two and fall to the ground. This earns them a round of loud applause from the crowd and an extra whistle from me. The photographer from the local news channel moves in closer, snapping photos of my girl and her business partner bestie, the two of them all smiles.

The girls step inside Bloom and begin welcoming their guests. For the next two hours there is a steady stream of people moving though their new flower shop with a drink in hand and a smile warming their faces. Everyone admires the perfectly arranged flowers on reclaimed wooden tables under a vintage chandelier in the center of the space. My Livy is at the center of it all, killing it.

She greets new faces from the community and catches up with both of our families, who have gathered around her with a surprise.

Jules hands Livy a large, beautifully wrapped package, a grand opening gift from both of our families. She unwraps it carefully to find a professionally framed and matted photo of the beach house, our special spot, to remind her of home and the people who love her.

"This is beautiful, and it means the world to me. I can't wait to hang it up here at Bloom. I will think of you all every day. Thank you all so much." Livy takes the time to hug each and every one of them with tears in her eyes.

"Honey, we are so proud of you." My mother rests her hand on Livy's shoulders, her eyes moving between mine and Livy's. "I'm also very happy you two found your way back to each other. It's a blessing to see how happy you two make each other. I knew it would work out, you just needed a gentle nudge in the right direction by someone who knew your two hearts were always meant to be together." My mom winks.

I look at Livy and for a minute we are both speechless, realizing that my mother had an ulterior motive the day she walked into Bloom to order flowers. She knew what she was doing all along, getting the two of us back together again, face to face, in the same room.

When everyone has left and it's finally just the two of us, I shut the doors to Bloom and wrap her in my arms.

"You amaze me, Livy. You were incredible today."

"Today was one of the best days of my life. Thank you for everything, Parker." She can't stop smiling and it's adorable.

"This was all you babe. You know me. I'm just the good-looking assistant at your beck and call," I tease her, pressing a kiss to her cheek.

In all honesty, we make a good team, and I can't wait to see where life takes us. We've already come so far. For now, it's just the two of us in Cape May. But one day soon, I am going to marry her, and we are going to have babies. I can't wait for the day when we are living back home in Reed Point, close to our families. But until then I have her all to myself, and that's fine by me. Actually, it's perfect.

I've never been happier, that much is true and it's all because of this woman in my arms. It took us eight years to find each other again and we are finally right back to where we started. I'm madly in love with Livy, I know she feels the same and I plan on spending every day of the rest of my life with her. She just doesn't know it yet.

"Time to go home, Livy girl?"

"Past time, baby. Take me home."

"I love you. So much," I whisper, brushing my lips along her forehead.

"I love you too," Livy breathes, reaching for my chin and pulling me down for a kiss.

I kiss her back and say the words that I will repeat to her all the days of our life.

"It's always been you, Livy girl."

"Always been you."

EPILOGUE

livia

Six months later.

It's been two months since Parker got down on one knee and asked me for forever. And of course, my answer was yes. It was the easiest question I've ever had to answer. I wasn't sure anything could ever top the seven hundred peonies he secretly ordered and surprised me with, but somehow, he did it.

Parker proposed on one of our many trips back home, at the beach house, of course. It felt perfect that the spot where we shared most of our firsts together was the place we committed to our future, too. I had arrived home after a girls' night out to a dimly lit house with a trail of candles leading to the patio. I found him waiting for me under the moonlight with a small blue box. It was romantic and sweet and everything I could have wished for.

I can't stop looking at the oval cut diamond on my finger. But more than that, I can't wait to be Parker's wife.

Tonight, our engagement is being celebrated with our friends and family at the Bennett estate. I told Parker I didn't need a party, that nothing could possibly make me happier than I already am. But Parker's mother wasn't having it. So, here we are, surrounded by both of our families. We just finished a delicious catered four-course dinner and the DJ, Parker's parents have hired has started to play our favorite songs.

I take a moment to let the night soak in. All of our favorite people are here tonight celebrating Parker and me, and my heart swells. My mother and father are dancing next to Parker's parents on the makeshift dance floor that is usually the Bennet living room and Kate and Jules are sitting together at a table in a fit of laughter. Our families have come together seamlessly and for a moment I forget what my life was like before Parker came back into it.

My eyes focus on Parker, who is across the room gazing right back at me in his navy suit and white button-down dress shirt. The man is ridiculously gorgeous and sexy and sweet and a million other adjectives that come to mind. I am the single luckiest girl on the planet. He's mine, he's all mine forever.

He crosses the room towards me and nuzzles his mouth into my neck. "There's my gorgeous girl. You smell as good as you look," He says in a voice only meant for me to hear.

He wraps a hand around the small of my back and pulls me into his hard body. The heat of his touch causes a shiver to roll up my spine. He kisses my neck and pulls back. He's looking at me in that way he often does, like he's seeing me for the first time and doesn't want to forget a thing. Like I'm all he's ever wanted. It feels so good to know it's me that makes him feel this way.

"Hi handsome."

"Hi." Parker lifts my left hand to his lips, his fingers fiddling with my engagement ring, and smiles. "Tonight has been amazing but I can't wait for the real deal. I want to marry you tomorrow, Livy."

"I want that too," I whisper, going up on my toes, kissing his mouth in a slow kiss. "More than anything. What do you say we pick a date and a venue this week?"

Parker smiles, and it reaches his eyes. It's pure happiness. It is love radiating back at me. There isn't a day that goes by that I don't count my lucky stars that he's mine.

He has been pushing me to set a date for weeks, but with moving into the Cape May rental and getting our second Bloom location up and running, I haven't wanted to rush into wedding planning. Getting my impatient fiancé to agree with me on waiting has been a whole other story. Parker wants what he wants, and he knows exactly how to go about getting it.

"I was kind of thinking we could get married here."

"My parents' house?"

"Yes. Unless you think they would mind?"

"I think my mom would be honored to host our wedding here. But I want you to have the wedding you've always dreamed of. Are you sure you wouldn't prefer a hotel or even a destination wedding?" Parker knows I wouldn't want anything lavish or too large, but he does want me to have the wedding of my dreams.

"I'm sure."

"Well then, it's settled! I love the idea. We can ask my parents tomorrow."

Parker and I are hosting a small brunch at the beach house before heading back to Cape May. We've invited both of our families and of course Ellie too. It's also an excuse to spend time with the people who matter the most to us, who we don't see as often as we would like to since our move.

I've gotten used to living in Cape May, away from my family and friends. It's not home in the true sense of the word but I've realized home is not a place. Home will always be wherever Parker is. And the home we have made together in Cape May is a dream. It also helps that we have the beach house to stay at whenever we feel that pull in our hearts to visit friends and family.

"Dance with me, Livy?"

I nod and Parker links his hand in mine, ushering us to the dance floor. He brings me in close, so his body is flush with mine, and I lay my palm flat on his chest. I nestle my body into his. We dance for a few minutes to a slow song before Kate and Ellie move in next to us. Miles and Liam join in, and the four of them form a circle around us, dancing to the upbeat song being played over the speakers. They are all smiles, singing along to the music, squeezing their bodies into us and laughing. Parker lifts me in his arms, my feet are in the air, spinning me around.

"You make me feel good, Parker," I say, looking down on him from high in his arms. His smile warms my soul, his love for me taking hold of my heart.

"You just wait. I'm going to make you feel really good later tonight."

My head falls back in laughter, which causes a huge smile to spread across his face. He lowers me to the floor.

In this moment, my heart is exploding. It's bliss, it's the life I've always dreamed about having but never thought was possible. Until Parker came back into it.

My first love, my soul, my eternity.

My every dream come true.

PARKER

Celebrating my engagement to Livy with my family and friends is surreal. Never in my wildest dreams would I have imagined this a year ago. Being here, engaged and counting down the days to make Livy my wife.

I'm fucking excited.

There's no doubt in my mind that Livy is the one for me. She is the only one for me in this lifetime and the next one after that. I think deep down I knew this the night we made love the first time in the bed of my pick-up truck. I realized it the second time years later on our drive to Mabel's, the day I played the part of her assistant. That was the day she began to open her heart to me. I had never seen anything more beautiful in my life when I looked at her in the driver's seat with the wind in her hair.

Being with her is what I crave. She is all my favorite things. She is light in the darkness, she is my peace at the end of a long day. She is my forever. Every day with her is better than the last.

Liam and Miles find me with three tumblers of whiskey, handing me one. We clink our glasses together, Liam proposing a toast to Livy and I and a long, happy life. I'll drink to that. The fact that my brothers feel such love for Livy and have welcomed her into our family fills me with a deep happiness.

"We are happy for you, Parker. You found a good one," Miles says through a grin.

"Thanks bro, that means a lot."

"I can't wait for you guys to make me an uncle. I'm going to spoil that kid rotten. Uncle Miles is definitely going to be the favorite."

"We'll see about that," Liam grunts, but he's smiling too.

"How about I marry her first, with you two at my side?"

"Really?" Miles questions me with a grin on his face.

"Definitely. Wouldn't have it any other way."

"Honored, man," Liam says, clasping his hand on my shoulder while Miles pulls me in for a bro-hug.

My attention moves across the room to Livy, who is talking to her dad. She has her phone out and they are looking at something on her screen. Their faces are full of happiness, her smile radiating across the room. Seeing her smile, an expression I know I will never get tired of, has me wondering if life could get any better than it is right now.

I watch her as my father joins the conversation. She turns her phone to him. Whatever the three of them are talking about has them all starting to laugh. I can't help but smile. She fits into my family. She fits into my life. Seamlessly.

"Who needs another? Have you seen the hot bartender? I think I need to reintroduce myself," Miles says, holding his empty tumbler in the air.

"I think he's over there," Liam says, nodding towards the bar. "I'm just glad you are finally being open about it. I want you to know I love you either way, little brother."

"Fuck off, Liam. There are two bartenders tonight, and the one I'm talking about is female and hot as hell. And you would know that if you could keep your eyes off of Ellie for more than five seconds."

Liam flips him off as Miles makes his way to the bar.

"Hey. Can I ask you something?" Liam looks different all of a sudden, like there is something weighing on his mind. "Can I talk to you?"

"Of course. Always. What's up?"

He motions me towards my dad's study where it's quiet, and I follow, taking a seat beside him on one of the two leather armchairs in front of the mahogany desk. It's unusual for Liam to ask to talk, so I'm curious as to what he has to say. He rubs his palm over his jaw and takes a breath.

"I need advice."

"Okay, shoot."

"It's about Ellie. I think I like her."

Now I see where this is going, and I'm pretty taken aback that my brother is actually falling for a woman. Happy as hell, but surprised to say the least. I assumed their hook-up at the party Livy and I hosted was a one-time deal. I guess I was wrong.

"That's great, man. Ellie is a great girl. What are you worried about?"

"I don't know. I mean, I guess I do. I guess what I'm wondering is... how did you know that you were ready for a commitment? I don't want to screw this up and make things awkward between us if it doesn't work out, considering she's Olivia's best friend and all."

"That's a tough question to answer. I just knew that I couldn't go a day without talking to her. I wanted to be with her every second I could."

It makes me think about how lonely my life felt before Livy. How much I was missing. She gives my life meaning, she makes my days brighter and I can't imagine going back to the way things were before her.

"I can't stop thinking about her," Liam admits. "She makes me laugh. There's just something about her."

"Well then, I say go for it. Take a chance. You'll never know what could come of it, if you don't give it a shot."

"Yeah, I guess you are right. I'm going to take your advice, but I reserve the right to blame you if it ends in disaster."

"Noted." I laugh.

"Thanks, Parks. I mean it." He clasps his hand on my shoulder as we both push from our chairs to standing. We make our way back to the party where I immediately scan the room in search of my fiancée. *My fiancée. I'm one lucky bastard.*

I spot her, looking sexier than hell in that pale pink strapless dress that hugs her curves in all the right places. Her long, wavy hair is swept back in a low ponytail.

My feelings for this woman have only grown stronger. I love how she makes me feel. I love her laugh, her smile and I love knowing that I'm the one who can drive her wild with just a look.

She walks towards me, and I reach for her hand. She kisses me - a slow, lazy kiss - and whispers my three favorite words. "I love you."

"Mmm… I love you too, Livy girl. I'll never stop."

A grin tugs at the corners of her mouth and I smile back against her lips. She's the most beautiful girl in the world. A lifetime with her will never be enough.

I scoop her up into my arms and carry her down the hall away from our guests.

"Parker!" She squeals as I carry her into the mud room at the far end of the house, before setting her down on top of the washing machine and closing the door.

I kiss her until she's breathless.

"You are a naughty boy, Parker Bennett."

"You haven't seen anything yet. I'm just getting started."

THE END

ACKNOWLEDGMENTS

First and foremost, thank you to our readers. To each and every one of you who took a chance on our book, we thank you from the bottom of our hearts.

Thank you, to our beta readers, ARC readers, bloggers and bookstagrammers. We thank you for every post, every mention, share and the continued support you have shown us. We are grateful beyond words. We hope you fell in love with Parker and Livy's love story.

Thank you, to our editor Carolyn De Melo, for never judging our spelling or the hundreds of commas that were either missing or put in places where no commas should ever go. You took our book baby and made it so much better. You are magic.

Thank you, Brandee, Erin, Natalie and Carmen, for believing in us. You have been on this journey with us since the beginning. Thank you for encouraging us to chase our dreams and for cheering us on every step of the way. Your feedback has meant the world to us. We are blessed beyond measure to call you our friends.

Thank you, Leah of Leah Anne Photography, for your patience behind the lens because lord knows you need it when you photograph us. You are such a talent.

Thank you, Melanie Harlow, for taking us under your wing and for being an endless source of advice and guidance. What we have learnt from you is invaluable.

Thank you, Alyssa and Tricia of LitUncorked, for introducing us to readers and book lovers around the world. Thank you for all of your hard work letting readers know Always Been You has arrived.

Thank you, Kim Bailey of Bailey Cover Boutique, for creating the cover of our dreams. It was a pleasure to work with you. You made the process so easy. You also give really great advice.

Thank you to a long list of friends, neighbours and co-workers who have shared in our excitement. Your enthusiasm and support have kept us going.

An enormous thank you, to our families, for making our lives so much better by being in it. How beautiful it is to wake up everyday and know we have your love and support. We hope we've made you proud. We love you.

XO Lily and Miller

Manufactured by Amazon.ca
Bolton, ON